THE SAGE'S WAR

KRYSTAL N CRAIKER

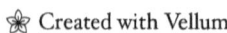 Created with Vellum

For the real Erenia, taken too soon

ACKNOWLEDGMENTS

How do you write the acknowledgements for the last book in a series? How do you adequately thank the people who have been on this journey with you for so long? I'll try but know my words can never do justice to my heartfelt gratitude for everyone one along the way.

Many people helped make this book a worthy final installment. My critique group, the Fiction Crafters, elevate my writing in ways I never thought possible. Through this group, I have made the most incredible writer friends. Michelle Monárrez, Mary Richards, Jennifer Black, and Casey Rafael are always there for motivation, brainstorming, pep talks, and honest critiques.

My loyal beta readers, Joseph Holt and Alyssa Boyett, love Elandria as much as I do and ensured this book made sense for the series. My editor Trisha Tobias not only improves the story but also leaves me comments that make me smile. Erin Olds at Salt & Sage Books is prompt, communicative, and understanding. And finally, Raven Tempestarii took my vague cover instructions and turned it into something beautiful.

My mother, Kathy, has always believed in me and been proud of me, even when I don't feel I deserve it. She embraces my creativity and lifts me up in so many ways. I wouldn't be who I am without her constant, unconditional love and support. (I kept my promise and didn't kill off her favorite character!)

And what is an author without someone to provide hugs and caffeine and tell everyone how they should read your book? Michael, you're not only my best friend and the love of my life, you're my hype man. You tolerate my late-night writing binges, my tears over fictional characters, and my random need to lay on the floor to work out plot points. Not only could I not have written these books without you, I never would have started if you didn't believe in me the way you do.

Finally, and this is surreal to write, thank you to my readers. My fans. Your reviews and messages and questions keep me going. I hope Quinn, Amarice, and Raymond make you proud.

-Krystal

MAP OF ELANDRIA

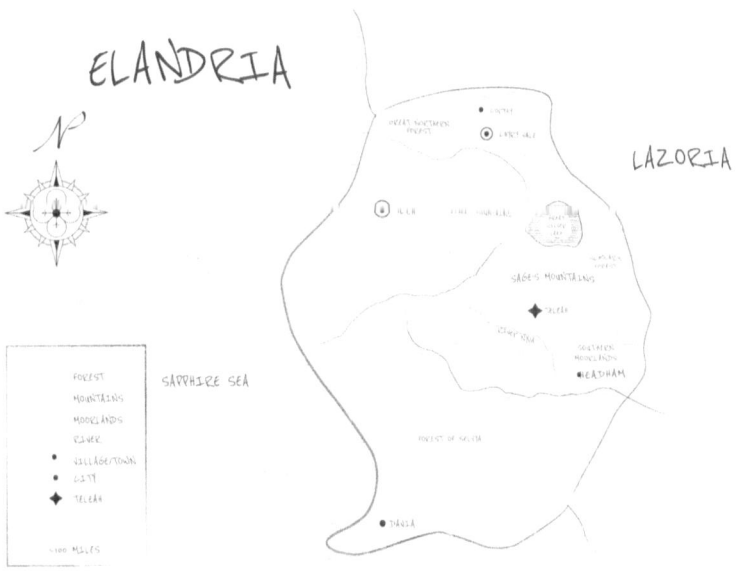

CHAPTER 1

QUINN

The shackles that bound his wrists scraped along the cold, stone floor as Quinn shifted to a more comfortable position. As if comfort were possible, he thought. He let out a dry laugh that turned to a wet cough. The dampness of the cell was not good for his lungs, and the bone-deep chill that never went away made it worse. His hazy thoughts remembered Jack's winter tonic; what he wouldn't give for a long swig of that vile, warm medicine coating his insides. If he were home, Amarice would send him straight to bed with a dose of the tincture. He'd wake up to a steaming bowl of Madge's chicken and lentil soup. He would groan as Amarice insisted he take another dose of the tonic before he fell back to sleep as she stroked his hair.

Amarice.

Tears would fall if he weren't so fatigued. Once a day, he got one cup of water with his one measly meal of gruel and stale bread to keep him alive. If it weren't for the gruel, he would have died weeks ago. Perhaps it would rain again soon. Last week, enough rain had leaked through the roof that Quinn was able to drink his fill. He could summon a storm if only he had the strength.

He had stayed drugged the entire journey to...wherever he was. The last thing he remembered was Amarice's faint screams of "Where's Quinn?" through the square as he drifted out of consciousness in the back of a wagon.

In his cell, he had been strong enough to replenish and focus his magic. He had cracked the ancient foundation and slipped away, taking down several guards. But the Chamberite soldiers were far too numerous. One took him down with a knock of his sword's pommel to the back of Quinn's head. After that, they bound him in chains.

Then some gruff, disembodied voice had called the guards fools. Too much of the poison could kill Quinn. Instead, they decreased his meals to the bare minimum to keep him alive. And now, he was too weak to summon any of his magic.

He could still sense the Gift of the Earth in the air, though, like a sixth sense. There was nothing tangible, but the magic was there in the same way his hearing and sight were. He was certain that meant he was still in Elandria; Scholars who ventured past Elandria's blessed borders reported drastic reductions in their powers.

The sound of waves crashed like thunder through the small window at the top of his cell. Other than the sound of guards changing shifts, the distant waves and crowing seagulls were his only companions. The air tasted of salt. Quinn had deduced that he was near the sea. But that hardly narrowed down his location, for all the good knowing it would do; half of Elandria bordered the sea.

He shivered.

The cell was frigid, as if the walls were coated in ice. It was so unlike Elandria, even in the winter. By his estimation, it was three or four weeks past Harvest Holiday. It shouldn't be this cold, unless he was in the—

South! He gasped at the realization, which launched him into another coughing fit. The hacking felt like dull knives in his lungs. When it passed, Quinn pieced together what he knew. The newfound revelation had cleared his mind and given him a glimmer of hope.

He was near the Southern Sea in some ancient building, a fortress or castle of some kind. He couldn't recall much of his first-year geography studies to narrow it down further. Amarice would know, if only he could reach her.

The Chamberites who held him wanted him alive for some reason. Perhaps they had offered him for ransom to the Sage, knowing she would pay a hefty sum for his return. But something about that didn't feel right. The Chamberites were backed by Azmar and Grellis, two of the richest Parliament members. And from what Raymond had said months ago, they now had the support of the Lazori government.

No, they didn't need money.

As sleep drifted over him, Quinn was no closer to figuring out the motive behind kidnapping him. He fell into a fitful slumber. Sickness and hunger did not keep the *tovari* dream magic at bay, and he witnessed the pain of his people through nonsensical images and faint screams.

His only comfort was knowing that Amarice saw it, too. That they were still connected, even through the horrors.

CHAPTER 2

AMARICE

Amarice sat cross-legged in front of the Consort's Tree, her brow furrowed in concentration and frustration. No matter what she tried, the two intertwined trees would bloom, but wilt in the next moment. She was covered in fallen leaves.

The tree sensed Quinn's absence.

Ludicrous, but true. No one would believe Amarice if she suggested it, but the Consort's Tree had not fallen to the seasons since Quinn's magical outburst two years before when he first arrived at the Villa. It stayed bright and lush through all of last winter. And by the time she had returned from Teleah without Quinn, every leaf had fallen. Despite her immense magic, it would bloom for only five minutes before covering the ground—and the Sage—in piles of red and gold and orange.

"She's been like that for two days," Amarice heard Daisy say in the distance. But she made no effort to turn back and see who her friend was speaking to.

Heavy footsteps crunched through the leaves moments later, and someone sat down next to Amarice.

"The leaves are a good look for you."

King Raymond's voice was gentle as he teased her. He nudged her shoulder with his, but she said nothing.

"No luck?" he asked, gesturing to the tree.

"I could ask you the same thing." Her tone was strained as she tried to bite back the acid in her words. Logically, she knew it wasn't Raymond's fault her Consort was missing. But she was growing impatient with his lack of information. Didn't he have dozens of spies at his command?

Raymond sighed. "Assuming the Chamberites haven't moved him to a new location at one of their latest captures, no. We still have it narrowed down to a dozen strongholds and are waiting for more information. My emissaries keep meeting...opposition. The roads are dangerous, and we lost another ten Messenger outposts in recent days."

Amarice nodded. The two friends sat in silence for several minutes. Twice, Amarice bloomed the tree and watched the leaves fall.

Raymond cleared his throat. "Amarice...are you certain that—"

"He's alive. I know he's still alive."

The king held his hands up in surrender. "That's not what I was going to say. If they wanted to kill him, they would have done it publicly."

Amarice narrowed her eyes at him.

"Sorry. That was insensitive of me." He reached for her hand, and she let him. "Your people need you, Amarice. I need you. And I'm not sure trying to fix this tree is the best use of your time or your powers."

She swallowed. A single tear ran down her cheek. "I'm lost, Raymond. Utterly lost without him. I feel as if my soul has been rent in two."

The king put his arm around her shoulders and pulled her close. "He's strong. He'll survive, and we'll find him."

Amarice said nothing. She was terrified for Quinn. Whatever he was enduring had to be awful. The Chamberites wouldn't have him put up in nice quarters with plenty of good food. But she was far more frightened of the prospect of living without him. Of fighting this war without him.

And she was terrified that she couldn't save him.

Raymond kissed the top of her head. "When did you last eat, Amarice?"

She groaned. "Not you, too. Don't worry. Everyone is forcing food down my throat. Do you think Madge or Daisy would let me go hungry?"

"No, not likely. It's odd, isn't it? The way we try to force people to eat when they're grieving." He squeezed Amarice's shoulders, hopped up, and brushed off the fallen leaves from his scarlet tunic. "Up you get, Amarice. I'm the king in the middle of a civil war. I need my Sage. I need my friend."

With a reluctant sigh, Amarice stood. She reached out a hand to brush the trunk of the Consort's tree one more time, then took Raymond's arm as he led her inside to her study. On their way through the northern gardens, they passed Elaine and Janessa. The two women brought their hands to their brows in deference. "My king."

Raymond flashed a friendly smile. "Hello, ladies. You don't have to address me as such, especially here. I come to the Villa to forget I'm the king. Well, I used to, anyway."

Janessa nodded, and Elaine blushed. "Sorry," she said, her eyes to the ground.

"Oh, it's all right. Please. I didn't mean to upset you. You're Elaine, correct?"

She looked up with wide eyes. "Yes." Raymond stuck out his hand. "Elaine. I'm not sure we've been introduced yet with how chaotic everything has been. I'm Raymond."

The mousy woman took his hand in hers. "Hello."

Amarice bit her lip to keep from laughing. "And you know Janessa, Quinn's sister by marriage?"

"Yes, we've met briefly. Hello, Janessa."

Janessa smiled, but it didn't reach her eyes. "Has there been any news about Quinn? Corbin is out training with the Deyoni, but I know he would want an update."

Amarice shook her head. "No. Nothing yet. I promise you will know as soon as I do." She swallowed hard, trying not to break down. It was hard to admit out loud that she was ignorant and powerless to save her lover. Janessa folded Amarice into a tight embrace.

"Well, if you'll excuse us," the Sage's voice quavered. "We have business to attend to."

In the study, Amarice plopped down on the sofa instead of the chair behind her desk. She curled into a ball. "What was that all about?"

"What?" Raymond asked.

"The lingering handshake, the dazzling smile."

Raymond sat down opposite her. "I don't know what you're talking about. I was just trying to reassure her that she doesn't have to act on ceremony." He looked at Amarice's stoic face. "You don't like her!"

"How dare you! Elaine is nice, if not a bit...dim. She's helpful around the Villa, and she's a good friend to Janessa. I have no reason to dislike her."

"You're jealous."

Amarice scoffed. "Please."

"No, you are!" He grinned. "You're jealous because Quinn loved her first."

"Perhaps." Amarice stared at her hands. "It's silly. And I'm just so angry all the time with him gone. But yes, it feels like she knows a part of him I never will."

"Oh, Amarice. It's not silly. It's natural, though you have nothing to worry about." He paused. "Well, you have plenty of things to worry about, but Elaine isn't one of them. But surely you loved someone before Quinn, too, yes? I know it wasn't me, not in that way."

Tears welled in her eyes. "Yes. I did."

She had loved someone once, long before Quinn. She didn't talk about Zayn much, and she had told no one how he had passed. But his dying face had haunted her in recent weeks, always morphing into Quinn's. Between those images in her waking hours and the tovari dreams of war in what little sleep she got, Amarice's mind was a prison of horrors.

When she offered no further comment, Raymond continued into business. "The Chamberites have purchased an army on credit from

Lazoria. As much as the Lazori king wants Elandria, he wasn't willing to risk his own army. So, these are mercenaries."

"Loyal to whoever pays them, then."

"Yes. Which, at a later time, could be advantageous to us." He gestured to Amarice's desk, where a map was laid out from hours of attempting to guess Quinn's location. Amarice stood and joined him at her desk. "They have pushed in from the north and are now approaching Beybrook, which means they'll control or blockade most of our trade. I've sent reinforcements, but I don't have a lot of hope they'll arrive in time."

The king moved his finger to the Sapphire Sea. "I have received word that they are also approaching by sea from the northwestern borders of Lazoria. I believe they mean to take Te'eh."

Amarice nodded. "Logical. Te'eh is already in complete disarray. Too many people are loyal to Sahra Azmar."

"And we believe Azmar is on board those ships. Grellis appears to be with the northern army."

"What about Samperian?"

Raymond tapped the southern part of Elandria. "We have no confirmation, but we believe if he isn't already in the south, he will be soon."

"If we lose Te'eh and Beybrook, we will be cut off from the rest of the world." The countries to the east of Elandria were no great military powers and were unlikely to send aid. And if they could not access Elandria's immense wealth, they would have no reason to be interested in the war at all. "This is dreadful news, Raymond."

"I know."

"Do you have troops in the west?"

He shook his head. "We have some new recruits, but not enough. They fucked me over when they bought half my army out from under me."

Amarice's head spun as she watched Raymond mark all the cities and villages that had fallen since his last update. "Fucked is right."

"Amarice, how many people do you have living in the mountains now?"

"Last estimate was eight thousand. More arrive every day."

"I need them. The able-bodied ones."

She sighed and sat in her desk chair. Though it had been her idea to train the Scholars and Deyoni, it was for defense. How could she send her people to the front lines? Many would die. Children left without mothers and fathers. Parents losing their grown children. More people she couldn't save. But if they stood any chance of defeating the Chamberites and their Lazori mercenaries...

"You will not conscript them."

"I'm not to that point. Yet." His jaw was clenched, but his eyes were pleading.

Heat rose in her cheeks, and her magic crackled under her skin. She tightened her jaw as she spoke. "I cannot send them to die. I was training them to defend themselves. But to send them off, to tear families apart like that. That's not what the Sage is. How can I tell my people—"

"They're my people, too! Don't doubt that for a moment, Amarice. But I cannot protect most of them without a bigger army."

She nodded, her lips in a thin line. "I never said they weren't. But our roles are different."

"Not anymore."

He closed his eyes and took a deep breath before he continued. "I want you to support me in recruiting them. They'll follow you."

"We aren't supposed to use our magic for war. Only defense."

"What's the difference at this point? They've taken so much from us. They struck first."

Amarice shook her head. It was different, marching to battle with magic. It was harsher, more intentional.

"Magic would turn the tide of this war. They need you, Amarice. Elandria needs you." Raymond reached across her desk and took her hand in his. "And it would give you something to do, to focus on."

She sighed. "I cannot stop you from recruiting people on my lands. But my intention is to keep them here, to protect them. I am not Brigitte." Most of Elandria may worship the first Sage as a heroine. But she had led the early settlers against the Deyoni. As far as Amarice was concerned, Brigitte was to blame for the precedent of violence and discrimination against the tribes.

"I'm not asking you to slaughter a race of people. I'm asking for your help in defending Elandria. Your support."

Amarice waved a hand. "As I said, recruit all you like. I will not oppose you publicly, but I will not support this either."

Raymond threw his head back and pinched his brow. "I fear it's only a matter of time before the war comes knocking on your doorstep, Amarice. You must continue training the Scholars."

"I know."

"It would give you something to do.

She nodded. "But at the first lead we have on Quinn—"

"Absolutely. You will go rescue him as soon as we know where he is."

A knock on the door interrupted them.

"Come in!" Amarice said.

Madge opened the door, face pale. "Amarice. We have a visitor. I'm not sure this can wait."

❧

AMARICE ENTERED the library with Raymond on her heels. Madge had cleared everyone out of the room before ushering in their guest. A tall, familiar man that the Sage had never met sat perched on a chair.

"*Drabekesala*! An honor!" Deben dia Gagiya leapt to his feet and brought his hand to his brow.

"Well, shit," Raymond whispered behind Amarice. "It's uncanny."

Indeed, it was. Other than the darker complexion and the black hair tinged with grey, Deben was the spitting image of Quinn. Amarice's heart lurched. She forced a smile. "Welcome, Deben dia Gagiya. My home is yours."

He grinned. "*Heyyana*. I am here for my son. As my tribe approached the border of Ilecin, I feared I would never see him again. I have forsaken my tribe and betrayed my *drabana*. But he is my only son. Where is he?"

Amarice took a deep breath and gestured for him to sit. Deben's smile faltered. Raymond stood in silence behind the Sage as she took a seat on a stool. She could not imagine the risks he took, traveling as a lone Deyoni through war-torn Elandria. She didn't want to tell him, but she had no choice.

"Deben... Quinn is missing. He was kidnapped at Harvest Holiday by the Chamberites."

The man froze as he processed the news. Then he let out a wail that rocked Amarice to her core. Raymond, too, judging by the hard squeeze he gave her shoulder. Deben sobbed violent earthquakes that shook his tall frame. Amarice placed a hand on his back, tears falling like rain from her eyes.

The door to the library slammed open. "Amarice? Madge said you sent for me. Is there news?"

The Sage wiped her eyes and looked up at Corbin. The sturdy, blond man was drenched in sweat from training. His blue eyes were wild with worry. She dreaded this; Quinn had put off telling Corbin the truth about their parentage.

"Of a sort. Corbin, this is Deben dia Gagiya. He is Quinn's real father." She patted Deben's shoulder. "Deben, this is Corbin. Eleanor's other son. Quinn's brother."

Corbin gaped as Deben looked up. Deben forced a watery smile at Quinn's little brother. "You look like her," he said.

Corbin puffed out his cheeks as he exhaled. "Well, that certainly explains a lot."

CHAPTER 3

RAYMOND

Raymond knocked his head against the door of his usual room at the Villa. He'd been king for only a few months, and his entire country was falling apart. Had he been so naïve to think banning the Chamberite leaders would solve Elandria's problem?

No, not naive, perhaps. But hopeful. He had inherited his father's damn optimism when he inherited the throne. Elandria was a peaceful country, with only a few conflicts of note in its long history. But now, the greatest threat in a thousand years was his to deal with.

He sighed, trying to push the self-pity aside. It served no one. When Daisy had sent a message to come to the Villa to pull Amarice from her state, he had left immediately. The Villa had always been a respite. But Amarice, his closest friend, was barely holding it together. He needed her strength more than she knew. He, too, was one of her people. And she wouldn't help him build their forces. He understood her side of it; she had sworn to protect the Scholars and had always been the savior of the Deyoni. But his soldiers were dying at a rapid rate. Even some of his spies and Messengers had been caught and killed.

Then Raymond had walked by Quinn's empty study to get to his room, and the grief about his missing friend had hit him like a punch to the gut. Although he had expended as many resources as he could in the search for Quinn, he felt as if he wasn't doing enough.

That was his general feeling about everything these days.

He needed a break. A distraction.

He looked at the clock on the bedside table. Two hours until dinner. That meant Daisy was likely around somewhere. He tried the Apothecary laboratory first, but Jack said she had gone to the baths a half-hour before. He checked the baths, which were—as per usual these days—packed with Scholars gossiping and laughing. It was as loud as the public baths in Teleah.

Raymond knocked on the door to Daisy's room, but there was no answer. He groaned and leaned against the wall.

"Raymond?"

He jolted upright. Daisy's long, red hair had been pulled into a wet braid. She looked exquisite in a silk emerald dress, so unlike the tunic and pants she wore when she worked. "Were you looking for me?" she asked.

"I was. I just wanted to see if you were busy now...or later." He winked at her.

She chewed her lip and looked at the ground. "Sorry, Raymond. Matthew and I have plans."

"That's why you look so ravishing. Anything I can tag along for?"

"No."

"Oh." Raymond furrowed his brow in confusion. He'd spent many entertaining nights with Matthew and Daisy at the Villa. "I see."

Daisy sighed. "Raymond, you know I care about you."

"That's never a good start to a conversation." He couldn't believe this was happening. Not today. "Why, Daisy? If I've done something, please tell me so I can make it up to you."

She shook her head. "No, of course not. But...you're the king now, Raymond."

"You're breaking things off because I'm the king?"

"Well, yes." She looked up at him. "We've had a lot of fun, Raymond. But at some point, you will need a queen. And that's not me. I don't want you to think it's me. Settling down, ruling, having children. That's not who I am."

He blinked. Had he ever given Daisy the impression that he wanted to marry her? He didn't think so, but they had become close. "I'd never expect that of you, Daisy. I like your company, but..."

"I started falling for you. And I can't. I refuse to give up the life I love for any man. I'm sorry."

Raymond nodded and stood straight. "Friends?"

She gave him a sad smile. "Always."

Daisy disappeared into her bedroom, leaving Raymond alone in the hallway. He stood there for several moments, trying to understand what had just happened. Self-pity started creeping back in. He needed a distraction even more now.

There were thousands of women in the lands surrounding the Villa. But he didn't feel like wooing and flirting, and the nearest brothel was six hours away.

"Fuck."

He shook his head and walked through the open archways into the courtyard. He stared at the ground as he moseyed through the large outdoor space, wondering if what Daisy had said was true. Would he have to settle down? Raymond had been philandering his way across Elandria since he was sixteen.

Amarice had done it. She had met someone that made her want to stop finding her way into a new bed every night. And look how well that had turned out, he thought. The most powerful Scholar in history reduced to anguish with her lover missing. That sort of heartbreak didn't sound like anything Raymond could ever stand.

Once, when he was younger, he had thought maybe that person could be Amarice. The two of them one day ruling Elandria side by side. That part might have come true, but Raymond knew now they were much better off as friends. And he had come to love Quinn like a brother. Those two were perfect for each other.

"Oh!"

Raymond looked up to find a shocked Elaine inches from him. He had nearly bumped into her and hadn't noticed her at all.

"My apologies, Elaine. I was lost in my thoughts. Are you all right?"

She smiled and tucked a loose strand of light-brown hair behind her ear. "I'm fine, my ki—Raymond." She cocked her head and studied him. "Pardon my asking, but are you all right?"

Raymond began to plaster on his best political smile, then faltered. He wasn't sure why; perhaps he just wanted to talk to someone who didn't know him. "Wallowing in self-pity. I'm fighting a losing war. One of my best friends is missing, and my other best friend is debilitated by sadness. And I was just dumped because I'm the king."

"Oof. That's quite the mud puddle to wallow in."

Raymond let out an unexpected laugh at the image of himself rolling around naked in a pool of mud. He hadn't expected Elaine to be witty, not from Amarice's assessment. It felt good to laugh, and once he started, he couldn't stop. He couldn't remember the last time he had had a good chortle. Or the last time he'd had a reason to.

Elaine stared in confusion as Raymond held his gut in laughter. But soon, a smile overtook her face. When Raymond composed himself, he thanked her. "I didn't know how much I needed a laugh."

"Well, I am glad to help. Thank you for making me feel like I have a sense of humor."

He raised an eyebrow as he took in her expression. "I have a feeling people underestimate you quite often, Elaine."

She blushed. Raymond studied her. She was short and built much like Amarice, though far more understated. Quinn had a type, he thought to himself. The restrictive Northern-style dress she wore hid much of her figure, and he wondered how she could breathe in so much fabric.

Off-limits, he reminded himself. She was an important part of Quinn's past, and Quinn was his friend. She was also not from a place where people hopped into bed together for no other reason than fun. It wouldn't be right. Raymond toned down his flirtatious stare, but he still didn't want to be alone. Tonight, he needed a friend.

"I'm off to find one of the Sage's most expensive bottles of wine. And I would love to hear some embarrassing stories about Quinn as a boy. Care to join me?"

Elaine's eyes widened, and a slow smile crept over her face. "I'd like that."

CHAPTER 4

QUINN

Quinn moaned as he woke from yet another dream. Since the war began, the dreams had become more frequent and more intense. He swore he could feel the violence happening to him, although he was chained here in this cell.

A tear ran down his cheek as he remembered this latest dream. They were never clear, but he could hear screams. Lots of screams. It was likely Deyoni, he realized. The Scholars were never massacred in groups. All the large groups of Scholars were residing in the mountains with Amarice to protect them. He hoped that it wasn't the Gagiya that had been massacred, that they had made it safely into Ilecin, and his father and extended family were safe.

Amarice.

He could feel her presence in the dream, meaning that hundreds of miles away, she too had been asleep. His heart ached, and he wished he could reach out to her, to touch her. Talk to her. Hear her voice.

He sat upright with an idea and groaned at the pain of the sudden movement. Chained up for weeks on a stone floor had left his muscles weak. But he breathed through it and focused on the first glimmer of hope he'd had in weeks.

Perhaps it was foolish, unreasonable. His mind was too clouded with sickness and exhaustion to logic his way through it. But he knew he felt Amarice in his dreams. As the only two *tovari*, they shared the dreams of the atrocities happening to magical peoples.

Could he reach out to her in his dreams? Were they connected through their magic this far apart?

He had to try. It was the only thing he could do, and he had to do something. But how? He had to be asleep for the dreams to occur, but he needed to be conscious enough to talk to Amarice. And something horrible had to be happening to Scholars or Deyoni at that moment. There were a lot of factors.

But it was something.

He calmed his mind as he laid on the cold, stone floor and focused on his goal. Perhaps she was still asleep, and he could fall back into the same dream. His stomach churned. That would require this latest massacre to still be occurring. Did that make him selfish for hoping it was? He'd have to moralize over that later.

It was a long time before he fell back to sleep. He was too focused on retaining consciousness during his dreams.

✦✦✦

THERE WAS FIRE, and yet there wasn't. Quinn felt himself blink in his dream. Whether it was literal fire, he didn't know. He looked around at the darkness, the rising heat burning his skin. He saw only an endless abyss. The fire was nothing more than a sensation.

It's a dream, he thought. Nothing is as it seems.

He needed to find Amarice, but his vision failed him. Dream Quinn closed his eyes and felt. He reached out with his magic, trying to find her. Maybe she was awake and wouldn't be here. He searched with his soul, panicking. More than anything, he wanted to reach her.

He felt light. When he opened his eyes, the abyss was lightening into the pale grey of dawn. The dream was ending.

No.

He tried to fight it, to stay asleep. But the burning sensation ebbed, and the grey faded. He would wake up soon, he knew.

The burning ended, and he felt himself swirl toward wakefulness. But at just the last moment, he sensed her.

◈

QUINN SPENT much of the next day sleeping, practicing conscious dreaming. Sleeping wasn't a stretch. His body was exhausted. He was sick, and he needed rest to heal. Assuming he would heal.

By the time night fell, Quinn's heart pounded with excitement. He was ready to see her. And when he fell into his dream, he did.

This dream was different. It was a world of Quinn's making. There was no screaming. No burning. He looked around. Though blurry, a few things looked familiar. Gooseflesh speckled his skin in the cool air, and though he couldn't see it, he could hear a babbling brook nearby. And there was a giant willow with a large, low branch reaching out to him like a mother's arm, calling him home.

It was his special spot in Corthy. A smile spread across his face as he remembered the night he and Amarice had spent there just a few months before. It seemed like a lifetime ago. He made his way to the tree, bare feet plodding across the wet earth.

A glimmer of light appeared on the branch. Quinn blinked, trying to make out the shape. A woman sat on the branch in a gown made of stars.

Amarice.

He crossed the last few steps and reached his arm to touch her, but his hand passed through her like she was made of steam. But he could see her. She wasn't looking at him, though. She gazed up into the sky.

He opened his mouth to call her, but no sounds came. Instead, he just stared as she looked around—and straight through him. But her brow furrowed as if she knew.

Dawn broke, and the forest faded into watercolor blurs. He mouthed her name over and over.

Just as she began to disappear, his voice appeared.

"Amarice."

She looked straight at him, startled.

And then she was gone.

CHAPTER 5

AMARICE

"Raymond!" Amarice pounded the door to Raymond's guest room. "Raymond, wake up!"

"Damn it, just a minute!"

Amarice tapped her foot as she waited on Raymond. His green eyes were thick with sleep when he threw open the wooden door. "It's five o'clock in the morning, Amarice. What in Brigitte's blessed name is the matter?"

"I saw Quinn!"

"What? Where? What are you talking about?"

"In my dream. He was there. And it wasn't like it usually is. But he was there."

Raymond raised an eyebrow. "So, you dreamed about him?"

Amarice shook her head. "No. He was there. He found me."

"That makes no sense, Amarice. You dreamed about him. You miss him, and you dreamed about him."

She flushed in anger at being misunderstood. "*No.* How do I explain?" She pushed past him into his room and sat on the edge of the crumpled bed. "I've told you about the *tovari* dream magic, yes?"

Raymond nodded. "Yes. Though I've never understood it."

"Neither do we, not really. But lately, I've sensed Quinn in the dream, too. We share the dreams, and it seems that we somehow exist in these dream worlds, witnessing these events. Well, not witnessing. Experiencing? It's hard to explain."

The king rubbed his tired eyes and placed his brown hand over Amarice's pale one. "So, you sensed him there."

"Yes, but...this dream was different. Nothing bad was happening. We were somewhere familiar that I can't place. Some place we've been. I was sitting in a tree. And I knew he was there, but I couldn't see him." She paused, thinking. She knew that place, even in its dreamlike state, but she couldn't quite recall. "And then just at the end, I heard his voice. He said my name."

"I see..."

"It was real, Raymond. We connected. I'm not sure why I never thought of it before. But if we share these dreams, perhaps we can communicate."

Her heart ached. She missed him, and to hear his voice—so clearly, so close—had pained her. She leaned her head against Raymond's shoulder. Warm tears rolled down her cheek.

"What does it mean?" Raymond asked. She could hear the skepticism in his voice, and it hurt.

She sighed and wiped her eyes. "I don't know."

The Sage spent the rest of the day in the library, trying to find any book she could about *tovari* magic. Though she and Quinn had turned the library inside out during his apprenticeship looking for anything on dream magic to no avail, she had a more guided question now.

But she found little. There had been so few *tovari*, and even fewer had written about it. The Deyoni rarely had children with anyone outside their kind because of how Elandrians treated them as a whole. And Scholar's blood was so rare that it was hard to find someone who was both. As far as she and Quinn knew, they were the only ones in generations.

Perhaps she and Quinn could explore this magic in more depth and write their own book for future *tovari*. Assuming they made it out of this war alive.

Quinn was alive. It didn't matter that Raymond didn't believe her. She knew the dream had been real. Quinn had reached out to her through their shared connection, that brilliant, brilliant man. And she was going to get back to him. She would find him.

And if she couldn't? Well, at least she could see him and hear his voice one last time, even if it was in their dreams.

⚜

AMARICE BOLTED UPRIGHT in her bed, her heart pounding in her ears. She let herself come back to the room, touching her blankets and blinking until the shape of her wardrobes and nightstands came into view.

She knew where Quinn was.

It had taken three more nights. Each night, Quinn's dream world became more tangible, though she still could not touch him. The second night, he had told her he loved her, but she couldn't respond.

She recalled the latest dream in her mind. The tree she sat in—the willow tree from Corthy, she had finally realized—felt real under her thin, glowing nightgown of starlight. She could feel the splinters and bark against her skin. Quinn stood next to her, and she could see the crinkle of his eyes with clarity.

"Amarice." When he spoke, he appeared next to her in the tree. She watched as he placed a hand over hers. She could see it but not feel it. Craving his touch, she leaned closer to him. How she missed his touch.

She tried to speak again, and a soft "Quinn" escaped her lips. He gave his signature half-smile.

"I've missed hearing you say my name, my love."

"I've missed everything about you," she replied, her dream voice getting stronger.

His brown eyes glistened with an ethereal magic. He was pushing his powers as far as he could, she knew. Her own magic hummed in her fingertips.

"I'm in the south, and I can hear the sea. It's some sort of cell in an old fortress or castle. It's ancient and crumbling. But I'm not in a dungeon. I'm high up."

Amarice nodded. She couldn't recall her geography now, in her dream. The darkness began to fade, and she knew the dream was ending. Quinn must have spent himself significantly.

Desperate for more, she tried to grab him, but nothing met her touch.

"I'll find you," she had said as Quinn faded from view.

In the darkness, Amarice pulled herself from her bed. She waved a hand at the lamp on her nightstand, and a flame burst to life, illuminating the face of the clock nearby. It was just after midnight.

She pulled a dressing gown over her nightclothes and went downstairs to her study. The fireplace roared to life at her presence, as if her magic knew she needed the light and warmth. She had work to do.

The Sage rummaged through her maps to find anything with details of the south. There was one in particular she knew she needed to find, one she had never studied since her own apprenticeship a decade before.

She laid out several maps on the floor in front of the fire and pored over them on her hands and knees. She rubbed her eyes over and over; they were still thick with sleep.

It felt like hours, but she eventually found what she was looking for. There were three ancient fortresses from the early days of Elandria when warlords ruled the south. They were in the Southern Mountains, near enough to the sea that Quinn would be able to hear it. She had learned about these in her military history class long ago, but she couldn't recall enough about them to deduce where the Chamberites had Quinn.

She spent the next few hours planning routes and calculating how long it would take to get there. She made lists of supplies to bring with her, wanting to leave fully prepared to rescue her Consort. There was no time to waste.

At just past six o'clock, Madge entered the study to set the fireplace.

"Amarice! I didn't expect to see you awake already." The plump head of house looked over the Sage sitting amongst piles of maps and paper, her grey eyebrows furrowed. "Is everything all right?"

"It will be." Amarice grinned, letting hope warm her for the first time in weeks. "Could you fetch the king, Quinn's family, and Jack? Tell them it's urgent."

Madge nodded. "Of course. Right away." She bustled out the door.

Amarice stared into the flames of the fire, soaking in its magical warmth. She would leave today if she could gather everything she needed.

Jack was the first to enter her study. "Amarice? What's wrong?"

Before Amarice could respond, Corbin and Janessa burst into the study, both in ragged dressing gowns and shivering from the cold.

"Is it Quinn?" Corbin asked through chattering teeth.

Amarice nodded. "Let's wait on the others."

Moments later, Deben and Raymond had entered the study. The five people closest to Quinn stood around her desk, anticipating the news.

"I know where he is," the Sage said.

"What? How?"

"That's fantastic news!"

"Where?"

"Amarice..."

The last voice was Raymond's, laced with skepticism. But Amarice didn't need his approval. She knew Quinn was alive, and she was going to rescue him.

She continued. "Quinn and I are *tovari*, half-Scholar and half-Deyoni. This gives us unique magic that others do not have. And we share dreams. Ever since the very first attack on Scholars years ago, when he was still at the Academy. A few nights ago, Quinn connected us through a sort of lucid dreaming."

Raymond frowned, but the others waited with bated breath. "Last night, he told me where he is. Or where he thinks he is. He's in the south in an ancient fortress near the sea. I've narrowed it down to three that are close enough that he could hear the waves as he said."

"We should leave now!" Corbin said. "Storm them all and find him."

Raymond studied Amarice with a raised brow. "I believe I know which three those would be. But Amarice...even if this is true—"

"Of course it's true."

"Fine. We knew there was a chance he was being held in the south, as that was where Samperian was headed. But you can't storm three castles to find him. You need precision."

She nodded. "I know. He said the cell is in a state of disrepair. He also said he's not being held in a dungeon, but in a tower."

The king's eyes widened. "He said that?"

"Yes."

"Citadel Kahyrst." He bent over the map on Amarice's desk and pointed. "It was built before Elandria claimed the south from the warlords. They put the prisons in the tower. It's the only one."

"Yes! The cliff on which it was built was too difficult to carve into. So, they built up," Corbin said with excitement. "I read about it in one of my architecture books."

"I know the place," Deben said in a low voice. "It is well-defended by the land and the sea."

Raymond nodded. "He's right. It's difficult to access, and if Samperian has an army there, they have extreme tactical advantage."

Jack shrugged. "Yes, well. They don't have a Sage."

Amarice smiled at him. "I've prepared a list of supplies that I'll need. If I ride Atsila, I can make it in eleven or twelve days."

"You can't go alone!"

"Raymond, with all due respect, you can't stop me. But I'm willing to take anyone with me. We'll need Messenger-stock horses, though."

"I'm going," Corbin said.

Janessa grabbed his arm. "Corbin, it's not safe."

"He's my brother, Nessa. I have to. He'd do the same for me." He looked at Amarice. "I'm strong, and I can wield a sword. I learned as a boy."

"Of course you can come, Corbin. Janessa, I'll take care of him, I promise." She hoped.

"I am coming, too, *drabekesala*," Deben said. "I must."

"Me, too," said Jack. "I've already lost one of my best friends. I'll be damned if I lose another."

Raymond pinched the bridge of his nose. "You're certain this is where he is? That this is real?"

"You said yourself it makes sense that he would be there." Amarice stared him down.

"I did." He nodded. "Very well. I can send you with a small company of my fine—"

"No." Amarice rose from her chair to make her stance clear. "You can't spare the numbers, Raymond. And I'd much rather have some of your finest soldiers defending the Villa in my stead. Without myself or Quinn's magic, you're relying on sheer numbers to protect my people."

"Amarice, you are powerful, but you are still only one person."

"She also cracked the foundation of a thousand-year-old structure with a tap of her foot," Jack said. "And didn't you kill your three kidnappers while you were injured and drugged?"

Janessa's mouth gaped.

"Yes," the Sage said. "I can do this, Raymond. But I also don't want us to draw attention to ourselves. If we went with a small army, a larger one could meet us. Or they could kill Quinn, knowing that we are coming."

The king sighed and threw his head back in defeat. "Fine. How many will you allow me to send? Ten?"

"Two."

"Seven."

"Three."

"Five."

Amarice groaned. "Five. Make sure you include Willum and Gracyn."

"Done."

"When do we leave?" Corbin asked.

Amarice glanced at the clock on the mantle behind her. "If we leave at lunchtime, we can make it past Teleah before nightfall. Assuming we can get the horses and everything packed."

"You have Atsila and Nivasi, yes?" Raymond asked. "I'll get you the rest. I may have to purchase some from the tribes here."

"I'll pack a Healer's bag," Jack said. "And we need to tell Madge about food."

"I will bring my Eleanor," Deben said. "She will hunt for us on our journey. And her claws are sharp when she does not like someone."

Raymond let out a sardonic chuckle. "Nine Deyoni horses, five soldiers, a falconer, an Apothecary, and a farmer. The Sage. And a killer bird. It's the start of a bad joke."

MADGE HELD AMARICE TIGHT. "Be safe, my dear," she said over and over.

"I will, Madge."

"And bring our Quinn home."

She extricated herself from Madge's embrace, and Daisy threw her arms around Amarice. "Are you sure you don't want me to go too? You only have one other Scholar with you. My magic can help."

"I need an Apothecary I trust here, preparing for the war. The soldiers across Elandria are counting on them. I can't take you and Jack away."

Daisy nodded and wiped her eyes. "Please take care of yourself, my friend. I'll have no one to gossip with if you die." Her words were joking, but her voice was thick with worry.

"Oh, Daisy. I love you. I'll be fine."

The Sage looked around at her ragtag company. Corbin was kissing Janessa. Deben was securing his hawk's cage to the saddle. Jack was already mounted and ready to go.

"We're ready, m'lady," Willum said. He gestured at the tenth horse that was serving as their packhorse. They had packed light so as not to tire the horses, but it was still a long journey. And this way, Quinn would have a horse to ride when they returned, assuming he was in enough health. Amarice pushed that thought out of her mind.

"You know better than to call me lady, Willum."

"Yes, well. My boss is right there." He jerked his head toward the king.

"Remind me to tell you some embarrassing stories about your boss."

At that moment, Raymond stepped up. He gave Daisy a small, sad smile, and Amarice wondered what that tension was about.

"Amarice, keep yourself safe," he said in a low voice. "I know you're powerful, but these Chamberites and their Lazori mercenaries...they're brutal."

"Trust me, Raymond."

"I do. I wish I could go with you."

She smiled and embraced her old friend. "I need you to take care of my people while I'm away. And you should return to your palace at some point and, you know, rule."

He laughed. "Probably. Be safe, Amarice. And if you see Samperian—"

"I'll kill the bastard."

"Good."

Amarice stepped away and mounted Atsila. She watched as Corbin hugged Elaine and kissed a sobbing Janessa one last time. Her heart grew heavy. It was one thing to save Quinn. She would do anything for him, morals be damned. But now she was responsible for these people, too. And the price would be great if she couldn't protect them.

She swallowed and rolled her shoulders back.

"Let's go."

CHAPTER 6

RAYMOND

Raymond sat at the breakfast table in the veranda the following morning. He squinted at his plate through the bright sunlight that fought late winter's chill. It was too quiet with Amarice gone. And Jack. Daisy was staring sullenly into her eggs, and Matthew was rubbing her back in comfort. Madge's cheerful demeanor as she served breakfast was gone. Her eyes were puffy, her face splotchy.

Elaine entered the veranda, hair pinned back in a tight bun, and she smiled at him. She took the seat to his left. "Good morning, Raymond," she said.

"Good morning. Did you rest well?"

She shook her head. "I stayed with Janessa, and she was too upset to sleep much. She fell asleep about an hour ago." She helped herself to some bread and butter. "And you?"

"I don't rest well at all these days." He lifted his coffee to his lips and drank the rich, bitter liquid as if it were his life-force.

"I'm sorry."

He waved a hand. "No matter. Do you like it here at the Villa?"

She buttered another piece of toast. "I do. It's just so different from what I have known my whole life."

"How so?"

She gestured at the table. "In Corthy, women and men had to sit on opposite sides of the table."

"Really? How strange."

She nodded. "I suppose it must seem that way. And the fashion here. I feel so out of place, but I'm not sure I could wear such loose, revealing clothes. Or pants. I've lived my whole life being told it was wrong."

Raymond thought for a moment. He couldn't imagine living such a restrictive life with so many rules. And he certainly couldn't imagine a place where women were treated as second-class citizens. "Do you believe it's wrong?"

"I don't know what I believe anymore."

He could understand that. King Roland had raised his son to become a king in a peaceful country. His military theory training had been just that—theory. Like other soldiers, he had been sent to the borderlands where occasional skirmishes popped up for a year. But the few he fought in could hardly be called battles. And there was his father. The man had taught Raymond integrity but cowered to blackmail in the last months of his life. And the logical, scientific magic he thought he knew was turning out to be far more complicated and irrational, if Amarice were right about the dreams.

"Have you been to Teleah yet?" He changed the subject.

Elaine shook her head. "No."

"I'm returning today. You could come with me and see the city. Although so much of it is abandoned with many of the Scholars here in the mountains. But I could show you the palace and take you to one of my favorite pubs."

She smiled. "Thank you. But I need to be here for Janessa. Perhaps another time."

"Of course." He flashed his best smile, hiding the hurt. It had been stupid to ask, but he was desperate for a friend, and all of his were gone now. And a large part of him worried they wouldn't make it back. "Another time."

He excused himself to finish packing for his return. As he walked past Amarice's study, his eyes welled with tears. He made it up the stairs, only to pass Quinn's study. And though he'd been there for days, in that moment, the emptiness of it threatened to swallow him. Once in his room, he slammed the door and slid to the ground, crying.

Hot tears leaked from his eyes, and his shoulders heaved. His breathing came in short, sharp pants between sobs.

He wasn't cut out for this. Ruling Elandria had once been an easy job for his father until Charles Chambers' influence spread like a sickness across the country. Before then, they had trusted Parliament to keep things running smoothly, though without sweeping and necessary change. Perhaps that was the crux of the problem. Parliament had run unchecked for too long.

Raymond had spent his twenties wooing women and drinking. Sure, he had done some diplomatic duties. He'd traveled to Ilecin and Lazoria to broker trade agreements. He'd made speeches to Parliament and sat in treasury meetings with his father. But nothing had prepared him for the intense loneliness of leading. He wondered if that was how his father had felt or if Raymond was fucking everything up.

He'd lost half his army to the Chamberites. Some because they had become zealots. Some because Grellis had paid them more. The damn military bill that had passed in the spring was nothing more than a ploy by the Chamberites to take control of Elandria. And now he was trying to rebuild. He could have an army of Scholars who could bend the forces of nature to their will, but Amarice wouldn't support it.

He understood why. It's not like he enjoyed sending people off to die. But he didn't know what else to do. Many of the young Deyoni men and women had joined up, but their numbers were still too small. And they needed training. At least other Elandrians who became soldiers had some weaponry training. But the Deyoni hadn't been allowed to carry weapons for hundreds of years.

He banged his head against the door, trying to knock some sense into himself. He couldn't lead if he was hiding at the Villa crying. And though the odds were stacked against him, he would not surrender his country without a fight. Raymond had always enjoyed gambling, but this time, there was more at stake.

He pulled himself off the floor and wiped his eyes. He poured water from the pitcher into the washbasin and washed his face. Then he threw his belongings into his satchel as he collected himself. He wouldn't let his men see him weak.

With one deep breath, Raymond grabbed his things and threw open the door. He made his way down to the stables to meet his private company of guards. They brought their hands to their brows when he arrived, and he nodded at them.

He mounted his horse, Sterling, a dapple-grey stallion. He'd had Sterling since the horse's first bit, and he trained the pony himself. He patted his old companion on the shoulder and turned to his guard.

"Ready?"

"We're behind you," the captain of the guard, Erenia, said. She nodded at him with a smile.

"For better or worse," he muttered under his breath. He nudged Sterling into a trot and headed to Teleah.

⚜

A FAMILIAR FACE greeted him at the palace entrance. He grinned at the lanky man, whose dark hair had turned grey in the years that he had attended to Raymond. Andin, his personal valet, had entered the prince's service on his thirteenth birthday, replacing the nanny who had helped the king raise him. Raymond listened as the older man listed the places in Teleah that had been repaired and the people who had visited the castle. He had Andin draw him a bath to wash off the dust of travel before dinner.

After a long soak in his private bath, Raymond sat at the small table in the front room of his chambers to read his correspondence. Andin had sent the most urgent matters to the Villa. These were less pressing, though equally devastating.

Final totals of casualties from previous attacks. Lists of buildings the Chamberites had destroyed across Elandria. The dwindling number of Messengers that still served Elandria and hadn't returned home in fear. Treasury reports. Calculations of harvest yields.

His head spun with numbers by the time he made it to the modest dining room. He ate alone, save the three servants who stood at the ready for his every whim. Ridiculous. He didn't need the ceremony or this many people waiting on him hand and foot. But if he dismissed them, they would be without work.

After dinner, he dictated letters to Andin and had them sent out for meetings the next day. There were a handful of loyal ministers still in Teleah, and he needed to update them. He also wanted to speak to the head of the Treasury about ensuring the safety of Elandria's vaults. He hated this tedium. It was necessary, but it felt close to inaction. If he could, he would lead all of his forces straight to the north to take out the bulk of the invading forces. Then he'd speed across Elandria with his army and force the rest of them to leave. He'd lead every battle himself, sword high above his head as he charged. But that was foolish and guaranteed to fail.

He pushed his hero fantasies out of his mind as he stretched out in his bed. The darkness was lonely. Even the moonlight through his curtains was pale tonight. Perhaps he could send for a couple of lovers from the nearby brothel. It would distract him. But it didn't sound fun. It sounded exhausting, and he wondered if he was falling ill or just getting old.

Raymond thought about Amarice and the others, who were surely camping in the southern moorlands by now. Amarice had selected a route off the main roads, avoiding villages they knew had fallen to the Chamberites. He wished he could be with them.

His thoughts shifted to Elaine and their conversation at breakfast. When Amarice returned, he'd have to tell her she was wrong about the Corthy woman. Elaine wasn't dim. She was lost and had been silenced her whole life, but she was sharp and witty.

She was also pretty. He wondered what she would look like if she let her light-brown hair frame her face. Maybe she would get comfortable with Elandria's fashions soon. She would look exquisite in a loose linen tunic and pants. She would look free.

He fell asleep and rested well for the first time in a long time.

CHAPTER 7

AMARICE

The journey across the south of Elandria was cold, wet, and miserable by the second day. Amarice and Jack, who usually used earth magic to warm themselves, piled themselves with cloaks to save their energy in case they needed it for an attack. Amarice could ease the storm, but it would take too much of her Gift. It provided cover, too, and kept curious eyes out of their way. The small party ducked their heads against the wind and rain as they rode. No one talked unless necessary, as they had to yell to be heard.

They had made it through the southern moorlands without incident. The villages in the south were sparse and far apart, so it was easy to avoid the ones taken by the Chamberites. Amarice stayed away from the loyal villages, as well, lest word of the Sage heading south went out. Nine days into their journey, Amarice pitched her tent two miles outside of one of the larger towns. Jack and Corbin had gone into town with a plain-clothed Gracyn to replenish their supplies. Willum helped Amarice stake down her tent against the biting wind.

"I hope they bring back some sausage," Willum said. "If I eat one more piece of jerky, I might die."

Amarice gave a dry laugh. "I'd be happy with some fruit. Atsila keeps giving me begging eyes, so she's taken all of my apples."

One of the other soldiers, Malena, swore, and Amarice looked over. "What's wrong?"

"I can't get the damn fire to stay lit in this fucking wind," the young woman said.

Amarice hurried over and waved her hands over the pile of logs. Large flames erupted from the wood. They consumed the dry kindling in an instant and emanated heat several feet out. This fire would burn until Amarice put it out herself, wind or rain be damned.

Malena's eyes widened. "Wow."

"Keep an eye on it," Amarice said. "Let me know if it burns out of control." She turned back and disappeared into her tent to make her bed.

She lay on her bedroll until she heard the others return with dinner. Sighing, she pulled herself up and dusted the earth off her traveling clothes.

"Amarice!" Jack's voice was almost as chipper as usual, after days of silent brooding. "I bought firewine!"

"Firewine?"

"The Feast of Fire is tonight," he reminded her.

"Is it?" How had she forgotten? She wondered if the Villa was celebrating at all. She hoped so. They deserved a celebration, and there were thousands of Deyoni and Scholars without homes who did, too. The Feast of Fire was about burning the griefs of your year.

Elandria had a lot to grieve.

"Did you get any chrysanthemums?" she asked Jack.

He rummaged in his sack and pulled out a small pack of seeds. "This was all they had left. The already bloomed ones were gone."

"That's fine. It should be plenty. Will you plant them?"

He grinned. "Of course."

She sat on a log and watched as Gracyn put a pan over the fire to prepare dinner. Jack dug through the hard, cold soil with his bare hands and buried the seeds in the ground. He waved his hands over the small earthen mound. Sprouts emerged and bloomed into vibrant yellow and red chrysanthemums.

This was like no Feast of Fire Amarice had ever celebrated. The nine companions passed bottles of firewine around the small pyre as they watched the sausages sizzle. Willum chewed with a look of contentment on his round face. Amarice stopped drinking when her head began to feel heavy. She would love nothing more than to lose herself to the numbness of the alcohol. But she needed to be sober enough to protect her companions should anything happen.

After they ate a dinner of meat, bread, and fresh cheese, Deben began to sing an old Deyoni folk song while stroking his falcon perched on his arm. Amarice closed her eyes, savoring his rich tenor voice and remembering how her mother used to sing it. She mouthed the words to the mournful tune, a story of lost love and regret. A single tear ran down her cheek.

Across the way, the dancing flames illuminated several tear-stained faces. She wondered if they could tell what the song was about even without knowing Deyoni. Perhaps it was just the sadness in Deben's voice. He had his own lost love, and he poured his soul into every note.

She glanced at Jack, who stared into the fire, deep in thought. He, too, had a lost love. Only Rafe had never known. Jack's family lived far away, and they weren't close. Quinn was the only family he had left.

She thought of Quinn and hoped he would appear in her dreams again tonight. He had a few times, but her sleep since they began traveling had been broken and sparse. It took effort to speak to each other, and when they did, Amarice woke drained of her magic. So, they sat in silence, letting their presence say what they couldn't.

When Deben finished the song, he threw three chrysanthemums in the fire, mouthing the names of Eleanor and two people Amarice didn't know. His parents, perhaps. The others threw their own flowers into the flames and watched them burn. Everyone tossed in a flower for King Roland.

Too many of Amarice's people had been lost in recent years. She would never remember most of the names, although she read the lists of every report of losses she received. She always spoke the names with an apology, but there were too many to recall now. People she couldn't protect. Couldn't save. Roland, who had been the only father figure she ever knew, had died trying to protect her. She let her heart speak the names instead as she threw the last of the chrysanthemums into the fire.

This year, the fire didn't feel cleansing. It didn't lift grief from her shoulders or lighten her heart. She went to bed, her soul laden with shame.

Her dream that night was the worst she had ever had. Dark mountains ran with rivers of blood. Her ears rang with ghostly wails and screams. The molten blood washed over her feet, and she couldn't move away. She opened her mouth to scream for help, but the sound died on her lips.

"Amarice!"

She turned her head. Quinn was rushing toward her through the red running rivers. He was here. He was here to save her. She reached out a hand as he came nearer. Their fingertips brushed, just as the darkness swept her away.

She woke with Quinn's name as a shout on her lips. Sweat poured from her brow and neck, as if the heat from the bubbling blood had been real. She sat up, panting and clutching at her chest.

Something terrible had happened. The worst thing to happen to Elandria yet. And what had it meant that Quinn slipped away? She couldn't bear it if their rescue mission failed. Once her breathing eased, Amarice curled into a ball and cried herself back to sleep.

TWO DAYS LATER, Amarice and the others pulled their horses to a stop at the edge of the craggy southern mountains that barred the rest of Elandria from the sea. A narrow mountain road laid two hundred yards in front of them. A three-hour ride down that road, and they would reach Citadel Kahyrst.

And Quinn.

They had made good time. Their horses were bred for hard riding, and the riders were determined to save Quinn. Their exhaustion could not compete with their motivation.

The air was frigid but still, and the sun shone high overhead. Amarice looked at the sky to determine the time.

"Two hours till sunset," she said to the others. "We'll camp here and get a good night's rest."

The rest of them set to work making camp. Amarice walked away from them toward the mountain road. She needed time to pull all her strength from the earth. It would not do to have her magic drain halfway through a fight.

She sat on a patch of grass near the road and meditated, clearing her mind and pulling the Gift of the Earth into her essence. After about an hour, she stood, letting the magic thrum through her veins.

She walked back to camp. Someone had set up her tent for her— Corbin, probably. Or Willum. The fire was already going, and a pot of stew was simmering. Deben was watching Eleanor fly and hunt. Amarice was certain they were facing more roasted rabbit tomorrow.

Amarice pulled a map from her saddlebag and spread it out on the ground. She placed small stones on the corners, then knelt over it with her brow furrowed. Willum and Gracyn came to join her, and they spent the next hour strategizing.

Once Raymond had told her which fortress Quinn was in based on his description, she had found a book about it in her library. She had spent several evenings of their trip learning the layout of the ancient building and figuring out where Quinn was being held. She sketched the grounds on a piece of paper and laid it next to the map before calling everyone over.

Corbin sheathed his sword; he had been practicing dueling with Malena and the other soldiers and was quite skilled. Jack was practicing using his magic as a weapon and had great control of the wind. He, too, had a sword, in case he drained too quickly or needed something sharp to fight with instead.

"We'll leave at first light," Amarice said. "We'll need time to get far enough away before sundown, and we don't know what condition

Quinn will be in to travel." Or if he'll be in any condition to travel. She pushed the thought out of her mind.

Gracyn pointed to a few spots on the map. "This is where we anticipate their scouts. If the weather is as clear tomorrow, the Sage will conjure storm clouds to cloak us in some level of darkness. But they'll still likely know we're coming."

"The prison cells are here," Amarice pointed at her drawing of Citadel Kahyrst. "We'll need to take out anyone in the way. Jack and Deben, you'll stay with three of the soldiers to keep anyone from coming after us. Corbin and I will go with the other two to find Quinn."

It wasn't a perfect plan. Amarice might be better off outside the tower, depending on how heavily guarded it was. It was more likely that the majority of the forces—however many there were—would be in other buildings. But she needed to find Quinn. To see him alive with her own eyes. And those guards would put up a larger fight. She couldn't be in two places at once.

"Willum and I will have your back, my lady," Gracyn said.

"Always, m'lady." Willum winked. "We'd follow you anywhere."

"I'll take point outside," Malena said. Gracyn nodded in agreement.

"Very well." Amarice stood and looked down at her companions. "We'll be outnumbered by dozens. But I will do whatever I can to keep you all safe. Get some rest."

CHAPTER 8

QUINN

Quinn let the cool water slide down his throat, quenching his thirst. He tried to savor it. Though they now gave him more water and food, it still wasn't much. He couldn't help but see the irony that it was Samperian who was saving him from dying of dehydration or hunger. It was also Samperian who had him imprisoned here.

The devout minister arrived a few days before and yelled at the guards who watched over Quinn.

"Fools!" he had shouted. "We need him alive! If he dies, we can't tell the bitch where he is."

From what he had deduced, Samperian had planned to reveal Quinn's location to the king's spies when something happened. He wasn't sure what they were waiting on, but they were counting on Amarice leaving the Villa to come rescue him. And that didn't bode well for the people who were residing there. The thought of how many people could die pierced his soul. But whatever Samperian was planning involved Quinn being alive, so his food rations had increased, as had his water. It wasn't enough for him to regain his health, but at least he didn't feel like he was about to die.

Maybe that wasn't a good thing.

The skies were dark today through the cracks in the ceiling. Ominous. He dreaded the rain that would leak into his cell, chilling him to the bone.

He slurped the gruel they had served him. It was bland and thick, but it was sustenance. He had stopped retching at the taste weeks ago. As he drained the last dregs from the small wooden bowl, he heard panicked shouts below.

And then the earth moved.

The vibrations rocked the surface of the tower and roared in Quinn's ears. Stones and dust fell from the ceiling, and Quinn had to cover his head with shackled arms. His heart pounded as the tower continued to shake. His weak, dormant magic prickled under his skin, calling to its other half.

Could it be?

The shaking stopped.

Screams.

The clash of swords.

Harried orders shouted by captains.

Moments later, five guards pounded up the spiral stone staircase to Quinn's cell and set a formation, blocking anyone from coming up.

He couldn't stop himself from asking, "What's happening?"

"Shut up, you insufferable bastard!"

He inched into the far corner. Standing was difficult, but he wanted to avoid as much wild magic as he could, in case Amarice really was here. He wouldn't let himself believe it until he saw her.

Through the high, barred window, Quinn saw lightning strike, and more screams echoed through the air, this time in agony. Wind swirled and roared, creating a cacophony of nature with the crashing waves of the sea. Earthquakes came and went, and he heard parts of the other buildings toppling down to the ground.

A mighty gust of wind swept up the tower, knocking several of the guards—and Quinn—off balance. He tried to pull whatever magic he could from it, but he feared he wouldn't be much help. And the irons around his wrists and ankles didn't help at all.

One guard looked back at Quinn in the cell. The weakened Consort saw fear written over the young man's face. He hadn't signed up for this, to face the Sage of Elandria in battle.

"If you surrender, she'll spare you," Quinn told him. His voice was hoarse. He had spoken little during his imprisonment.

The young soldier trembled but shook his head. Whether it was pride or embarrassment or zealotry, Quinn wasn't sure. Whatever it was would be his downfall.

"By the Mother and Father," he heard another guard say. "Save me. Save us all."

Quinn felt heat rising in the stone tower, heat with the distinctive flair of Amarice's magic. Fire. Whatever the guards could see must have been terrifying. Their armor rattled as they quaked. Sweat from the ascending swelter beaded on Quinn's forehead. His heart thudded like it was trying to escape his chest, to find its way to her.

He heard her voice.

"Open his cell and give him to me, and I'll let you live."

No one spoke.

"Give me the keys, then. And run."

Silence, though Quinn could hear their breathing come in heavy pants.

"Very well."

A whoosh. And a scream. Quinn had never heard a sound like that in his life. The agony of the soldier hit Quinn in his stomach. The young guard closest to Quinn vomited at whatever he saw. When the screaming stopped, there was a long pause.

"Y-you burned him alive," a guard said. "You're a bloody witch."

The man charged. Swords clashed, and a loud crack sounded. A thud. More shouts. More swords. The air crackled with magic, and the tower shook. Amarice cried out.

"No!"

"You fucking asshole!" a familiar voice yelled.

There was lightning. There was lightning inside, and Quinn didn't understand how that was possible. The smell of burning hair and burning flesh singed his nostrils even in the corner of his cell.

His ears became numb to the screams of agony. The young guard in front of his cell curled into a ball on the ground. Quinn crawled toward him.

"Do you have the keys?"

The boy shook his head. Quinn reached through the metal bars and touched his shoulder. The soldier jumped. "Do you know who does?"

Slowly, he extended an arm and pointed at a fallen comrade. In the staircase, battle still raged on.

"Get the keys. Get the keys, and I'll protect you. I promise." Quinn squeezed his shoulder weakly; his hands were raw from the cold. "You can do it. Get the keys."

He watched as the guard got to his knees. The smell hit Quinn; the young soldier had soiled himself. He didn't blame him. Shaking, the boy inched his way to the fallen body of his fellow soldier. His hands trembled as he removed the keys from the belt.

"Good. You can do it. Just a little farther."

The soldier was too scared to stand, but he crawled over and handed Quinn the keys through the bars. Quinn grasped the cold metal and fumbled with the keys. He stuck several in the locks of his ankle shackles, trying to find the right one. When he found it and removed the irons, blood rushed into his feet, and it hurt like a thousand tiny daggers. But he pulled himself to standing and unlocked the manacles around his wrists. He shook his hands out and felt magic spark under his skin.

Interesting. He wasn't sure whether the iron had dulled his magic or if it was the rush of being free, but there was no time for magical theory. He reached through the bars of the prison cell that had been his home for the last few weeks and put the largest key in the lock.

It turned with a loud click.

Quinn pushed open the metal door with effort. It groaned against the stone floor. He took a tentative step out, worried his feeble legs would crumble underneath him. He looked at the solider on the ground, who was rocking back and forth, his eyes wide with fear.

"Thank you," the Consort said. "You'll be all right. Stay here."

"He b-burned."

"I know."

Quinn peered down the staircase at the cluster of fighting bodies, trying to find Amarice. He could see a flash of long, brown hair, but that was it. He had regained some of his magic, but he couldn't try much, in fear that it would be wild and cause damage he didn't intend.

Blood spurted from wounds and men moaned. The staircase wasn't wide, and Amarice couldn't make it farther up the stairs until the handful of guards either surrendered or died. Bodies lined the steps.

Amarice was pinned against a wall. Quinn could only see the top of her head, but she was surrounded by three soldiers. She swore, and the walls shook. He had to do something.

He picked up a dead soldier's sword. In his frail state, he struggled to lift it. Then Amarice screamed, and he found residual strength. He charged down the steps and stabbed a guard from behind, straight through his back and into his bowels. The guard crumbled.

"What the fu—?" But Quinn silenced the next soldier before he could react. He took out one more before he fell, unable to continue.

It worked, though. The soldiers surrounding Amarice looked away, giving her a chance to gain the upper hand. She cracked the foundation of the stairs, and they fell, dropping their weapons. She took a dagger from her belt and sliced their throats.

"Quinn!"

She leapt over bodies. Blood-stained face and matted hair, with slices on her arms and her tunic in tatters, Quinn had never seen something so beautiful. He couldn't believe she was here.

"Oh, my love." She grabbed his hand and pulled. "You need to stand. Can you stand? We have to get out of here."

Quinn nodded and got to his feet.

"Careful now." She kicked a body out of the way. "A few steps are missing."

He kept his hand in hers, savoring her touch, not wanting to ever let her go again. A familiar man stood in front of them, parrying a stab from a guard. "Corbin?"

Corbin turned, and the soldier narrowly missed him. "Quinn!"

Amarice let go of Quinn's hand and conjured a ball of fire from thin air. The soldier fighting Corbin dropped his sword and ran down the stairs, pushing the others out of his way.

"Gracyn!" Amarice said. "Move!"

Gracyn plastered himself against the wall, and the Sage launched a ball of flames down the stairs. It caught one of the fleeing soldiers, and the others ran away screaming. Quinn held down the bile that crept up his throat at the sight of the burning man. He fell to the ground, and Amarice waved her hands. The flames disappeared.

"We have to go," Amarice said. "Hurry!"

"But Willum!" Gracyn's face was pained. Quinn looked down to see his old traveling companion dead on the stairs, cold eyes staring up at him.

"Willum." A tear ran down Quinn's face. His friend had died rescuing him.

"I need you to fight," Amarice said. "I'm sorry, Gracyn. We can't take him."

Quinn knelt down and closed Willum's eyes. He didn't have the strength to carry his friend out, either.

Gracyn nodded and wiped the blood from his face. "Burn him. Please. I don't want them touching his body."

Amarice waved a hand and gentle flames caressed Willum's body. Quinn looked away.

"We must go and help the others," Amarice said.

Quinn looked to the top of the stairs. The young guard was still there, cowering. "Corbin," he said in a hoarse voice. "There's a guard. He helped me. I told him I'd protect him."

"I'll get him." Corbin took the stairs two at a time.

"Quinn, my love. We have to leave."

With one final glance at Willum's burning figure, he took Amarice's hand and followed her down the stairs.

CHAPTER 9

AMARICE

Amarice blinked in the sunlight as they exited the tower. Her earlier storm had dissipated; she hadn't had the magic to maintain it while fighting inside the prison. Quinn squeezed her hand, and she took a deep breath. He was safe.

So far.

Deben and Jack were still standing, along with Malena. The other two soldiers had fallen. These three had somehow kept the rest of the Chamberite soldiers from entering the tower. Deben's hawk was clawing out someone's eyes while Deben fought another one. Melena was fighting three soldiers. And Jack had his hands in the air, manipulating the wind to launch stones at the enemy.

Samperian stood on the ruins of a small storehouse, screaming at his soldiers to advance, and his soldiers tried. Dozens of bodies lined the courtyard. Large cracks in the foundation and the earth had taken several victims in the earlier onslaught.

"Quinn, our horses are a half-mile away. We have to get past these soldiers. Can you make it?"

"I don't know," he said.

She glanced around. Corbin had helped the young guard out of the tower. The soldier had scrambled away to safety. "Corbin, help Quinn. Keep him safe."

Jack turned. His face was white, and his hands shook with the effort of his magic. "Amarice, I can't do much more."

"Just a bit longer, Jack. I need to focus."

He gave her a weak nod.

Amarice was draining, too. But she could go on. She had to.

"Move forward," she shouted.

She stamped her foot on the ground, and a forceful rumble came from the depths of the earth. She poured her magic into it, forcing it to ripple outward. The surrounding tremors pulled everyone to the ground. Sweat dripped from her brow, and her head throbbed.

The tower cracked. Stones fell from the top, and Amarice narrowly dodged one. But she pressed on. Soon it began to crumble faster, and all around her, she heard the thunder of other buildings of Citadel Kahyrst begin to fall.

The ancient prison tower imploded on itself with a reverberating roar, burying Willum and the dead Chamberites in the rubble. Amarice released her hold over the earth. She doubled over, spent.

"Amarice." Quinn's voice was gentle in her ear. A refuge amidst the echoes of destruction that surrounded them. "Amarice. You can do it."

She melted into his touch, his hand on the small of her back, and she straightened to see his face. Streaks of dirt marred his pallid complexion. But beyond the dark circles beneath his eyes, bright brown flickered in the sunlight. Her magic pulled to his, like a lodestone in a broken compass finding its way back to true north. His gaze seared through her, waking the embers of her dwindling magic like bellows. She found the last of her strength in him.

Always in him.

"Fire," she whispered.

He nodded with a spark in his eyes, and she knew he understood her completely. Her magic—the magic that destroyed the centuries-old fortress—flowed through him, forcing his own into action. A warmth rushed through her veins, urgently spreading to her Consort. He gripped her hand, and they faced their enemies together.

Amidst the tumbling stone towers, the Chamberite force was in disarray. Some screamed in agony from injuries, and others ran. Some were trapped under fallen rubble. From his higher ground, Samperian still barked orders that most of his men ignored.

Together, Amarice and Quinn summoned fire and razed Citadel Kahyrst to the ground.

A blaze erupted. The fire consumed everything in its path. Amarice controlled the flames into a barrier between the Chamberites and her small retinue. Black smoke filled the air, stinging her eyes and singeing her nose. But with Quinn's complementary magic, she maintained control. A path through the fire led to the sea beyond the fortress.

Samperian's icy hatred could be seen even through the smoke. Fear and fury sizzled from his stare as he ran past her, yelling for his men to retreat. The fire followed them to the sea.

"I should go after him," she said once all the Chamberites had fled the grounds of the fortress. But Quinn fell to the ground. He was too weak, too sick, too depleted. "Oh, my love. All right. We're almost safe."

The fires burned and spread, and she needed to get the remaining company to safety. She didn't think she had the magic to contain the fire should it burn out of control. With great strain, she waved a hand and cleared one small path toward the mountain passage.

Deben and Corbin pulled Quinn to his feet and led him out the gate to the road. Malena and Jack followed behind, swords still drawn. Gracyn gazed at the fallen tower, his face wet with blood and tears. Amarice took his arm and led him away.

❧

THE HALF-MILE WALK to the small crevice where they had left the horses was the longest walk of Amarice's life. She was mentally, physically, and emotionally drained. Her magic was completely depleted for only the second time in her life; the last time, she had been able to curl up in the woods and fall asleep after killing her kidnappers.

No one spoke. They had lost three of their company. Willum had been a friend, and she hadn't been able to protect him. Her throat constricted at the thought. One more person she couldn't keep safe. One more person lost on her watch. She kept her eyes on Quinn's back as he ambled, supported by his father and brother. At least she had saved him. She could handle anything with Quinn by her side.

Their horses glanced up at their approach, unaware of the devastation that had just occurred. No one had touched them during the fight. Amarice had taken out the handful of scouts with strikes of lightning and gusts of wind that knocked them from their lookout positions in the mountains. Nivasi chuffed and stamped her hooves when she saw Quinn. She had missed her master.

"I think we're safe to stop for a few minutes," Amarice said. "I want to assess Quinn."

Corbin helped Quinn to a large boulder. But he stood and held his arms out to Amarice. Amarice let herself fall into his embrace. She clung to him. Unable to stop the tears from falling, she cried into his shoulder. His arms, so much thinner than she remembered, held her close, and he rested his head on top of hers.

He coughed, and she pulled away. "How long have you been sick?"

"Probably since the second week," he said.

"I have something for that," Jack said. He rummaged in his saddlebag and pulled out a glass bottle. He handed it to Quinn. "Take a swig. Twice a day for a week, and you'll be back to normal."

Quinn drank, then pulled his friend into a hug. "Thank you."

"I couldn't lose you, too." Only Quinn and Amarice heard his whispered words.

Amarice and Jack fussed over Quinn, forcing water and various tinctures down his throat, while Deben and Corbin embraced him and told him how glad they were he was safe. They ate a bit of jerky and apples until Amarice decided it was time to go.

"Can you ride, my love?"

Quinn nodded. "I should be fine."

Deben helped Quinn onto Nivasi. Corbin took on one of the now riderless horses and pulled one of the others behind him. Malena led the group out through the mountain pass, and Amarice brought up the rear.

When the path widened, Quinn pulled Nivasi alongside Gracyn. Amarice listened to their conversation with a heavy heart.

"I'm sorry about Willum. He was a good friend."

Gracyn gave Quinn a sad smile. "Me, too."

"Thank you. For coming with Amarice."

"I'd follow her into the abyss. Willum would, too. He would have been proud of dying trying to protect the two of you."

Quinn nodded. "I know. But I'm still sorry he's gone, noble death or no."

"Yeah. I'll be lost without him." He said nothing else, and Quinn didn't either. Behind them, Amarice took a deep breath. She could hear their guilt, but it was hers to bear. She had promised to protect them all.

The sun was high when they left the narrow, craggy road in their wake. But Amarice wanted them to make it farther before stopping for the evening. She knew Quinn must ache from riding for three hours after weeks of imprisonment. But she didn't want to run the risk that Samperian would lead his dwindling forces after them. Another hour, and they would be near the woods. They could hide.

As they rode on the open plain with the southern mountains behind them, Quinn fell back to talk to Amarice.

"They were planning something. They wanted to lure you away from the Villa."

Amarice nodded. "The thought crossed my mind. But why did they keep your location a secret if they wanted me gone?"

Quinn shifted in the saddle. "They were waiting on something. I don't know for what or for how long. But Samperian made it sound like it was a matter of weeks. Perhaps."

"Well, hopefully, you threw their plans off by reaching me in our dreams." She smiled at him. "Brilliant, by the way."

"I was delirious enough not to talk myself out of it with rationality."

She laughed a little. Quinn extended his hand to cover hers where they lay on Atsila's reins. "You saved me, Amarice."

"Did you doubt me?" She winked at him.

"Of course not."

"I would do anything for you, Quinn. My soul, my magic—it's not whole without you."

She halted Atsila, and Quinn pulled on Nivasi's reins. She leaned over in her saddle and placed a gentle kiss on her Consort's lips. "I love you."

"I love you, too."

"Never get kidnapped again."

CHAPTER 10

RAYMOND

The king had taken to pacing the halls of the palace. As a boy with too much restless energy, he'd spent hours climbing up and down stairs and exploring every nook and cranny of the castle. He never had a destination in mind. He just liked to move. Coddiwomple, his nanny called it. Walking without a purpose. Very unkingly.

When he was a little older, he would ditch his nanny and explore Teleah. Everyone knew who he was, but even if they didn't, Teleah had always been a safe city. He continued his habit through his four years at the Academy and his apprenticeship year in Parliament. He liked the freedom to think while he walked.

But Teleah wasn't safe now. Most of the Scholars had fled the city. Though the capital wasn't in open rebellion, there were too many pockets of Chamberites hidden throughout the ancient city. And there were those who didn't care about the political aspect of the war; they just wanted to loot the abandoned businesses.

So, Raymond spent hours wandering the halls of the palace. He'd read his morning updates with breakfast, then wander. Have meetings, then wander. Eat dinner and relay correspondence to Andin, then wander. He worried about Amarice and the others. He still wasn't entirely convinced that Amarice's dream had been real. But it was specific, and they had deduced Quinn was likely in the south. He hoped they wouldn't run into any trouble on their journey and wished again he had sent more troops with them.

He paused in front of the coronation portrait of his father, King Roland. Roland had been young when he'd taken the throne, losing his mother the queen to a horseback riding injury at twenty-three. Raymond was born the next year, and Roland's wife died in childbirth.

"How do I know if I made the right choice?" he said to the painting. That's what plagued his thoughts most these days. He made many choices, none of them easy. And he constantly second-guessed himself.

The painting of his father didn't reply. Raymond continued wandering the halls. He had a meeting with two ministers later in the afternoon. One of them was acting as a spymaster for the western part of Elandria, and she had news from the spies in Te'eh. Raymond glanced at his watch. He still had an hour and a half. Wandering the halls wasn't a great use of his time. He headed down to the inner courtyard where he knew his private guard was training.

Staying sharp with a sword was important, so he decided to join them for practice. He would need it before the war was over. He made his way downstairs and threw his tunic on a bench before pairing up with the captain of his guard.

They bowed to each other and began their fight. It wasn't long before Raymond was dripping in sweat.

"Don't go easy on me, Erenia!"

The captain laughed through heavy breaths. She wasn't going easy on Raymond, and they both knew it. "Just wouldn't want to hurt your majesty's precious royal skin."

Raymond parried and darted away, forcing Erenia to spin on her feet and nearly lose her balance. The king thrust his sword, and Erenia avoided the jab by an inch. They continued for a while, matched in both skill and good-natured insults.

After several minutes, Raymond managed to sneak up on Erenia and knock her to the ground. Erenia yielded, and Raymond pulled her to her feet. "Good match."

"Indeed, your highness. I'll get you next time."

Raymond smiled and wiped his brow on his loose undershirt. "I'm sure you will." He looked at his watch and bade the others goodbye. It was time for his meeting.

RAYMOND WOKE the next day to the first light of the sun. A lovely woman lay next to him, her curly, dark hair splayed out on his blue silk pillows. He pulled himself quietly from the bed so as not to wake her. He dressed and tiptoed out the door to the front room of his chambers where his valet was waiting.

"Good morning, sir," Andin said.

"Morning. What's on the agenda?"

"It's the Feast of Fire, sir. I have overseen arrangements at your request. It will just be members of the staff and your personal guard and their families. The feast begins at seven o'clock."

"Excellent." He took a sip of coffee. "Andin, what do you make of the news from yesterday?"

"From Te'eh, sir?"

"Yes."

"It is odd that Azmar would return only to leave her city again. Te'eh would make a good base of operations for the war."

"I agree. I wonder where they will set up. Beybrook, perhaps. Or the south." If the Chamberites increased forces at the southern fortress, that did not bode well for Amarice and the others. Even the Sage could not defeat an entire army by herself. He pinched his brows. "I'll head down to breakfast. Make sure to tip the lady well, please."

"Of course, my lord."

Raymond ate breakfast alone. It would be his first Feast of Fire without his father, and it hurt. Tonight, he would throw a chrysanthemum in the flames for the lost king. He had dreaded this night and had hoped Amarice and Quinn would be there to support him. He had never felt more alone. No one should spend holidays without their loved ones.

He wondered what the Villa would do for the Feast of Fire. It was always a spectacle when the Sage was there, with her Deyoni dance magic and powerful Gift of the Earth. And Madge's feast was a delight. He thought of Elaine and wished that her first Feast at the Villa could be amazing. But it wouldn't be, not with Quinn missing and Corbin gone. He imagined the Deyoni tribes in the mountains would celebrate with acrobatics and dancing and song. The Scholar refugees would enjoy it. The two groups had moved past their tentative acceptance to friendship in recent months. It was what Amarice had dreamed about, uniting the magical peoples of Elandria. But he also suspected that is what kept more people from joining the military. Now they had more loved ones to keep them from running off to war.

His recruiting campaign two weeks ago had only gotten them three hundred Deyoni men. No women, and no Scholars. If their numbers didn't increase soon in the territories they still held, he would have to resort to conscription. And he didn't want to do that.

It may have been a holiday, but he was the king, and it was wartime. He locked himself in his study after breakfast to catch up on his correspondence. Andin was busy overseeing holiday arrangements, but Raymond didn't mind. He enjoyed the silence.

He wished he could receive a letter from Amarice. But with the Messenger numbers dwindling, they couldn't risk her letter falling into the wrong hands. He had only told his closest advisors that the Sage had left the Villa, but he imagined her absence had been noted by the people camping in the Sage's mountains.

He wandered the halls awhile, then soaked in a long bath before the festivities started. He let himself cry a little for his father before he dressed in his finest red-and-gold tunic and headed downstairs for the feast.

The staff had opened the large dining room for as many of the palace guard and their families as could fit. Though not feeling social, Raymond chatted with his loyal soldiers and cracked jokes with their children. The families of the castle staff were in the ballroom, and he made a point to stop by and visit them before the bonfire started.

There was no Scholar to light the bonfire with magic. Raymond's magic wasn't strong enough, and the rest of the people were regular Elandrians. It took a long time for the bonfire to catch and grow large enough. When it did, Raymond gathered a bundle of yellow chrysanthemums—his father's favorite color—and placed several in the fire to honor all the innocent Elandrian lives lost.

He stared at the last flower, the heat of the fire drawing beads of sweat from his forehead. He heard whispers behind him, and he knew he was taking too long. He cleared his throat.

"King Roland. Father," he said, loudly enough that those nearby could hear him. Then he threw the flower into the flames and watched it burn into ashes.

Many flowers would be burned for the king tonight. He hoped his father knew how many people had loved him. Raymond stepped back into the crowd. Someone handed him a glass of firewine, and he watched as others stepped forward to burn their own griefs.

He went to bed early and tired. He didn't drink much, and he thought Amarice would be pleased that he was trying to keep a clear head. But for the first time in a long time, he fell asleep in a matter of minutes, drained from the emotions of the holiday.

A loud rapping pulled him from his sleep, and he bolted upright, bleary-eyed and confused.

"My lord!" Andin shouted through the door. "My lord!"

"Come in!" Raymond said. "Brigitte's tit, what is the matter, man? What time is it?"

Andin stood in the door's entry. "The Villa has been attacked. A battle is underway now."

Raymond leapt from the bed and fumbled in the dark for his pants to dress. "Send word to rouse the troops and ready my horse. I need my armor."

"Right away, sir." The valet rushed away.

Raymond lit the lamp on his dresser and blinked as his eyes adjusted. The clock read two thirty in the morning. The fastest anyone could make it from the Villa, at the speed of a Messenger, was two-and-a-half hours. He hoped someone had come at the first sign of attack. Still, there was a chance the battle would be long over before he arrived.

Long over and lost.

Andin returned with Raymond's armor. He helped dress the king in a hurry and followed him downstairs as Raymond barked orders for him to do once he left.

The king's guard was ready and waiting outside the front doors of the palace by the time Raymond made it outside. He mounted Sterling and kicked the stallion into a run.

"Be safe, my lord," he heard his valet shout over the thunder of fifty horses' hooves.

Raymond sped to the northern gates of the city, leading his guard. The rest of his troops wouldn't be far behind. Dying bonfires still illuminated the town outside the city gates, lighting the road they traveled on. The cold wind carried the smell of smoke, burning his nostrils.

He bent low over his horse and charged toward the Sage's Mountains.

CHAPTER 11

AMARICE

Amarice woke the next day, happy for the first time in weeks. The thoughts of losing Willum and the others hadn't entered her sleepy mind yet. But when she roused, she was able to curl against Quinn's warm body in their tent. She placed a hand on his chest, feeling the rise and fall of his breathing. He was alive. Weak and sick, but alive. Once they had made it to the woods and set up camp, Amarice and Jack had assessed his health in more detail. He had an infection in his lungs, but he would recover. He had some wounds from the pressure of the shackles, but the salves would treat them easily.

Amarice was certain that if Samperian's forces hadn't found them by now, they must have left by way of the sea. She decided to give her group a day to rest.

And grieve.

She swallowed the lump in her throat. Willum was gone. He was so young, so full of life. And now he was dead, lost to the abyss. Tears stung her eyes but didn't fall. She blinked them away.

Quinn stirred. She smiled as she traced her fingers in patterns on his chest. Part of her had thought she would never touch him again, never study his face in the early morning light. She raised her head to see if he was awake. The last dregs of sleep blurred his big brown eyes, but upon seeing her, a grin spread across his face.

"Good morning." His voice was hoarse from coughing through the night. "How did you sleep?"

"Better, now that you're by my side. Although I woke up when your fever broke. Your skin was a fire."

Quinn raised a hand to wipe his brow. "Explains why I'm so sweaty. Jack's tinctures work fast."

"Don't think you're getting out of your next dose," Amarice said. She lay her head back down on Quinn's shoulder. He shifted to put an arm around her and pulled her close. "I'm so glad you're all right."

"Me, too." He kissed the top of her head. "Me, too."

Empty words hung between them as they lay in silence. There would come a time when they could talk about their fears, about their experiences without each other. But not today. They stayed in their tent, not talking, until Amarice heard a rumble from Quinn's stomach.

"Let's get you some food," she said.

"No chance you brought me a change of clothes, is there?"

She sat up. "Of course. What do you take me for?"

Once dressed, they crawled out from their small tent. Amarice knew she'd miss her large, Deyoni tent soon now that Quinn was with her, but she didn't care right now. A sweet and smoky smell wafted toward them. Deben was cooking squirrels over the fire. His smile at the sight of Quinn brought tears to Amarice's eyes.

"Come, sit! Sit! The food is almost done. Eleanor and I woke early to hunt so that you could have fresh meat."

"Thank you, Father." Quinn sat, his face twisting in pain from the movement. Amarice studied him with concern. He needed something else for the pain. Poppy tea, perhaps. She'd ask him later and turned toward Deben.

"Where is everyone else?" Amarice asked.

"Still asleep. It is very early, and yesterday was a long day." Deben handed her a tin plate of meat and waterskin, and she inclined her head in thanks.

"Indeed, it was." She chewed the tough, nutty squirrel meat. Squirrel wasn't terrible when it was slow roasted with butter and seasonings, but this was dry. She took several sips of the cool water to wash down the meat. It wasn't her breakfast of choice, but it would be good for Quinn to regain his strength.

Quinn, on the other hand, devoured the meal and asked for more. Amarice reminded him not to overeat, lest his body reject the sudden uptick in food quantity. He slowed down a little.

Jack was the next to wake, and he threw his arms around Quinn from behind. "I was worried that I'd dreamed you were alive and well."

Quinn laughed, which turned into a cough.

"'Well' might not be the best descriptor," Amarice said. "He needs more medicine. And perhaps poppy tea for the pain?"

"No." Quinn shook his head. "No poppy tea. I spent too many weeks drugged. I want a clear head."

Over the next half hour, the others awoke. Gracyn's confident posture was gone, replaced by hunched shoulders and red eyes. Amarice's heart ached for him. Malena acted fine, though Amarice noticed her staring off into the distance, lost in her thoughts. Amarice wasn't sure how close she was to the other soldiers, but losing your comrades was never easy.

Amarice announced that they would rest and leave at first light in the morning. She made Quinn lay down to rest. Most of her motivations were pure; she wanted him to heal, and his body needed sleep. But she also wanted time with just him, away from the others. She stretched out next to him and studied the maps in the filtered sunlight of the tent.

Not hearing any news from Raymond or the Villa was bothering her. She hadn't focused on it much during the journey to rescue Quinn. Her thoughts had been too consumed by their goal. But now that he was safe, and they were headed home, she worried about what would await her on their return. And that dream from a few nights before— what did it mean? What had happened?

But she couldn't know. Not until she returned, or perhaps gathered some news when the others went into a village. She looked at her map and made calculations in her head. They could take a slightly slower pace, but she didn't want to be away much longer. She was the Sage, and her people needed her. And Quinn needed to be home, where he could sleep in a comfortable bed and eat plenty of nutritious food.

"What's wrong?"

She jumped. She hadn't noticed that he had awoken. "Just trying to calculate how long it will take to return home."

"Two weeks or so?"

"Yes, fifteen days at most. I don't want to push you too hard, but..."

He sat up and looked her in the face. "I'll be fine, Amarice. I can already feel my strength returning. My magic returning."

"Well, sleeping on the ground will connect you to your magic quickly." She took his hands in hers. "I can't believe you managed the fire in the state you were in."

"It was your magic. I pulled from your power, I think."

She cocked her head and contemplated this. She had been so drained at that point, and she couldn't believe what she had done either. But she had felt a familiar magic with hers—Quinn's.

"I might have pulled from yours. I was nearly drained. But that doesn't make sense, either."

"It appears we make each other's magic stronger," Quinn said. "This *tovari* magic, it's so much different from Scholar magic. So much more complex."

"One day, when all of this is over, you and I will study this properly. We'll do experiments and collect data and write a book!"

Quinn's eyes lit up. "Yes! And we'll rewrite every theory about magic that exists. Can you imagine if there were more *tovari* and what that would mean for the future of Scholars?"

"And Deyoni. Maybe—just maybe—Scholars will overcome their bigotry against the Deyoni, and the Deyoni will integrate into society."

Quinn stretched and rolled his neck, cracking it. He was too tall for the tent while sitting. "I've missed this. I've missed our theories and our talks and dreams."

Amarice nodded. A tear ran down her cheek, and Quinn wiped it away with his thumb. "I was so scared, Quinn. So scared, and so lost."

She should be strong for him now, after what he had suffered these last few weeks. But it had been too long since Amarice had been vulnerable. Quinn was her haven, and she was almost ready to crack. He folded her into his arms, pulling her against his chest. She let the tears fall as she listened to his steady heartbeat.

They were far away from the Villa, but she was home.

CHAPTER 12

RAYMOND

He nudged his horse along, whispering encouraging words in his ear. He knew Sterling was getting tired, but they were almost there. Fires and smoke were burning in the distance, and he could hear screams.

How he wished for faster travel. The roar of stampeding horses echoed behind him on the mountain road. Dawn was breaking over the horizon, casting phantom shadows on the hills and trees like ominous fingers pulling Raymond closer to destruction.

Ten minutes, maybe fifteen, he calculated. His heart thudded in his ears in time with the stallion's hoofbeats, worry and fear and anticipation mingling into a general feeling of surrealism. He didn't know what awaited them, didn't know how bad this attack had been. And why had they attacked? Had they somehow known that the Sage was away?

From a tactical standpoint, it was a smart move. No one would expect an attack on the most sacred night of the year. People would be sleepy and drunk, unprepared. Not that they were all that prepared, anyway. Though they trained in defense, no one had thought the

Chamberites would dare attack where the Sage lived. They had to know she was gone.

He swallowed hard as he guided the horse around the last major bend of the mountain road. He was leading his men into battle, and they would look to him for guidance. And though they trained their whole careers, none of them had ever fought in an actual war. Only a small skirmish or two at the borders. The last time Raymond had fought was when he, Amarice, and Quinn had taken down Charles Chambers in his church. But this was different. He knew deep down that no number of books and theory could prepare him for what awaited them.

The first camps appeared with sobs and screams. He slowed down to survey the situation. No one was fighting here, but there were dozens of injured people—men, women, and children. His stomach roiled.

"Where are they?" he shouted to the nearest people.

"Northern side. We've pushed them back to the edge of the camps."

"Hyah!" Raymond kicked the horse into a gallop to where the battle raged.

He bypassed the Villa itself on the eastern edge, weaving in between tents, cooking fires, and—he forced himself to choke down the bile that burned his throat—dead bodies. Ahead, he could see Deyoni and Scholars wielding swords and hoes and whatever they could find to fight off a large force of Chamberites. The air buzzed with magic, and the wind swirled with flames and rocks and branches as the stronger Scholars tried to fight with their magic. He squinted as he neared. No Lazori mercenaries, which was good. That meant these soldiers used to be his, and they were only as well-trained as the men he brought with him.

He drew his sword and charged into the fray with a shout. His guard shouted behind him. He knew the rest of his forces from Teleah would be just a few minutes away, giving them another three hundred swords. If they could just hold the invading forces back until the mounted reinforcements arrived...

Sterling tried to buck away from the yells and frenzy, but Raymond forced him into the throng of people. He swung his sword, taking down two soldiers in seconds. None of the others were on horses, giving his guard an advantage.

He sliced.

He stabbed.

He screamed.

Blood sprayed from necks, and guts spilled over the ground. The metallic taste of blood and magic was in the air, mixed with the smells of smoke from the Feast of Fire and excrement from the fallen. This was the smell of death. Sweat dripped into Raymond's eyes, obscuring his view, even as the fiery sun rose higher in the sky.

Time stopped and rushed forward all at once. He didn't know how long he'd been there, barely noting when the rest of his forces arrived. His horse trampled over corpses as they faced more and more soldiers, forcing them farther north into the mountains. His armor and being mounted kept his injuries slight, but he had a few deep scratches from desperate swords.

He lost count of the lives he ended. His blade dripped scarlet. But he didn't have time to think.

Stab. Parry. Dodge. Slice. Stab. Parry. Dodge. Slice. His actions beat in a rapid drum that matched his heart rate.

After minutes or hours, he heard shouts for retreat. The Chamberites that remained standing turned and ran. Stunned, he stopped and watched as one of his companies ran after them, forcing them farther away.

He panted and blinked. He had to give the orders to stop. His shouts got stuck in his throat when he opened his mouth. But he forced himself to yell, "Fall back!"

"Fall back!" his captains echoed, and his troops turned. They lined up in formation at the front until well after the last of the Chamberite soldiers disappeared from view.

It was over.

His captains rallied around him, waiting for orders. The rush of battle fading, Raymond now felt grossly underqualified and unsure of what to do next. He looked into the eyes of the men and women that he led, their faces covered in blood and dirt.

He swallowed and nodded to one of his captains that led a company of seventy-five. "Send scouts. I want to know that they're gone. And set up a watch around the perimeter in case they return."

She nodded and rode away, shouting for her troops.

He gave more orders to collect the dead and set up funeral pyres for the Chamberites. The Elandrians would wait until families and friends could claim their own loved ones among the Deyoni and Scholars. He told more officers to gather initial estimates of injured and dead and to get accounts of what had transpired before they arrived.

He led his personal guard back to the Villa. Every corner was packed with crying children and Scholars tending to wounds. He looked around for anyone familiar.

"Elaine!"

She was carrying bandages and a basin of steaming water on her hip. "Raymond! Is it over?"

"Yes. Elaine, what happened?"

Her brown eyes welled with tears. "It was awful. They arrived at midnight, a thousand of them or more. Many of us were in bed already, but some celebrations were still going on. No one noticed them until they were in the camps. We thought...we thought the first shouts were just from the Feast."

She broke down into sobs. Raymond pinched his nose between his eyes. A headache was forming.

She hiccupped, then continued. "They never made it to the Villa. The Deyoni rushed as many of the children and elderly in as they could, but..."

Raymond gave her an abrupt hug, and her basin splashed over both of them. He wasn't sure whether he was comforting her or himself. It was all too much. He didn't know how to deal with any of this.

She patted his back, and he pulled away. She handed him one of the wet cloths from the basin, and he wiped his face. He felt sick as he looked at the blood-stained fabric. So much blood. And so much wasn't his own. "Thank you," he said.

She nodded. "I have to get this to one of the Healers upstairs."

She hurried away, leaving Raymond in the middle of the courtyard. People pushed past him, not noticing him, as they hurried to attend to more dying patients. Madge found him a few minutes later and led him into the Sage's study. He took a seat at Amarice's desk and stared into the fire, waiting on reports from his captains.

Someone brought him food and coffee. He didn't look up to see who it was. But once they left, he realized he was ravenous. He ate three sandwiches in quick succession without even tasting them.

The first report came from the scouts. The Chamberites were badly injured and had stopped to care for their wounded three miles away. They estimated a company of three hundred or so, half of whom were in terrible condition. They didn't show any plans of regrouping, now that they were so vastly outnumbered.

The next report was the number of dead Chamberites. Five hundred, most of whom had been slain in the last hour when Raymond had arrived. That meant that about eight hundred had attacked. A small number against the eight thousand who resided in the mountains, but they were well-armed, trained, and organized. They also had the element of surprise.

The king let the Healers organize a field hospital as they saw fit, knowing he was not at all skilled in that knowledge. They could assess who needed the most urgent care and who could wait. Half of the Apothecaries were helping administer medicines, while others began brewing more potions and tinctures. Thankfully, Jack and Daisy had been stockpiling medicines for months.

It was early afternoon before Raymond received his most dreaded report. Fifteen hundred loyal lives had been lost. Most had died in the first onslaught of battle. They were mostly Deyoni, as their camps were on the outer edges of the land. Two hundred children had been killed. It was that number that made Raymond sick.

He retched into a trash can, the acid scalding his throat. His captains waited for him to finish without a word. They, too, were barely holding it together. Erenia, who gave the report, had broken down in tears when she started reading off the numbers. He had never seen her cry.

The number of injured was less precise but was estimated at around four hundred. At least there were a few hundred Healers. Raymond knew that all of it could have been even worse. If the Chamberites had any more soldiers, the surprise attack could have claimed hundreds more lives.

And yet...this was the worst thing Elandria had experienced in hundreds of years. Even in past wars, when the casualties were this high, they had been on a planned battlefield full of trained soldiers. This was far past a massacre. It was a slaughter.

It was genocide.

Raymond dismissed his captains and told them to help in whatever way they could. He made his way to the baths to clean up, but they were full of injured patients. He found a member of Amarice's staff and asked for a basin and some spare clothes and locked himself away to make himself look presentable. Kingly.

He looked in the mirror. He had scratches on his face; he was unsure where they came from, as he had no memory of getting them. A gash on his arm had stopped bleeding, and he tied it with a cloth. He needed to get something from the Apothecaries to prevent infection.

He made his way down to the Villa's Apothecary laboratory. Daisy was barking orders, her hair escaping her bun. When she saw Raymond, she stopped and threw her arms around him.

"I heard you were here. Are you all right?"

He sighed. "About as expected. I need some melaleuca salve. Then I'd like to help. It's been a long time, but I wasn't terrible at medicine."

She gave him a small tub of thick cream, and he plastered it over his wounds. There was no room in the laboratory for anyone but the highest trained Apothecaries. But she sent him out with a crate of medicines to deliver to Healers.

King Raymond took a deep breath and went out to care for his people.

CHAPTER 13

QUINN

Quinn started the morning fire with ease, glad that his strength and his powers were returning. They were a week into their journey home, and Quinn had finished his final dose of medicine the night before. His cough had subsided, and his lungs no longer ached. He could still feel his ribs when he ran his hands along his side. And while he didn't feel well enough to go for a run yet, he woke up early to take a short walk each morning before breakfast.

They had no news from the capital. In these outlying villages, no one seemed keen to speak to Corbin or Gracyn when they went to buy food. Even gregarious Jack couldn't make these people chat, although one woman had told him they hadn't received newspapers in two months. Quinn had to admit their suspicion of outsiders was for good reason.

But Amarice and Deben stayed in the camps with him whenever the others went into town. Amarice and Quinn could be recognized, and Deben was Deyoni. Even Jack removed his Scholar's pendant before venturing into a village. It was impossible to know who were loyal Elandrians and who were Chamberite sympathizers.

On this day, Deben returned with Eleanor and two rabbits. As he skinned the lean hares, he told Quinn a story about when he was younger and had gotten into trouble for stealing a rabbit from his father. He wanted to keep it as a pet, and he tried to hide it in his sleeping roll. He laughed as he recalled his mother's reaction.

"You would have loved your grandparents," Deben told him. "And they would be very proud of you."

Amarice was the last to wake. She greeted Quinn with a kiss, then bit into an apple. He watched the juice slide down her chin, and a familiar feeling fluttered in his stomach.

"There's a brook about a hundred yards that way." He jerked his head to the east. "Private, lots of trees, if you'd like a bath."

"Brigitte's tit, that sounds wonderful. And I could wash some of these clothes." She looked at the others. "What do you say? Shall we spend a few hours here?"

"I think the horses would appreciate it," Malena said. "We rode them hard yesterday."

The others nodded in agreement.

"Very well," Amarice said. "We'll leave after lunch."

She gathered some of her clothes and a bit of soap from the tent and planted a peck on Quinn's lips. "I'll see you soon."

"I'm coming with you, love."

She grinned. "All right."

They held hands as they made their way to the stream. Amarice asked how he was feeling, and he was glad to tell her he felt good. She'd fretted over him every day, making sure he ate and drank just the right amounts and tending to the wounds on his wrists and ankles. But those were little more than scratches now.

At the creek, he stood on the bank and watched Amarice undress. His heart pounded at the sight of her. His hand ached to touch the curve of her hips, her breasts. She splashed into the water with a shriek. "It's cold!"

He pulled his shirt over his head and watched her close her eyes as she submerged herself up to her chin. Knowing that she had warmed the water to a bearable temperature, he slipped off his pants and waded in. The gentle water lapped against his skin, washing away the grime and aches of his imprisonment. He sighed as his magic jolted to life inside him, filling him with an invigorating rush.

Amarice stood, and he was distracted from the refreshing sensation of the river. The water only came to her waist, leaving Quinn with a gorgeous view of the top of her body. She washed herself with the soap, running her hands over her arms and stomach and below the water. And she didn't know how much she was teasing him.

She groaned, and Quinn felt it in his soul.

"That feels so good," she said.

That was it. He splashed toward her and captured her lips in a passionate kiss. He pressed against her, and she whimpered into his mouth.

"Quinn," she whispered. "Are you sure that you're feeling up to it?"

"I've never wanted anything more. Are you?"

She responded by running her hand along his torso to his swollen member, eliciting a gasp from him. He lifted her under her buttocks, and she wrapped her legs around his waist. They nearly slipped a few times, but he carried her to the banks and laid her on the soft grass.

He placed kisses on every part of her soft skin that he could reach. Her back arched in pleasure as he touched her the way he knew she loved. He moved his mouth from her neck to her round breasts, bringing her to the edge over and over again.

"I want you," she half-begged as she ran her hands through his hair.

He shifted until he hovered over her, his hands on either side of her head. He sheathed himself in her with a moan. His lips crashed onto hers, kissing her as they moved together. She shuddered around him, and he came with her name on his lips.

They lay naked and intertwined on the banks for some time, savoring their privacy. It was easy to forget everything in that moment. It was easy to forget that just a week before, Quinn had been imprisoned. That had his illness continued unchecked, he could have died. That they had lost a friend, and that elsewhere in Elandria, a war raged on.

After a while, they rose and washed their clothes. Quinn heated the surrounding air to dry the sopping garments faster while Amarice washed her long, brown hair and braided it. It was lunchtime when they rejoined the others, relaxed and replenished. They ate a meal of rabbit and stale bread before packing up and heading further north.

Just a few more days and they would be home. As excited as Quinn was to see his loved ones at the Villa, he knew that their days would become frantic with war preparations. He decided to savor this week and pretend that the real world was far away from him and Amarice. At the back of his mind—and Amarice's too, he knew—was the dream from the night of the Feast of Fire. Whatever news awaited them would be terrible. He often watched Amarice as they rode, her face strained, lost in thought with a thousand burdens on her shoulders.

But he was back. Whatever plagued her, whatever challenges this war brought, she wouldn't have to face them alone any longer. He was her Consort, and he would follow her into the darkness.

CHAPTER 14

AMARICE

Teleah stood in the distance, the palace on the hill a white speck overlooking the valley. The Sage's mountains were a pale green blur on the horizon. The sun beamed down in the bright winter sky, warming the riders without the need for magic. She was almost home.

"Is that Teleah?" Corbin asked.

"It is. We're nearly there. We should reach home by tomorrow afternoon." She glanced at the sun's placement in the sky. "We could stay the night at the palace. Or we could press on and be there tonight."

The last part of their journey would be in the dark, but the road was well-maintained. And she wanted to be home.

"I vote we press on and sleep in our own bed tonight," Quinn said.

He winked at her, and she grinned. Their own bed was not only plush. They also wouldn't have to steal away to have time alone without Quinn's father and brother overhearing them. Yes, she could make it seven more hours on horseback to return to her home. And it would feel like home again, now that Quinn was back.

The others were just as eager as she and Quinn to end their journey, and they agreed to continue. They stopped for a brief lunch to stretch their legs and let the horses rest. Then they continued north, planning to bypass the capital rather than going through. Though it added distance, riding through town usually came with delays.

It was at sunset when Jack started singing happy songs—and some randy ones. The sky was painted in vibrant shades of orange and pink, and owls hooted in the distance. The others joined in the songs when they knew the words, excited to have made it this far without incident. Their cheery singing seemed to lighten the horses as well. Hours passed like minutes.

But a thick stillness met them in the mountains. It wasn't just the impending darkness. Something felt...off.

"Something's wrong." Amarice shot a concerned glance at Quinn and kicked Atsila into a gallop. She patted her horse's side, whispering that she could rest soon if she would just get them to the Villa fast. Atsila pushed herself as if she knew, too, that something terrible awaited them.

The moon shone overhead, illuminating the mountains in a spooky glow. The whistling wind had silenced any sounds of life. Dark tree branches spread over their path like bony hands, grazing their heads and shoulders and pulling them toward something they didn't want to see. Amarice shivered, but she refrained from warming herself in case she needed the full strength of her powers when she arrived.

Her magic buzzed under her skin, reacting to her emotions, her fear. She silently thanked the moon and stars for their light. If she had used fire magic to light their way, it might have burned out of control. She forced her magic to stay inside.

She slowed as she reached the edge of the camps. Fires dotted throughout, casting ghostly shadows on the tents. She breathed in the smell of staleness and waste. It was still early—it couldn't be later than seven o'clock, but there was little sound coming from the people.

Until they spotted her.

"It's the Sage!"

"*Drabekesala!*"

"Is that the Consort? She rescued him!"

"They're back!"

She slowed Atsila to a trot. They seemed happy to see her, but she knew something wasn't right. She could stop and find out. But she needed to see the Villa, to see Madge and Daisy and Matthew and know they were all right.

"What happened here?" she heard Quinn holler to someone behind her. She slowed to hear the answer.

"We were attacked, my lord. On the Feast of Fire. We...we lost many."

The air escaped Amarice's lungs as if they'd been punctured. Her thoughts swirled in violent stains of red and black. No. No, it couldn't be. She had left them alone, unprotected. And they had been attacked.

There were shouts, and she turned. A fire nearby roared, and flames leapt from the pit. People stomped on the grass, trying to put out the blaze. She froze.

Then the fire shrank. Quinn. He rode up beside her.

"Amarice," he said in a calming voice. "Take a deep breath."

She inhaled a sharp, desperate breath. Maintaining control was vital for everyone's sake, and she reminded herself that she had mastered her earth magic long ago. She grabbed Quinn's arm to steady herself. She took another breath and looked at his face. His eyes, glimmering in the starlight like amber, were warm with concern.

She nodded and continued on the road to the Villa.

News of their arrival had reached the Villa, the massive alabaster building shining in contrast to the devastation that had occurred. In the front garden, a crowd awaited them. She pulled to a stop in front of Madge, Daisy, Raymond, Janessa, and Elaine. What was Raymond doing here? Had he been here during the attack?

Daisy embraced Amarice in a tight hug. Madge sobbed into Quinn's chest as she embraced him.

"There now," she heard him murmur to the older woman. "I'm all right, Madge."

"You're too skinny." She sniffled.

A stablehand took Amarice's horse, and she patted Atsila's rump. She deserved sugar cubes and a good night's rest. She hugged Madge while everyone else bombarded Quinn with affection. Corbin and Janessa hadn't stopped kissing in several minutes. She let herself smile just a little.

"I'm glad you're safe," Raymond told Quinn. "All of you."

"We lost Willum," Quinn said. "I'm sorry."

"And the others," Malena added.

Raymond's face fell, but he nodded. "I'll write to their families myself."

"Raymond." Amarice hated to ruin Quinn's reunion, but she had to know what had transpired in her absence. "We heard there was an attack?"

"They're calling it the Fire Massacre."

"How many?"

The king looked at the ground. "You should come inside."

Quinn took her hand, and they followed Raymond into the Villa. Cheers erupted in the courtyard, and residents embracing them slowed their path to the study. Bittersweet, she thought. And she dreaded knowing just how bitter it would be.

Several minutes later, she sat on her sofa in her study with Quinn beside her. Raymond leaned against her desk, which was littered with maps and missives.

"I've been using your study as my own these last few weeks. I hope you don't mind."

She waved her hand. "Of course not. Can you stop evading my questions, though?"

He sighed. "A Chamberite force of about eight hundred attacked around midnight at the Feast of Fire. It was a complete surprise."

"Were you here?" Quinn asked.

The king shook his head. "I arrived at the end. We pushed the last of the forces into retreat." He cleared his throat. "It was...terrible. Like nothing I'd ever seen."

"How many?" Amarice asked. She rubbed the ache in her chest.

Raymond crossed the room to sit across from the Sage and the Consort. "The Scholars and Deyoni did well. They were surprised, but they rallied and wiped out half of the Chamberites before I arrived with my troops."

"How many, Raymond?" Her tone was glacial.

He swallowed, his throat bobbing. "One thousand six hundred and fifty-three."

Amarice's eyes widened. "One thousand six hund... I lost that many of my people?"

"Yes."

Her stomach roiled. Quinn grabbed her hand, to steady himself or her, she wasn't sure. She had lost over sixteen hundred people that she had sworn to protect. "How? How did eight hundred soldiers kill that many?"

"It all happened so fast. People thought the shouts were just end-of-the-night celebrations. To be honest, it's amazing it wasn't more."

"Amazing?"

"Surprising," the king corrected himself. "It was the worst thing that's ever happened, but it could have been far, far worse."

Madge knocked on the door and carried in a plate of fruits, cheese, and roasted chicken. She smiled sadly at Amarice and left the room. Quinn reached for some food, but Amarice didn't feel hungry in the slightest.

"And the injured?"

"I had the evening report from a Healer before you arrived. There are still five people that are touch-and-go. The rest are healing well."

Amarice buried her head in her hands. She had promised refuge to these people, promised them she could protect them. And she had failed. Quinn rubbed small circles on her back, comforting her, but she didn't deserve it. Those deaths fell on her shoulders.

Raymond continued. "We've begun building a wall with guard towers. We've made great progress, but we'll need your help to restore the forest. My latest intelligence suggests that the Chamberites' army is at Beybrook. Grellis is there, and Azmar has probably arrived by now. She left Te'eh two weeks ago. We still don't know where Samperian is."

"He'll head there, I'm sure," Quinn said. "He had just arrived before Amarice rescued me. They fled back to the sea, where I assume they had a ship waiting."

There was silence. Amarice lifted her head to see Raymond bent over a map on her desk. "Depending on where they made landfall, he is probably a day or two away. If he took a boat down the river, he's already there."

Amarice stood, and Quinn followed suit. "I need to see what's happening with the injured. Or the wall. Or...something."

"Amarice. I say this as your friend." Raymond's voice was gentle. "Your people need you rested and healthy. My soldiers are here keeping watch. You've been on the road for a month. There will still be a war tomorrow."

She wobbled on her feet, feeling lost. She looked at Quinn, who said, "He's right, my love. A good night's sleep will have you feeling much more certain about what you need to do."

She nodded.

Raymond embraced her. "I'm glad you're back, Amarice. I needed you."

His kind words stabbed her in the heart. So many people counted on her. She had needed to rescue Quinn, but she had failed so many others. How could she face the injured and the other survivors?

Raymond bade them goodnight, and she let Quinn lead her into their bedroom. Nothing seemed real. She moved through a fog as she climbed the stairs and undressed. Quinn held her in bed, stroking her hair. He knew her well enough by now. He knew when to say something and when to leave her alone with her thoughts.

It wasn't long before he drifted off to sleep. Amarice stared at the ceiling for a long time before her dreams claimed her. The guilt threatened to suffocate her. Her sleep was restless and broken, though Quinn slept soundly beside her, his weariness getting a true reprieve. She bolted upright in a panic more than once. Every time, Quinn reached out to calm her. Even in his sleep, he knew when she was upset or scared.

And when she awoke, she awoke from a dream about Zayn.

CHAPTER 15

QUINN

It took a moment for Quinn to orient himself upon waking. He blinked several times, and the room came into view. The oak wardrobes, the blue chaise lounge, Amarice's clothes from the night before on the floor. He smiled.

It was good to be home.

He reached out his right arm, but Amarice's side of the bed was empty. Odd. He rarely slept in past her, unless she couldn't sleep. Then he remembered.

Over sixteen hundred Scholars and Deyoni were dead. Slaughtered. A moment of clarity hit him. That's what Samperian had mentioned to the guards, why they were keeping Quinn alive. They were waiting to lure Amarice away.

He thought back to the day he had seen the minister. His lanky form and greasy hair had towered over Quinn. He had kicked Quinn awake and questioned him about the Sage and the king's plans.

"How should I know? I've been here for weeks," he said between coughs.

"Well, just a few more weeks, and it won't matter." Samperian spat at him and left the cell before yelling at the guards about the state of Quinn. The next day, Quinn began receiving more food and water. And a ratty blanket which was far more useful as a pillow.

They had been waiting to lure the Sage away. They knew she would come after Quinn herself. And then they planned to attack. But eight hundred soldiers against eight thousand refugees wasn't much. They must have been waiting on more troops.

Raymond was right. It could have been much, much worse.

He groaned as he stretched his aching muscles. Thankful he didn't have to ride a horse today, he stood and glanced at the clock. Seven o'clock. He picked up Amarice's clothes off the floor and threw them into the basket by the stairs for Madge.

Amarice was sitting at her desk, reading through papers. She glanced up when Quinn entered from their chambers. Dark circles surrounded her grey eyes. She had thrown her hair into a loose bun, and stray strands escaped from every direction. He furrowed his brow in worry.

"Good morning, my love," she greeted him. "How did you sleep?"

"Better than you, I'd say." He crossed the room and sat in the chair opposite her. How often he had sat here, first as her apprentice and then as her Consort. The familiarity made his chest ache.

She forced a smile. "I managed to get a little sleep. Not much. I'll be fine with some coffee."

"What are you reading?"

"Raymond's reports. I figured if he left them on my desk, they were fine for me to see."

"And?"

"Two hundred and four children. Children, Quinn."

Bile rose in his throat. He couldn't fathom it. And after so many centuries of relative peace, no one else could either. This was uncharted territory. He thought of little Melya, the Deyoni girl he had met on their travels earlier in the year. He hoped she was safe. At least his father's tribe—his tribe—had fled the country. That meant his cousins and aunts were alive.

He looked at Amarice. She wasn't crying, and she didn't look angry.

Shock, he was sure. He was shocked, too. He didn't think he'd believe it until he left this room and saw the damage himself. But there was something else.

"Amarice, you know this wasn't your fault." He proceeded to tell her about his revelation. "They'd been planning this. There was no way you could have known."

She shook her head. "I promised them refuge."

"Amarice."

She sighed and forced another smile. "Come. Let's eat breakfast."

AFTER A SATISFYING BREAKFAST of meats and fresh fruits, Quinn took a walk through the Villa and its gardens. He wandered the halls and stopped in front of the room he had used as the Sage's apprentice. Amalla, the Healer they had met in Yaana, now occupied it.

The Villa had felt like home the moment Quinn arrived. For the first time in his life, he'd had the sense that he could belong somewhere. The Sage's Villa was that place for many people. For centuries, it had been a haven for Scholars. When Amarice became the Sage, she had opened her doors and lands to everyone, Deyoni and Elandrian alike. And the Chamberites had tried to take it away.

It was the ultimate betrayal.

He ran his fingers over the familiar wooden door before walking away. He soon found himself in the northern gardens. At the edge, overlooking the camps in the distance, stood the Consort Tree.

The limbs were barren, reaching out with desperate fingerlike twigs. Tears burned Quinn's eyes as he made his way to the intertwined trunks.

"What happened to you, my friend?" he said. He caressed the tree.

The moment his fingers grazed the thick, ridged trunk, the Consort Tree burst to life. Vibrant green leaves bloomed, and the dull bark turned to a rich, earthy brown.

Quinn smiled. "Welcome back."

LATER, Quinn went with Amarice to the makeshift hospital on the east side of the Villa. The Deyoni had put massive canvas tents together to make a comfortable-sized space for the Healers to work. Low travel beds lined each long wall of the tent. Quinn didn't want to think about where they got all the extra beds. Healers and Apothecaries bustled about, cleaning wounds, administering medicines, adjusting pillows. Some were cleaning workstations or scrubbing laundry against washboards. Patients sat up at the arrival of the Sage and the Consort. They waved and chatted amongst themselves, excited to meet Amarice and Quinn in person.

There was an unexpected amount of life in that tent.

With a silent glance, Amarice went to one side of the tent, and Quinn went to the other. He greeted each patient with a smile and asked how they were feeling. Each reaction was a little different.

Some were wide-eyed at the chance to visit with the Consort and *shesakesalo*. One teen Scholar girl flirted with him while her older brother blushed and buried his head. She was fighting off an infection in her leg, but the Healers expected to release her the following day. Others didn't say much, just thanked him and said how glad they were that he was safe, while still others told him their whole life story. Some told him their detailed, harrowing accounts of the attack. Those were the hardest.

He kissed Amarice's head as they passed each other to switch sides. Amarice wanted to make sure she saw every patient and heard their story. By the time Quinn had seen the nearly forty patients, he had to stifle yawns from the emotional exhaustion.

At the far end of the hospital tent was a flap. A stench of death and sadness filled the air near it. Inside were the five patients who were fighting for their lives.

The Healer that Raymond had appointed as the head—someone Amarice knew but Quinn did not—filled them in on the cases in a whisper. Two of them had a chance to pull out of this. The other three she expected to pass within days.

"It's amazing they've held on this long, my lady."

Amarice reached for Quinn's hand before she pushed back the flap. It was dark in here, and Quinn blinked to adjust his eyes. There must be layers of tent fabric and skins keeping the sunlight out, he realized.

Amarice knelt at the bed of the first patient, a young Deyoni man that couldn't be older than Corbin. His skin glistened with sweat. His mother ran wet cloths over his skin, but the man was unconscious and didn't respond. Quinn watched the labored rise and fall of his chest. Amarice took a linen from the nearby basin and began helping the mother soothe the man's burning skin.

The next person was awake—an elderly Scholar woman that grasped Quinn and Amarice's hands with a weak smile on her face. She tried to speak, but most of her words were nonsensical babble. Her son, an old man himself, sat next to her and assured them that this was just her age, not her injury. She was fighting internal bleeding and a broken hip, as she had fallen in the rush of the onslaught. They had her on a high dose of poppy tea, so she didn't seem to be in much pain. She was nearly a century old. She had lived a good life, but the Healers said she could still pull out of this.

They moved to the next patient. Amarice took a seat at her side. It took Quinn a moment to make out the woman's face in the darkness. He gasped.

"Oh, Sarah. No."

He fell to his knees and grabbed the Scholar's hand. Her skin scorched with fever. Tears welled in his eyes, and his lip quivered.

"You knew her?" Amarice whispered.

He nodded, and with his next words, the tears fell. "We were friends. And almost more."

A strange feeling mingled with the grief in his gut. Guilt. He had ignored her advances for all the years they were at the Academy, mostly out of his own obliviousness. They had shared one night together, the night before Quinn came to the Villa to begin his apprenticeship. He had been such a hungover ass the next morning as he rushed away.

He had never apologized. But she had met a Healer at the hospital and fallen in love, he had heard. And she had been a good friend. Funny, smart, kind. He hadn't even known she was here in the mountains. He wondered when she had left Teleah.

As if she could read his mind, the head Healer spoke in a low voice. "She only arrived a few weeks before. I worked with her at the hospital in Teleah. She stayed as long as was safe. Arsonists set fire to her apartments, and that was the last straw."

"How terrible," Amarice murmured.

"She saved many people the night of the massacre. She was bleeding from a stab wound in her shoulder, but she didn't stop. Her patients always came first. By the time she slowed down enough to tend it, the infection had already set in."

Quinn brushed a loose hair from Sarah's face. She didn't deserve this. No one did, but especially not a person like Sarah.

"I'm so sorry," he whispered to her, though he knew she could not hear him. She was hours away from death. "I'm so sorry."

He needed to tell Jack to see her before she died. Dazed, he followed Amarice to the next two patients. He barely noticed their wounds or the states they were in; he kept stealing glances back at Sarah.

"Let me know when she passes," he told the head Healer. "I want to be here."

He was silent as he and Amarice returned to the Villa. Amarice leaned against his arm as they walked. They went straight to their chambers, avoiding everyone. Their faces must have said everything, as no one attempted to stop them to talk.

He sank on the sofa downstairs and buried his head in his hands. He couldn't believe it. Not Sarah. Amarice sat next to him and stroked his hair while he cried. She, too, cried. Quinn knew that she needed him to be strong, but this was the first person he knew who had been claimed by the massacre.

The Chamberites had taken too many people he loved. Rafe. His mother. Willum. He swallowed, his throat thick from crying. A new feeling appeared, burning through him like the fever that was taking over Sarah.

Rage.

"They have to pay." He lifted his head and looked at Amarice. Her tear-stained face was swollen and red. "They have to pay for this."

"They will."

CHAPTER 16

RAYMOND

The king sat in Quinn's study, looking over the latest figures from his captains. Now that Amarice had returned, Raymond had given up her study. Quinn offered his, saying that he could work alongside Amarice. Raymond appreciated it. It was quiet up here, and it was next to the bedroom he used at the Villa.

It was starting to feel more like home than the palace.

The palace had become cold and lonely after his father died. It was duty that kept him there. But after the massacre, he had only returned for two days. The people in the Sage's Mountains needed him while Amarice was gone.

And he had made progress. Once the shock of the attack had worn off, anger set in. He had nine hundred new recruits. They had all but demanded swords and armor, wanting to fight back against the murdering Chamberites. More were joining every day, Scholars and Deyoni alike. His own guard was overseeing their training. Now that Amarice was back, he supposed he should return to Teleah. But he could receive messages from spies and other captains across the country here, too. He decided to write to Andin and request for him to bring more clothes. He was more useful here.

Someone knocked on the door.

"Come in," he said.

"Are you coming down to lunch? Or should I bring it up to you?"

He looked up and saw Elaine standing in the doorway. She wore an apron over her russet dress. With all the extra mouths to feed, Madge had welcomed her help in the kitchen.

He smiled. "Am I late again?"

"No. But I knew you'd work straight through lunch if no one reminded you. It's a chicken and citrus pie. Quinn's favorite. Smells amazing."

"I'll come down," he said. He sat the papers on the desk and stood. He stretched, sore from hunching over the desk for hours. "Thanks, Elaine."

"Of course."

He followed her out of the study and down the back staircase. She asked him how his work was going and seemed interested in the reports. A strand of brown hair fell in front of her eyes. Raymond couldn't resist the urge to reach up and brush it behind her ear. She blushed at his touch.

"Are you joining us for lunch?" he asked. He hoped she would say yes.

She bit her bottom lip, thinking. "I suppose I could, if Madge doesn't need me."

"Madge needs a lunch break, too."

Elaine smiled, and it reached her warm golden-brown eyes. "I'll go ask."

Raymond whistled as he crossed the courtyard to the veranda. He took his usual seat across from Quinn. He noticed both Quinn and Amarice were staring into their pies, their forks barely moving.

"What's wrong?"

It was a stupid question. He had just told them about the massacre last night, but he had hoped they could at least enjoy Quinn's return a little.

"We visited the hospital," Quinn said.

"A friend of Quinn's is dying," Amarice added.

Raymond frowned. "I'm so sorry."

"Thanks." Quinn stood. "Excuse me."

Raymond watched Amarice's face as she stared after Quinn. She set her fork down with a sigh. She turned to gaze into her plate as if it would give her answers. Raymond reached over and patted her hand. Her grey eyes were full of sadness when they met his. She gave him a quavering smile before leaving the veranda herself, her steps slow and heavy.

He forced himself to take a bite of the pie, but it tasted flavorless. His thoughts ran in circles, so fast he didn't know what he was thinking about. He tried rubbing the tension from his neck to no avail.

Elaine took a seat across from him. Janessa was on her other side. She glanced at Quinn and Amarice's neglected plates. "Where is everyone?"

Raymond shrugged, unable to speak. Janessa whispered that she would tell Elaine later. She nodded, and Raymond regarded her as she filled her plate. Watching her grounded him. It gave him something to focus on. The way she got a bit of everything on her fork. The movement of her dainty wrist as she brought the bite to her soft lips.

She looked at him and raised an eyebrow, and he realized his staring had crossed an uncomfortable line. He smiled and cleared his throat, then went back to eating.

⚜

QUINN'S FRIEND, Sarah, passed the following day. Raymond attended her funeral alongside his friends. He'd been to every funeral here in the mountains since the massacre, yet the sight of bodies on pyres still made him nauseated.

Some Scholars preferred burial, to return their bodies to the earth that blessed them. Others preferred their essence to join the air and spread throughout Elandria. Sarah had loved fire and had manipulated it well, so her lover had requested cremation.

The skies were overcast with billowing clouds, and the air was humid and thick. A bone-deep chill made Raymond shiver, a reminder that spring was not yet here. Her friends shared memories of Sarah's life, eliciting wet chuckles from the crowd. Past patients told their tearful stories of her compassion as a Healer.

Jack's eyes were puffy and red. He stood next to Quinn, who stared past the pyre into the horizon. The Consort's diadem rested atop his head, stones dull in the grey light of day. Raymond cursed their stations on his friend's behalf. Quinn should be allowed to cry, to grieve alongside his peers. But here he was, maintaining his composure.

Raymond knew the feeling too well.

Gut-wrenching wails broke through the symphony of sniffles. Sarah's partner, a Healer from Raymond's year at the Academy, fell to his knees at the foot of the pyre. He screamed and begged for her to return, to wake up and not leave him here alone. Other loud sobs broke out, crying as much for the man's pain as Sarah's death.

Raymond swallowed hard against the raw lump in his throat. He wanted nothing more than to run back to his room and collapse on the bed. He wanted to put a pillow over his head to drown out the noisy tears and screams that haunted him every moment.

It was Amarice who knelt beside the man, whispering words in his ear that no one could hear. He leaned into her and cried, his shoulders heaving. She wrapped her arms around him and eased him away from the pyre.

She glanced up at Quinn and nodded. Raymond turned to see the Consort step closer to the stack of wood where Sarah's body lay. He outstretched his hand, and a ball of flames the size of a large chicken appeared, hovering above his flesh. Raymond couldn't help but gasp. Sometimes he forgot how powerful his friends were. Conjuring the fire appeared to take no effort whatsoever.

The flames leapt from Quinn's hand onto the oil-soaked wood. The blaze spread quickly, and soon no one could see the body anymore. Fire burned the herbs that had decorated her final resting place, an ancient Elandrian tradition to cover the smell of flesh. Soon, an earthy, floral scent mingled with smoke filled the air—the smell of a life leaving this world too soon.

CHAPTER 17

AMARICE

The moonlight shone through the curtains, which moved in the gentle breeze. Amarice sighed. She looked at Quinn lying next to her. His brow furrowed in his sleep, and as she wondered what he was dreaming about, she kissed his forehead.

She glanced at the clock on the table beside her bed. Two o'clock. Another sleepless night. She didn't think she could stand another night tossing and turning, trying to find sleep. And she didn't want to get up and do any work.

Most people were probably asleep, and she wasn't sure she wanted company, anyway. She rose from the bed and slipped a shawl over her nightgown. She padded down the stairs, barefoot, careful not to make a noise and wake Quinn.

The baths were empty. Just what she needed. They were usually crowded now that the Villa was full to the brim. She lit the furnace with a wave of her hand, then slipped off her clothes. She found the rose soap she loved in a basket at the back of the room. Steam rose from the water in ethereal tendrils. She dropped in with a splash.

Her mind wandered as she scrubbed at her skin, the rose scent in her nose. She loved roses because of Zayn. For years as a young girl, she had called them overrated, though she thought they were beautiful. But on her fifteenth birthday, Zayn had brought her half a dozen from his mother's garden. It had been a joke—he knew she claimed to hate them. But he told her she was just like a rose—beautiful but prickly. And not afraid to draw blood, he added. She had punched Millie in the nose the week before, and the teacher had sent her home from school early.

Millie had deserved it, though all these years later, Amarice couldn't recall why.

That was her last birthday with Zayn. He died a few months later. She had grown a rosebush at his grave.

She sat the soap on the side of the bath. Her muscles ached as the warm water woke them. The insomnia was catching up with her. Quinn was worried, she knew, and she decided to ask Daisy for a sleeping tonic tomorrow. She supposed just a few days of taking it wouldn't hurt. Amarice flexed her fingers under the water, trying to calm the magic that tingled in her hands. Yes, she needed to get some sleep. She was the Sage, and she shouldn't be fighting so hard to control her magic from going wild. She closed her eyes; her head leaned against the edge of the bath, wet hair pooling around her on the stone floor.

"I thought I might find you in here."

Amarice jumped, water splashing over the side. She must have dozed. Finally. She blinked, clearing the sleep from her eyes, and looked up to see Quinn standing at the door to the baths. He leaned against the doorframe.

"What time is it?"

"A little after three."

Less than an hour, then. She stretched and turned her whole body to face him, folding her arms on the edge. "What are you doing awake?"

He shrugged. "Woke up, saw you weren't there. You weren't reading downstairs or working in the study. I checked the library before coming here."

She could hear the worry in his voice. She smiled at him. "Care to join me?"

He closed the door and slipped off his pants. He folded them and placed them on the shelf. Amarice smiled and rolled her eyes. Her own nightgown and shawl were in a pile on the floor.

She studied him as he approached the bath. He was filling out again; she could only see a couple of ribs. Some muscle was returning to his arms. They had been back a week and a half, and he had started his daily running again. He ate a lot at meals, which was easy to do with Madge's cooking. He still hadn't talked much about what he had experienced. In time, she would ask him.

He splashed her face and pushed through the water to reach her. Then he pulled her into his arms and placed his chin on the top of her head.

"Are you all right, Amarice?"

"I'm fine."

"No, you're not. You don't have to pretend with me."

She sighed and pulled away. "I know. But...it's not your burden to bear."

He gave a sidelong glance. "Yes, it is. You named me Consort, Amarice. It is."

"But you've been through so much, and—"

"And so have you. Amarice, let me help you shoulder whatever is weighing you down. I know you're not sleeping."

"I will ask Daisy for a sleeping tonic today."

He nodded. "But Amarice, that's not all. I don't know what you're thinking. I know you're hurting. And I can feel your magic wild around you."

"I have it under control."

"Amarice..."

She kissed him, wanting to stop the conversation. She would be fine with some sleep. He needed to focus on healing—his body and his mind. He had been through unspeakable horrors, and it took her far too long to rescue him. And he was helping her. He was training Scholars in their magic and how to use it in battle. They were growing trees in the forest to replenish what Raymond's forces had cut down for the wall. He handled everyone who came requesting an audience, taking their concerns and reassuring them.

The loss of lives wasn't his fault.

"You're distracting me from the conversation," he said against her lips. But he didn't pull away.

"Is that a problem?" Her voice was low, seductive. She bit his lower lip.

He moaned and kissed her again, pushing her against the back wall of the bath. "No."

"Good." She put her arms around his neck.

"We'll talk about it later."

He set to work, diverting her from the thoughts that plagued her.

⁂

A BRAND-NEW TREE stretched above her, and she smiled at it. Growing trees was much harder work than growing some vegetables or flowers, but it was also far more satisfying. The forest was full of chattering Scholars, even though the work drained them. Scholars belonged among the trees. The woods invigorated their magic.

She and Quinn moved much faster at filling up the forest, but the wall took a lot of trees. She appreciated as much help as she could get. The Scholars with the strongest powers of earth helped every day. Quinn was getting to know them well. He was training the most powerful Scholars in creating concentrated earthquakes. They weren't much, but they were enough to knock a few people off their feet. It would be useful in a fight, in case the Chamberites attacked them again.

She watched him laugh with a group of men and women, and her heart swelled with pride. How far he had come since the shy young man who wouldn't meet her eyes!

Amarice turned back to the forest floor, where a sapling waited for her. She knelt, placing her bare hands on the ground for more direct contact. Though, in theory, touch didn't make her magic stronger, it was far easier to control. She inhaled, letting the earthen scent wash over her. Her Gift of the Earth pulsed through her veins. She imagined the tree growing, growing, growing.

It began to grow.

The magic poured into the soil, nurturing the roots with its warm energy. The sapling grew, and the trunk thickened. Branches spread, grazing Amarice's head with their scratchy fingers. Leaves bloomed as the trunk soared ever higher.

Several minutes later, Amarice stopped. She pulled her hands away and sat back on her heels. She gazed up at the towering sycamore. Ten trees today. A new record.

She closed her eyes and took a deep breath, focusing on the energy that ran through the earth below her hands and feet. She imagined pulling it to her, funneling it into her body, filling the well inside her.

It would take a longer meditation to fully replenish, but at least she wouldn't faint upon standing. She stood and dusted the dirt off her emerald gown. Quinn met her eyes from a few yards away and smiled. He, too, looked exhausted.

She jerked her head toward the deeper part of the forest, letting him know she was going for a walk to regain her strength. He nodded. She knew he would head for the river. As water was his strongest element, it was much faster for him to replenish with a swim.

Amarice couldn't very well walk into flames.

So, she walked barefoot into the woods, past the new trees and the tree stumps, until she reached the old part of the forest. It was still here, save for the birds. Sunlight filtered through the leaves, casting long shadows. She slid against the trunk of a sturdy oak, savoring the roughness that dug into her back. She placed her feet flat on the ground, her hands on either side of her, and closed her eyes.

But unbidden images kept appearing. Quinn, sick and weak at the top of the stairs of Citadel Kahyrst. She pushed it away and cleared her mind. The young Deyoni man and his mother from the hospital tent. She sighed and cleared her mind again.

Sarah, as she lay on the funeral pyre. Her partner, sobbing. Quinn's tear-stained face as he lit the pyre.

"No," she said aloud.

Her mind cleared.

The funeral of Rafe and the other young Scholars from almost two years ago. Roland's smiling face. Thousands of faceless Deyoni and Scholars swirling around her.

Zayn.

She leapt up. She couldn't be alone with her thoughts. Not right now. She hurried through the forest, tears burning her eyes, not stopping until she reached her chambers in the Villa. She climbed the stairs, unstoppered the bottle of sleeping tonic, and downed the syrupy sweet liquid in one go.

Then she collapsed on the bed and cried until sleep claimed her.

CHAPTER 18

QUINN

"Hey, Quinn. You busy?"

Quinn looked up to see Jack brush his curly red hair out of his eyes. The Consort glanced down at the Villa budget—he had taken over that duty from Amarice a few months before—and set down his pencil. "Glad for a break. Come on in."

Jack entered the study and sat on an overstuffed green armchair. Quinn rose from the small desk that he had set up in the corner and joined Jack in the sitting area.

"What's going on?"

Jack shrugged. "Nothing major. Well, besides everything." He waved his hands. "We haven't gotten to visit much since we returned."

Quinn felt a pang of guilt. He hadn't talked much to anyone but Raymond and Amarice at all. He visited with the Scholars he trained, but it was little more than small talk. "You're right. I'm sorry."

"Oh, I'm not saying it's your fault! I've been spending every waking hour in the Apothecary lab."

Daisy and Jack were running the entire scene for the Apothecaries.

Daisy was spending a lot of time out in the gardens cultivating ingredients while Jack supervised the actual making of medicines and tinctures.

"How are you doing?" Quinn asked. "With Sarah and...everything."

Jack's smile faltered. "It doesn't seem real, you know. How are so many old schoolmates just gone?"

"I don't know." Quinn ran a hand through his hair. "This had to be coming for a lot longer than just Chambers. One man who stayed mostly anonymous doesn't throw a country into a civil war in less than two years."

"We've lived in a bubble," Jack said. "A tower at the top of society. We think we know everything, but we're just on the outside looking in."

Quinn studied his friend. Jack was smart. He had always known that. But other than his rants about apothecary theories, their conversations in school had been lighthearted. Jokes, stories of Jack's escapades and lovers, gossip about their classmates. Rafe was the politically minded one. Quinn, too, though he was far more introspective than Rafe.

But everything had changed. Rafe was gone, and his death had changed Jack. He wondered how he would feel if he lost the love of his life, then quickly pushed that thought away. "You're right. But I don't know how we change that."

"I don't either. I'm just a lowly Apothecary." He smiled, just a little. "How's Amarice?"

It was Quinn's turn to shrug. "She's surviving."

"Aren't we all?"

They were silent for a few minutes, their unvoiced thoughts accompanied by the ticking of the clock. Quinn thought back to the night a few months ago when they had all gathered in the courtyard for some drunken singing and fun. Things were bad, but it all seemed so far away. Now there was little escape. He stood and crossed over to the cabinet where Amarice kept a stash of imported liquors. He poured himself and Jack each a tall glass of a dark, smoky-sweet alcohol from an island off the coast of Ilecin.

Jack took his glass, and they clinked them together. Quinn sat back down and took a sip.

"Do you remember the night of my farewell party?" he asked Jack.

Jack snorted. "Barely."

Quinn laughed. "You had a lot to drink that night. Ugh. So did I."

"If I recall," Jack said, "I spent the night with two third-years. I think they were a couple."

"Not the whole night! You were in my bed when I made it back to the Academy."

Jack guffawed. "That's right! Brigitte's tit, I was so nauseous on my way back to my room that I stopped at yours and Rafe's. I didn't think I could make it down the hall."

Quinn slid down on the sofa and leaned his head back. "I can imagine Rafe's face when you knocked on the door."

"He was mad. Some blonde ran out of the room." He grinned into his drink. "Can't say I feel bad about interrupting that."

"I got sick in Bucky's bushes that morning. Worst hangover of my life."

"Oh, yeah. That was the night you and Sarah…" His voice trailed off. Quinn took another drink. "How did that finally happen? I don't think you ever told me."

Quinn thought back. His memories from that night were hazy. "She started hanging all over me, and I let her. Thanks to all the drinks you gave me before we even went to dinner. We kissed. Rafe was dancing on a table, I think." They laughed. Rafe had a tendency to do that when inebriated. "And then she told me she had rented a room from Bucky, so I followed her upstairs."

Jack nodded. "It only took you four years. That girl had her eye on you from the beginning. You were so dense."

Quinn shook his head. "At first, maybe. But once I realized it, I was just too shy to do anything about it. Oh, and I was such an ass that next morning. Just ran out on her to catch the carriage to the Villa."

"And look at you now."

"Look at me now. The target of high-profile kidnapping and the man doing the stupid budget for the Sage's Villa." He chuckled.

"I lost a bet, you know. Rafe and I had bet on when you'd sleep with Sarah. I said it would never happen. I was so close."

"Sorry," Quinn said, not sorry at all. "Such great friends I have."

"And now things are...different."

"Yeah."

The somber mood returned. Quinn glanced at the clock. It was almost dinnertime. He wondered where Amarice was. She'd been spending more and more time in the forest, and he was worried about her. But she was usually back by now. He stood. "I need to get cleaned up before dinner. I'm glad you came by, Jack."

Jack pulled himself from the armchair and folded Quinn into a warm hug. "Me, too."

۞

AMARICE WAS LATE TO DINNER. She gave Quinn what he assumed was supposed to be a reassuring smile, but he didn't buy it. For days now, she had been quiet around him. Tentative. As if she didn't want to upset him. It pained him because he knew she was hurting, but she wouldn't allow him to help her.

Now that several weeks had passed since the massacre, dinner was returning to its old liveliness. It was strange how a bit of time made tragedy seem so far away. Amarice still didn't speak much, but she answered questions that people directed at her.

After dinner, Raymond grabbed Quinn by the arm. "Have you got a minute?"

Quinn glanced at Amarice, but she was talking to Madge about the new schedule for the kitchen staff. "Of course. What's going on?"

"Not here." Quinn followed Raymond out through the open veranda arches into the long path of ivy-lined archways. Raymond looked around, then leaned his head in close to Quinn's.

"Is there anything I should know about Elaine?"

"What? What do you mean? Is something wrong?"

Raymond shook his head. "No. I just mean...well, are you two still close?"

Quinn stared at the king. He was nervous, almost boyish. "No, not really. We hadn't spoken in years until this summer in Corthy."

"Why, uh, why did you end things with her?"

"Well, I didn't. Not exactly. We made love, and the next day she confessed our sins in front of the whole town at church. I was already a pariah for being a Scholar, and that was the last bit of shame I could take. I left for Teleah that night."

Raymond crinkled his brow. "Wow. I didn't know. I'm sorry."

Quinn shrugged. "It was a long time ago. I've moved on. She's moved on. Raymond, why are you acting so strange?"

The king raised a dark hand to scratch the back of his head. "I'm not. I was just curious."

"Right." He folded his arms and leaned against a trellis.

"Fine!" He sighed. "Would you be upset if I was interested in her?"

"Interested in her? Really?" Elaine was far from Raymond's type.

"Yes! But if it would cause any conflict between us, I'll drop it."

Quinn cocked his head. "And she's interested in you, too?"

"I don't know! It's...I can't tell. I don't know how to let her know I'm interested."

Quinn found that hard to believe. Raymond could wink his way into any bed in Elandria if he wanted. He used to envy him for it.

"I used to be jealous of your history with Amarice. Now, I just want Elaine to be happy. And you. But Raymond, things are very different in Corthy. If this is just a passing fancy, she might not be all right with that. I don't want to see her get hurt."

Raymond nodded. "I know. But it feels...different."

"Why her?"

"I feel like I don't have to try around her, like I can be myself. I haven't felt that way since..." He rubbed his face with his open hand. "In a long time."

Quinn smiled. "If you can't figure out how to flirt with her, you should just tell her how you feel."

"Probably." He sounded dubious. "Thanks, Quinn."

He turned back to the Villa, leaving Quinn alone in the moonlit garden. What a strange day, he mused. He ran his fingers over the ivy that ran along the archways, lost in thought.

Amarice came out a few moments later. "There you are!"

He held his arms out to her, and she stepped into his embrace. He breathed in her rosy scent as she buried her head in his chest.

"I just had the strangest conversation with Raymond."

"Oh?"

"He likes Elaine."

"Well, she's nice enough. Wait, what do you mean 'likes her'?"

He laughed. "Exactly what you think I mean."

"Odd. She's not his type." Amarice laughed. "How can he even see her through all those layers of fabric?"

Quinn stepped back and looked at her. "You don't like her?"

She looked down. "She hurt you. I don't like people who hurt you."

He kissed her on her forehead. "It was a long time ago, and she was a victim of religious brainwashing. We've seen what that does to people. I forgave her. She's a good person."

"All right. I'll try to like her."

Quinn laughed. "You know, I used to be jealous of Raymond because he had you before I did. It's not unrealistic for you to feel the same."

She lifted her chin. "I have no idea what you're talking about." Then she gave a small, sheepish smile.

He grinned and put his arm around her waist. "Let's go inside."

CHAPTER 19

RAYMOND

Raymond paced his bedroom floor. Maybe Quinn was right last night. He should be direct with Elaine. But what if she wasn't interested? That would be embarrassing. It could make things very awkward at meals.

But he had been flashing her the most charming smiles. He had placed gentle touches on her hands. She had to know. She probably didn't like him in that way. She was too nice to turn him down. Telean women had no problem telling men to get lost, but Elaine was far too polite.

He groaned. He hadn't been this nervous about a woman since he was fifteen years old and had a crush on his much-older maid. Of course, that had gone nowhere. Maybe he'd just talk to Elaine when he got back from Teleah. He was returning to the capital tomorrow for a few days.

No. He could tell her now. And then maybe she'd want to visit the capital with him. He wouldn't push her. He knew things were different where she came from, but the palace had plenty of bedrooms. And he enjoyed her company; she was a nice reprieve from the stress of being king during a civil war.

He steeled himself and opened the door. He made his way down the back staircase to find her. She wasn't in the kitchen, but Madge handed him a fresh-baked lemon muffin. He bit into the soft, sweet bread as he went to check the library. She enjoyed reading, and he had recommended a few of his favorite books to her yesterday.

But as he walked down the open hallway, a loud voice rang across the courtyard. "Your highness!"

It was the captain of his guard. Erenia's eyes were wide as she ran toward Raymond. Amarice and Quinn stepped out of their study at the commotion.

"What's wrong, Erenia?" the king asked.

"My lord! It's the palace. It's been taken."

"Taken? What do you mean?"

Erenia panted as she stopped in front of the king. "Teleah has fallen."

⊗⊗⊗

HE LISTENED to the reports in Amarice's study. Well, he tried to listen. His eyes had glazed over. Everyone's voices sounded far away, like echoes down a distant tunnel.

He wasn't sure how it had happened, although he should be after hours of meetings with the troops from Teleah and palace staff who had escaped.

He knew the basics. There was no invasion. An organized riot started on the high street. A mob stormed the palace. Many of his staff had died. There were hundreds of them, and they set fire to whatever they could touch. Rather than retaliate, the captain of the unit left behind made the decision to save as many people as they could. They couldn't do both.

It was the right choice. The one Raymond would have made. More people were arriving in the mountains in a matter of hours. Not just Scholars anymore. Regular, loyal Elandrians whose homes had been destroyed or who feared Chamberite rule. How had this happened? Someone had to know how depleted the forces were in Teleah and that Raymond would be returning with more troops soon. And somehow, the Chamberites had known when Amarice had left the Villa to rescue Quinn.

He had a spy in his confidence.

"Get out."

The soldier who was speaking stared at the king in shock.

"Raymond?" Amarice said, concerned.

He cleared his throat. It wasn't like him to be so rude to his soldiers. "Thank you for your report. I need to speak with the Sage and the Consort."

The soldier nodded and hurried out of the room. Raymond looked up at his friends, the only two people he could trust. Quinn was leaning against the mantle of the fireplace behind Amarice, who sat at her large mahogany desk.

"I have a spy in my midst. Someone who knows everything that's going on. It's the only explanation."

Amarice nodded. "Yes, I had the same thought. Any ideas who it could be?"

He shook his head. "No. I can't fathom who would betray me. Who would betray Elandria? But whoever it is also knew when you were away. And they knew that there weren't enough troops in Teleah to fight back and get people to safety."

He buried his head in his hands. How many people in his beloved city had fallen to Chamberite rioters? How many people in his employ? He thought of Andin, his loyal valet. Of the chef and of the maids and butlers who had been there since he was born. Of his father's portrait that might have fallen victim to the flames. He might never lay eyes on his father's visage again.

"Fuck!" He clenched his fists and pounded them against his thighs. "Fuck!"

"What do you need from us, Raymond?" Amarice asked.

"I don't know. I don't know what to do. We're fighting a losing war, and every day, it gets worse." He stood and pinched the bridge of his nose. "I have to figure out who is leaking information to the Chamberites."

"How?" Quinn asked, speaking for the first time in a while.

Raymond shrugged. "Not a clue. Excuse me."

He stormed out of the study and slammed the door. Several sets of eyes turned and stared, but no one said anything. He looked like a fool. A complete failure of a king. He took a deep breath, then turned toward the back staircase. "Raymond!"

He turned around halfway up the stairs at the sound of Elaine's voice. Her honey eyes were wide with worry. She met him where he stood and embraced him. He froze at the unexpected touch, unsure if he wanted to be comforted right now. But he softened and wrapped his arms around her.

"Oh, Raymond. I'm so sorry. I can't imagine how much you must be hurting."

A lump grew in his throat. He was devastated, tired. So very tired. He didn't think he could stand to hear another report about how unprepared he had left Teleah. He didn't want to hear about any more of his people dead at the hands of the rebels. A single tear slid down his cheek.

Elaine let go of him and gazed into his eyes. "Can I bring you anything? Anything at all?"

He shook his head. He wanted nothing more than to get pissed on firewine and fall asleep. And he had half a bottle in his room. It wouldn't get him drunk, but he didn't need to lose his mind right now in case he was needed. In case more terrible reports came in.

But he could be alone. And alone sounded good. "I'm just going to go...process everything, I think. Thank you, Elaine."

She gave him a watery smile and squeezed his hand. "If you need anything, let me know. Even if you just need to talk or want some silent company. My room is just two doors down, you know."

He hadn't, somehow. But that explained how she was always around when he hoped to see her. "Thanks."

He shut himself into his bedroom. He looked around. He was glad it felt so homey since he didn't know when he'd see his real home again. If ever.

He pulled the firewine from the cabinet and drank straight from the bottle. Then he collapsed onto the bed and threw an arm over his eyes, his other hand dangling off the bed with the bottle.

For the first time in weeks, he let himself cry.

CHAPTER 20

AMARICE

"One day, we'll be out of this stupid place." A teenaged Amarice skipped a rock on the pond. "We'll be far away in Teleah. You and me."

Zayn handed her another rock, and she threw it harder this time, not trying to skim the surface, not caring about ripples and waves. She imagined a fish narrowly dodging the rock under the surface of the water, swearing in an unknown fish language at the intrusion. She giggled.

Zayn looked at her in confusion at the sudden shift and shook his head. He was used to her antics and her moods. He knew the way her mind wandered by now. They'd been friends since they were five years old. Amarice smiled at him in fondness.

"Let's go for a swim," she said.

"It's freezing!"

She rolled her eyes. The chill was slight; the air smelled like spring was around the corner. "I've gotten good at warming the water, I promise."

"The last time you said that I nearly lost my bollocks to frostbite."

She huffed. "Come on, Zayn! That was two years ago. You never swim with me anymore."

"I can't."

"Why?"

"I can't, Amarice."

"But why?"

He groaned and rubbed his eyes. "Are you five or fifteen with all these whys?"

She shrugged and tugged on his shirt. "You've never given me a good answer. You've avoided swimming with me for a long time."

"Stop, Amarice."

She pouted. "Please, just tell me why."

"Because...ugh, stop giving me that look. I'll tell you."

"I'm listening." She grinned and batted her eyelashes.

"It's because I don't want to get undressed with you anymore. It was fine when we were kids. We're older now, though, and you're...and I'm..."

"Oh." Zayn found her so repulsive that he wouldn't even swim with her? Her eyes welled with tears as she stared at the ground. "You think I'm ugly?"

"Brigitte's tit, no! No, quite the opposite!"

She cocked her head and wiped away her tears. "I'm confused."

"For someone smart, you're dumb sometimes." But there was no malice in his voice when he said it. "I don't want to go swimming with you because you're beautiful, and I'm afraid of..."

Understanding dawned on Amarice. "Ohhh." She was no stranger to that sort of reaction. She'd just pulled a boy behind the schoolhouse this afternoon. "Well, that's ridiculous. It's nothing to be ashamed of."

He sighed. "Amarice. I know you don't like me that way. I don't want to mess up our friendship."

She opened her mouth to respond but found herself without words. Did she really not like him in that way? Or had she just never considered it because it was Zayn? She studied him, his long blond hair loose around his face. He was taller than her, which wasn't saying much. He had crystal blue eyes that sparkled. And he was kind. So very kind, when so much of Daviya was not.

For their whole lives, it had been the two of them. The only two Scholars in the school. And their teacher hated Scholars. Well, she hated Amarice—that much was certain. She and Zayn had become fast friends, as their old bat of a teacher had tried to turn their classmates against them. When the bitter matron had harassed Zayn that second day of school for messing up his numbers, Amarice had defended him.

He was like a brother. He was at her house more than his own, and for good reason. His mother was a cold woman. Amarice's mother and grandmother had all but adopted him at age seven, when he turned up with a black eye, crying.

But could he be more? Amarice didn't like a lot of people in Daviya. But she loved Zayn. Like a sibling, like a friend. And now she looked at him, wondering if they could be something deeper.

"Stop staring at me like that. You're acting strange."

Amarice smiled. "Sorry."

Then, "We could, you know."

"Could what?" he asked.

"We could...be more. If you wanted."

Hurt spread across his features, and she didn't understand. Isn't that what he had just said he wanted?

"Zayn, what did I say wrong?"

He shook his head. "Amarice, I love you."

"I love you, too."

"No. I'm in love with you. And I know that we could tear off our clothes and kiss and all of that. But I know you. It means nothing to you. And I don't want..." His voice trailed off after a pubescent squeak. "I want my first time to mean something."

He turned away.

"Zayn!"

"I'll see you tomorrow, Amarice." He didn't turn around.

A GENTLE—AND wet—touch on her thigh jolted Amarice out of her thoughts. Her eyes flew open to find Quinn, half-submerged in the river, staring at her with concern.

"I didn't mean to startle you, love."

"It's all right." She gave him what she hoped was a reassuring smile.

"What's wrong?"

She leaned forward and planted a quick kiss on his lips. "I'm fine. I'm always fine when I'm with you."

He arched a skeptical eyebrow. "Right. And at some point, you're going to tell me what's been bothering you, yes?"

"I'm just stressed with everything going on." Stressed at all the lives that had been lost, lives that rested on her shoulders.

"Then let me help you, Amarice. I'm your Consort."

She put a hand on his wet cheek. "You are helping. With the forest and the training, and all the day-to-day tasks at the Villa. And you've been through so much."

He sighed. "You'll tell me if you need more from me?"

"Of course."

There was nothing he could do, anyway. Amarice watched him swim away. She kicked her feet in the river and watched tendrils of steam from her magic rise from the surface like fingers of the dead. There was no way she could put this burden on Quinn. If he knew how guilty she felt for being away during the attacks, he would blame himself for pulling her away. Quinn swam for a few more minutes before Amarice reminded him they were meeting with Raymond soon. He pulled himself onto the banks and dried himself before dressing in his linen pants and tunic. The air was just starting to warm again, hinting at the spring ahead—so like that day with Zayn all those years ago.

"I wonder what sort of mood Raymond is in tonight," Quinn said as they walked toward the Villa.

Amarice wondered, too. It had been three days since Teleah had fallen. Outside of meetings with his captains or themselves, he had sequestered himself away in his room. Elaine was bringing him meals. He spent most of the meetings sullen and distant but also had random periods of hysterical laughing. She hoped he wasn't drinking.

"How do you feel about him liking Elaine?" she asked. She took his arm and leaned against his shoulder.

"It's strange. I was worried at first, you know. I guess I'm still a little protective of her. But she's a grown woman now."

"You're not jealous?"

He was quiet for a moment, thinking. She loved that about him. His responses were careful and well-considered unless he was angry. Amarice had a tendency to blurt out the first thing she thought, although she was getting better with age.

"No, not jealous. Not of her. Sometimes I still get jealous thinking about his past with you. That he had you first."

"Many people had me first, but you have me last."

He smiled down at her. "That's right. I do. And you have me in every way that matters."

He took her hand as they approached the arches in the east garden. Scents of gardenia and lavender kissed their noses. She breathed in the deep floral aroma.

"I still have trouble liking her. I know it's silly."

He chuckled. "Jealousy is not an emotion I ever expected from you."

"I'm not!" He gave her a sidelong glance. "Fine. Maybe a little."

"You know, the more I think about Raymond and Elaine, the more I think it could work. She could ground him, you know. There aren't many people who can get away with telling Raymond to calm down or take a break."

"He'd be good to her," Amarice said. "When he loves, he loves with his whole heart. He would never intentionally hurt her."

"It's the unintentional I worry about. He's never been one to be tied down. Of course, this isn't Corthy. Maybe Elaine wouldn't want to be tied down. I don't know her well anymore."

"Raymond might present as a philanderer like most Telean men. But I think deep down, he just wants someone to dote on."

He had wanted that from Amarice, she knew. He never said it, but he showed it. Amarice never wanted a life like that, she had thought. She enjoyed going from lover to lover, having fun while guarding her heart. She was certain her capacity for falling in love had died with Zayn.

But then she met Quinn.

"I love you, Quinn. I love you more with each passing day."

CHAPTER 21

QUINN

"The important thing is to know your strengths. I don't mean your strongest element, but the easiest to control. Your strongest is likely not your easiest element to control." A group of about twenty Scholars sat in a semi-circle around Quinn, hanging on his every word. This was a group of the newest Scholars to enlist in the military. They were strong enough to fight with their magic. Amarice was still adamant that their goal was self-defense, but Quinn knew an offensive battle was nigh.

"That doesn't make any sense," a young man said. He must be a second or third-year student. "The strongest is the one we have the most control of. That's what we learned in Viridion's class."

"That's the common belief. But let me ask you a question. Which element can you control the best?"

"Water."

"Which element can you control the least?"

"Air."

"And when you have bursts of wild magic, which element most often appears?"

The man opened his mouth, then closed it. He furrowed his brow. After a moment, he said, "Air."

Quinn watched the other young Scholars nod as they realized he was right. It had been less than a year since Amarice had told him the same truth. And what a wild year it had been.

"But can you learn to harness your strongest element?" a young woman asked.

He nodded. "With lots of practice. And to a degree. It will always be stronger than you, and it will drain you faster."

"What's yours, Lord Consort?"

He smiled. "Water."

He enjoyed this—the teaching, answering questions. It was nice being an expert on something. He cleared his throat. "As I was saying, you should stick to the elements that you can control the best when you're defending yourself. It will keep you from draining your Gift too quickly, and you'll fight with more precision.

"But today, we're going to practice replenishing your magic while using it. This requires great focus, at least until you get more used to it. Even then, you'll need to have one part of your mind dedicated to pulling your magic in."

He stood, and the others stood with him. He walked them through a meditation to pull the Gift of the Earth in through their bare feet. Then he gave each a handful of wildflower seeds from a leather pouch. He challenged them to grow each small germ from seed to mature plants one at a time.

By the fifth seed, many students began showing signs of slowing down. He told them to divide their minds and replenish without stopping the growth. It was a difficult skill to master. Scholars were trained to focus when they used their magic. It was just Amarice—and now Quinn—who used it with little thought and without weakening. The students struggled; they were unlearning everything their professors had taught them.

By the end of an hour, the group of students was splayed out on the ground, exhausted. But about half had refilled their Gift a small amount. Quinn instructed them to keep practicing, and he'd check on them in a few days.

He angled his face to the winter sun. The day was clear, and the sun beat down with some warmth on his skin. Spring wasn't far away. With a satisfied sigh, he put his hands in his pockets and began walking back toward the Villa.

He stopped along the way, chatting here and there with faces that were becoming familiar. He practiced his Deyoni with some children. Joy was returning to the people of the mountains. It was both heartening and terrifying—he knew it could not last. Though Raymond's armies were winning some battles, this war was far from over. The last report said that Samperian had arrived in Beybrook with Azmar and Grellis. But the Elandrians were close to reclaiming Te'eh. Teleah was another matter altogether.

He stopped at the edge of the northern garden and ran his hand along the twisted trunks of the Consort Tree. It hummed with magic under his touch. The green leaves were vibrant against the winter landscape. The pile of leaves that had rested under it on his return were turning into mulch. Whatever grew in it this spring would be hardy and plentiful, with his and Amarice's magic infused into it.

A familiar hawk swooped down and landed on a branch above his head.

"Hello, Eleanor." He reached his hand up, and the massive bird nuzzled her feathered head against Quinn's knuckle. "Where's Father?"

She opened her beak in response.

"Sorry. I don't have any treats."

"My son! That is not what I expected Eleanor to find, but I am pleased." Deben walked up and patted Quinn on the arm. Another of his birds circled over his head. "How is your today?"

Quinn grinned. "It's going well. And yours?"

Deben nodded. "Quite well. The birds have hunted much meat. I was about to return them to their cages."

"I'll go with you."

He'd been so busy that he hadn't seen his father and brother much, except at meals. He watched as Deben called his birds to him. Eleanor perched on the leather brace on his left arm, and the other bird—

Quinn couldn't recall the name—landed on his right. Quinn lifted a leather bag full of the hunted animals. He was sure Madge could turn them into something delicious, although Deben often hunted for the people in the mountains.

"When all this is over, will you return to the Gagiya?" Quinn asked. It was a question he had wondered about, and one he wasn't sure he wanted the answer to.

Deben thought for several moments. "I miss my family. My sisters. The children. But I am enjoying learning to be a father."

Quinn felt a lump grow in his throat at the kind words.

Deben continued. "In a perfect world to me, you and Amarice would come home with me. You would have many children, and I would be a jolly *hala-shesalo*." He looked at Quinn with a grin. "But I know that is not the case. I want to be your *shesalo*. I want your children to call me *hala*. I would leave the Gagiya for that."

They reached the stables where the cages sat in an empty stall. He returned the birds to their cages with gentle words and pieces of meat. When he finished, Quinn pulled him into an embrace. Perhaps it was selfish to want Deben to leave his life behind, but Quinn was happy his father was considering it.

"Come, come." Deben patted Quinn's face. "I promised to meet your brother and tell him a story about your mother. Can you join us?"

Quinn glanced at the sun. He still needed to finish some correspondence for the Villa. But that could wait. "Of course."

He spent the rest of the afternoon in the library with Deben and Corbin and Janessa. Deben first told them of the day he and Eleanor—the woman, not the bird—visited the tribe together. He told them how his sisters tried to teach Eleanor to dance. Quinn and Corbin laughed until they cried.

"You mean to tell me that our mother danced like a Deyoni?" Corbin said between guffaws.

"Well, she certainly tried. She was unsuccessful but lovely in her attempts." Deben smiled at the memory.

Quinn snorted. He couldn't even imagine such a thing. His mother was so quiet and straitlaced his entire life. Timid, and never happy. His smile faltered at that thought. His heart ached for her. Part of him had hoped that one day she could be with Deben, though it had been nearly twenty-eight years since they last saw each other. But his mother was dead, yet another victim of this senseless war.

Quinn's face grew somber. Deben switched his stories to a story from his youth. Amarice joined them at some point, tucking herself under Quinn's arm on the sofa. Elaine came in looking for Janessa and settled on the floor. Raymond came by looking for Elaine and sat cross-legged next to her. By dinnertime, Deben had shifted to Deyoni folk tales. Janessa and Corbin hung on his every word. Quinn watched the scene with a full heart.

Family.

He had wished for a scene like this his whole life. When Madge came to collect them for dinner, Quinn kissed the head-of-house on top of her head. She was family, too. He thought his mother would appreciate someone looking out for him, making sure he was well-fed. At dinner, he sat next to Jack and across from Daisy. The two bickered with no malice, as if they were brother and sister.

War raged on. Miles away, the world was falling apart. But here, in the warm glow of the dinner table, Quinn was happy. Here, the people he called family were alive and laughing. For now, it was enough.

CHAPTER 22

AMARICE

"Any word on the spy?" Amarice asked.

Raymond shook his head and poured himself a glass of wine. He sat the bottle on the table and sank into the armchair. He propped his feet on the small table, ignoring Amarice's disapproving glance. She sat behind her desk. Quinn was splayed out on the chaise with one arm thrown over his eyes. Poor Quinn. Training the Scholars for hours a day was taking its toll on him. Amarice had been working with the more advanced Scholars, while he had taken on the ones who were still students.

"The captain of my personal guard has been interrogating everyone who knew sensitive information, but there've been no results."

"And you trust Erenia?"

Raymond shrugged. "I have to. I've questioned everyone's loyalty, save the two of you. But I do trust her, I think. She's been my friend since we were kids."

The three friends were quiet for a while. Amarice sipped her own drink, an ale that Marian had brought months ago and saved for the

Sage. After several long minutes, Raymond spoke again. "Let's say that we win this war. What comes next?"

Amarice cocked her head. "What do you mean?"

"I mean, we win the war. We defeat the Chamberites. Lazoria's mercenaries leave. What do we do?"

It was a good question. The last time any major conflict had occurred in Elandria was three centuries ago. The Elandrian army had squashed the Deyoni rebellion, and the queen of the time had taken more of their rights away. Amarice recalled the earlier history of her country. She knew how the wars ended, and she knew the general changes that happened. But history books always glossed over the specifics of how those changes came about.

"Well," she said, "first, we'll have to figure out what to do with the soldiers from the Chamberite army. Do we try them all for treason?"

Quinn sat up and joined the conversation. "That seems like a lot of trials, assuming we don't kill them all in battle."

"But that's also a lot of pardons," Amarice countered.

"And if they lose, there will still be Chamberite sympathizers." Raymond sat his drink down and leaned forward with his elbows on his knees. "How do we ensure there is no further uprising?"

"Their religion is the issue. The idea that men should rule and magic is evil," Amarice said.

"Should we ban their religions, then?" Raymond asked.

Quinn shook his head. "No. You can't stop people from believing something, and they'd just resent us more for it."

Amarice agreed. "You know how well it goes when you try to tell someone not to do something."

"Fine. We can't ban a belief system. We could ban churches, though."

Amarice sighed. "Again, they'll resent us more. Quinn is right about that. They'll continue to meet in secret, and that's dangerous. They'll feel they have more of a cause to rebel."

Raymond groaned and leaned back in his chair. "So, we can't make them hate us more. Fine. How do we keep them from gaining power again?"

"Bar them from Parliament?"

"You're both missing the point," Quinn said. "You can't take away rights. That's what they're angry about in the first place."

The king and the Sage turned toward the Lord Consort. Quinn had sat up. His jaw was set, and red crept up from his neck. Amarice raised her eyebrows in surprise. "What do you mean?" she asked.

He took a deep breath. "Their religion is problematic with most of Elandria's views, I'll give you that. But that's not the issue. Azmar and Grellis don't believe in Samperian's gods. Azmar certainly doesn't believe in a patriarchy."

Amarice nodded. He was right.

"Most of their supporters don't believe the theology. But they blame magic for their problems. It's a scapegoat, but the real issue is the entire way our society is structured. It's inherently unequal."

Amarice let out a shrill laugh and glanced at Raymond. His fists were clenched at Quinn's accusation.

"Unequal for the Deyoni perhaps," Amarice said. "But I've spent my whole life fighting for their rights. No one discriminates against the Chamberites. They do most of the discriminating."

Quinn stood and paced as he talked. "But they are. There is much of our society that is designed to favor Scholars. Let me ask you. Why don't we allow regular Elandrians to come to the Academy?"

Raymond scoffed. "Because it's the Academy for Scholars. We learn how to use our magic."

"That's one class a year. The rest of the time, we learn healing and history and government and engineering. Why is that reserved for Scholars?"

Amarice spoke without thinking. "Scholars are more intelligent."

"See! That's exactly the mindset they're fighting against!" A vein was throbbing in Quinn's neck. "Do you believe that, or is that just what you've always been told?"

She opened her mouth but said nothing, instead biting her lip and crinkling her eyebrows.

Raymond responded with a weak retort. "It's well-documented."

"By whom? Scholars! But let's be honest with ourselves. Azmar is a brilliant woman. A genius strategist. She's no Scholar." He stopped by Amarice's desk and looked her in the eyes. "Your mother. You've said yourself she was the most gifted Healer you've ever seen. Your father, Raymond. He was no fool."

He looked away and rubbed his forehead. "Corbin understands engineering and architecture in a way I never will. It doesn't take magic to learn healing or law. Yet we keep people out of these fields for no good reason."

Raymond stood this time, raising his voice. "What are you suggesting, Quinn? That we overhaul the structure of our society after a war to please a bunch of zealots?"

"I wasn't suggesting anything! I was just pointing out why they're upset. And it's not just zealots! Think of the Scholar's taxes that passed. They're angry at being second-class citizens!"

"Oh, please. What you're suggesting is ludicrous! They vote. They're in the government. In fact, they make up most of Parliament!" Amarice stood and slammed her hands on her desk, her voice a half-octave higher as she tried to control her temper.

"But can they sit on special counsels to the king? Do they make trade agreements and meet with foreign dignitaries?"

"We're trained in that!" Amarice was almost shouting. "At the Academy!"

"Who says they can't be trained, too? This elitist thinking is what caused this mess."

"How dare you!" Raymond roared. "How fucking dare you suggest that we caused this! Not after all the deaths at their hands!"

Quinn put his hands up in front of his chest. "That's not what I'm suggesting. I know they started the violence. Brigitte's fucking tit, Raymond. They kidnapped me! They almost killed Amarice two years ago! But the discontent—that's centuries of Scholar elitism festering." He shook his head. "We won't get anywhere by screaming at each other. You asked what comes next. I answered. We need to address the problem at the root. You can't cure an infection by placing bandages on it." He turned to Amarice with a bitter smile. She could see him swallow hard. "I expected you to see this more clearly. With more empathy."

He stalked out of the study and slammed the door behind him. Off for a late-night run, Amarice was certain. Her head ached from clenching her jaw. She downed the rest of her ale in one go.

Raymond let out a long string of curses. "It's horse shit, right?" he asked when he calmed down.

Amarice shrugged and collapsed back into her chair. "Honestly, Raymond. I don't know."

"Of course you'd say that. You'd do anything for your precious Consort."

"Don't you fucking dare, Raymond. I have always been my own person and had my own mind." She rubbed her eyes with the heels of her hands. "But Quinn is my Consort because he challenges my mind. I'm not saying he's right. But perhaps I should think on it."

"Great. When you get your shit together and come to your senses, let me know. I could use some help."

He stormed off and slammed the door a second time. Amarice threw her empty glass against the door. Then she buried her pounding head in her arms and wept.

IT WAS hours before Quinn returned. Amarice lay in bed on her side facing away from the stairs, the night breeze from the window cool on her back. She wasn't asleep. Sleep wouldn't come.

She listened as Quinn undressed and folded his clothes. She knew it so well, she could picture his motions in her mind. He pulled the covers back and slipped into the bed next to her. She smiled as he kissed her temple.

"You're awake," he said. "I didn't disturb you, did I?"

"No." She turned to face him and tried out a small smile. "Did you have a nice run?"

He bit his lip. "Yes. Then I went to the camps and drummed with a group of Deyoni for a bit."

"Good."

Quinn stroked her hair. "Are you still angry with me?"

She shook her head against the soft pillow. "No. Are you still angry with me?"

He smiled. She loved his smile. "No. Not angry. I can't stay mad at you. But maybe a little disappointed."

"I know. I've been thinking all evening. You're right, I think. But it's hard for me, Quinn. It's hard for me to change the whole way I think about everything."

He nodded. "I thought a lot while I was at Citadel Kahyrst. There wasn't much else to do. And I had to figure out *why*. What was I missing, you know? These men that were holding me weren't evil. Well, most of them."

"It's easy to villainize people, but life isn't a storybook."

"No, it's not."

Amarice flopped onto her back and stared at the ceiling. "I was so despised as a child. And I know you were, too. But I grew to resent them, everyone who wasn't Deyoni or Scholar. I didn't have a brother or an...Elaine."

"What about that boy you've talked about in passing? Zayn?"

A lump grew in her throat. "He was a Scholar. The only other in the school. We were supposed to go to the Academy together. Take on the world together."

"He died?"

"Yes."

He reached out a hand and placed it over Amarice's. "How?"

She shrugged one shoulder. She didn't want to talk about it. Saying it out loud brought it all back, made it too visceral, too real. It had been almost fifteen years.

"All right, that's fine. You don't have to talk about it." His voice was gentle. He shifted, put an arm over her stomach, and nuzzled her hair. "I love you."

"I love you, too."

"Do you think Raymond will come around? It's not good if the three of us are at each other's throats."

She smiled. "He will. He's quick to anger and quick to forgive. And

I think...once he thinks about all you said...I think he'll come around to a new way of thinking. It just takes some of us longer."

"Stubborn, the lot of you." But Quinn's voice was teasing.

"Indeed. That's why I have you. No one else can deal with my stubbornness."

He kissed the side of her head. "I like your stubbornness."

CHAPTER 23

RAYMOND

Two weeks had passed since Raymond had lost his home to the Chamberites. He had decided not to retake Teleah yet. A force of the Lazori mercenaries was approaching. He couldn't risk any troops in what would be a very bloody battle. So, he made the Sage's Villa his permanent base of operations.

It was a good day, considering. He wasn't as angry at Quinn this morning, and the two had been cordial at breakfast. When the anger subsided last night, he started to see some truth in Quinn's words, especially when he thought of Elaine. But he didn't know if those truths were enough to turn his country inside out.

The day was off to a positive start. He had just received word of two successful battles with minimal casualties. The Chamberites had also stopped murdering Messengers, realizing they were far more useful alive. This led to an odd, tentative peace. The Messengers delivered letters for both sides, as they had sworn to be impartial in times of conflict. However, most were loyal to the throne, and many passed off information to Raymond's troops. He hoped these unlikely spies were only helping his side.

He jaunted down the stairs, deciding it had been far too long since he had taken a walk. His earth magic was itching under his skin at its disuse. Though he wasn't powerful, he was still a Scholar. He ran into Elaine in the garden. She knelt on the ground, unearthing potatoes from the fertile soil and placing them into a basket. Her pale brown hair was loose, as she had taken to wearing it lately. She wore a thick cotton dress of vibrant blue, but Raymond was confident she wasn't wearing a corset. Life outside of Corthy was starting to take effect on her.

He smiled and stopped several paces behind her so as not to startle her. "Good morning!"

She turned and grinned at him, pushing the hair out of her dirt-stained face. "Good morning! You're in a good mood."

"I suppose I am." He walked closer. "Do you need any help?"

She shook her head. "No, I think I've gathered just enough. Thank you, though."

He glanced down at the basket of potatoes. There had to be twenty-five in there, which meant it would be heavy. "Let me carry this for you."

Elaine stood. She wiped the dirt from her knees to no avail, then dusted her hands off. "Are you sure? I mean, you're the—"

"Stronger person of the two of us? Yes. Even a king can carry potatoes." He winked. She blushed.

He followed her down to the kitchen and placed the potatoes on a worktable. He picked up two scones from a platter and handed her one. "I'm going for a walk to get some fresh air. Use my sorely neglected magic. Want to tag along?"

Her eyes lit up. "I've never seen you use magic!"

He shrugged. "Don't get your hopes up too much. It's nothing impressive. My Gift of the Earth is weak. It's nothing like watching the Sage or the Consort."

"Well, I'm not sure anything is quite like that. But yes, I'd love to join you."

They walked out the western side of the Villa. There were no camps on this side. The aqueducts ran in from a nearby tributary, and the forest line was just a few hundred yards away. Raymond offered his arm to Elaine, and she took it.

A cool breeze was blowing, whipping Elaine's hair. She shivered. Wanting to impress her, Raymond pushed his own warming magic out to embrace her. She looked confused for a moment at the sudden temperature change. She looked up at him with a smile when she realized.

"It's amazing that the forest has grown up so much. I can't wrap my head around Scholars growing trees," she said as they neared the edge of the woods.

"Have you seen them do it?" he asked. She shook her head. "I'll bring you out tomorrow. Quinn made them take the day to rest. It's draining. I think they've moved to the northern boundary."

"I haven't explored the lands much." She bit her lip. "It's silly, I know, but I'm a bit frightened. I was told my whole life to fear Scholars and Deyoni. I can't shake some of that fear, even though I know it was all lies."

"That makes sense. It's hard to unlearn something you thought you knew."

She tucked a strand of hair behind her ear, and he fought the urge to run his hands through her silky locks. "Can you grow a tree?"

He laughed. "Not even if I used every drop of my magic. I can sprout a seedling, and that's about it."

"Why does everyone have such different levels of magic?"

He thought back to his magical theory classes over a decade ago. "The leading theory is the strength of the bloodline. The royal family has traditionally not had many Scholars. It's not a hard and fast rule, but we think it's hereditary. Amarice knows a lot more about it than I do."

They stopped when they reached the trees. He touched the grizzled trunk of an oak. Though it looked old, he could feel the newness of its life. He bent down and picked up some small rocks, then turned to face Elaine.

He tossed them in the air. The wind bent around him, and he

swirled them in spirals and zigzags. Elaine laughed and clapped her hands in delight.

"Amazing!"

He slowed the air and reached out to catch the tiny stones in his hand. He took a bow. "I'm glad you're impressed. Most Scholars can do that by about age ten."

"You're modest."

He chuckled. "I think you might be the only person to ever describe me as modest."

"You are, though! I see you doubting your leadership, your decisions. But you're a great king, Raymond. A great man."

He stepped forward to close the distance between them. She drew in a sharp breath as he stared into her deep-golden eyes. If he leaned forward anymore, his chest would brush against her. His heart pounded erratically in his ears.

His voice was a whisper. "Can I kiss you?"

She nodded slowly, her eyes never leaving his. He placed his hands on either side of her face. He lowered his head and closed his eyes, letting his lips brush hers. When she parted her lips, he deepened the kiss.

Kissing Elaine was like no other experience Raymond had ever had. And Raymond had kissed many people. There was a tentative curiosity in Elaine's kiss, but there was also a spark of fiery passion. He swiped his tongue across her bottom lip, asking for silent permission. She let him in. He moved a hand into her loose hair, pulling her closer, and felt her shiver against him. He worshipped her mouth with languid strokes and gentle pecks. He lowered his other hand to the small of her back, pulling her into him.

She let out a small whimper and jerked away, clapping her hand over her mouth. He smiled as a red blush flooded up her neck.

"I'm sorry," she murmured.

He chuckled. "For what? That precious little sound?" She nodded. "Never apologize for enjoying something, Elaine."

She smiled back and looked at the ground. "It's been a long time since..."

"That's all right."

He pushed her chin up with two fingers, bringing her gaze to meet his. "I have wanted to do that for a long time now, Elaine."

"Why?" Her words were so quiet, she almost didn't make a noise.

"Because I think you're incredible. I think you're beautiful and witty and intuitive."

She shook her head, but he held her cheek in his hand to stop her. "I'm not. I'm certainly not fit for the king."

"Oh, darling. You are, though. I wish you could see yourself the way I see you. And me? I'm a mess. I'm moody and sullen half the time. The rest of the time, I don't know how to be serious enough. I'm only king because of my birthright, not because I deserve it."

She placed her hand on his wrist and pushed her head into his hand. "You don't give yourself enough credit."

"I could say the same to you."

She smiled. "Then maybe we aren't all that bad of a match."

He bent his head to kiss her again. The curiosity was still there, but with more confidence. He fought to keep himself controlled when all he wanted to do was kiss her with more heat, more intention.

They parted, breathless. He placed his forehead against hers as they caught their breaths. She tasted sweet like honey, and he wanted more. But he was a gentleman—or could be, at least.

"I could spend all day kissing you," he said. "But tell me to stop, and I will."

"Don't you dare!"

They spent the rest of the afternoon walking and kissing and talking and kissing some more. Raymond hadn't felt this giddy since he was a teenager. He just wanted to be close to her, to touch her, to taste her.

As afternoon waned, they sat with their backs against the wall of the aqueduct, listening to the rushing water above their heads. She leaned her head against his shoulder. Their hands intertwined, and Raymond couldn't stop looking at the way her small, pale palm fit so well in his large, brown one.

"I'm nervous," she said.

He looked at her face. She was chewing her bottom lip. "What about?"

She sighed, and he could see her choosing her words carefully. "I know that you probably have...expectations. You're from the city, and..." She took a deep breath. "I don't know what you know about Quinn and me, but that was the last time—the only time—that I have ever..."

He squeezed her hand. "I know. And I have no expectations."

She gave him a dubious look. "Really?"

He laughed. "Desires, yes. Expectations, no. I'm not going to pressure you into anything, Elaine." He watched as she chewed her lip again. "What do you want to ask?"

She blushed. "How did you know I want to ask something?"

"Because I've paid attention."

Elaine pulled her hand out of his and crossed her hands in her lap. His heart skipped a little at the sudden loss of her touch. Just like a schoolboy, he chastised himself. He watched as she twiddled her thumbs.

"But what if you...have needs?"

"Are you asking if I'm going to sleep with other people?"

"I know that it's customary in the cities. I mean, my room is next to Matthew's. I hear things."

He placed his hand over hers to stop her wringing out her thumbs. She looked up at him, insecurity in her eyes. "What do you want me to do?"

"I don't know." She laughed a little. "Having the romantic interest of the king of Elandria is not a situation I prepared for."

"That's fine. Until you let me know one way or the other, consider me loyal only to you."

"You'd do that?" Her eyes widened.

He paused. It was terrifying, how strong his feelings were for this woman. "For you, Elaine, I think I'd do just about anything."

CHAPTER 24

QUINN

Quinn watched as Amarice stirred her coffee absentmindedly. She had taken to long periods of distraction, and he had no idea where her mind wandered. Though his Sage was often deep in thought, this was different. She was hurting, and she wouldn't let him help.

Raymond joined the breakfast table with Elaine close on his heels. He often saw the two of them with their heads bent together, talking and exchanging small touches. He wanted to ask Raymond how that situation was progressing, but they had only made peace from their argument a few days prior. Things were still tentative between them.

"Good morning," Raymond greeted him with a cheery grin.

"Good morning," Quinn replied. Amarice said nothing. He wasn't sure she even noticed Raymond's arrival.

Raymond nodded toward the Sage and raised an eyebrow. Quinn shrugged and changed the subject. "Any news?"

Raymond sipped his coffee. "Nothing from the fronts, but I have received new counts of our recruits here in the mountain. I have enough to form several more companies. I'm planning on promoting some of my lieutenants to captain today."

"What?"

Quinn and Raymond looked at Amarice. The gaze she fixed upon Raymond was stony. Quinn took a deep breath, waiting to see how this would play out.

"Nice of you to join us, Amarice," Raymond said, teasing.

"Where are these recruits coming from?"

"Here. In the mountains."

Her voice raised an octave. "My people?"

The rest of the table fell silent. Raymond sighed. "They're my people, too. But yes, Scholars and Deyoni. Some Telean refugees."

"And what do you plan to do with these new companies?" she asked with acid in her voice.

"Fight. They've been training."

"To defend themselves!"

Raymond lowered his voice. "You can't still believe that, Amarice. This is war. We are finally gaining the numbers we need to turn the tide."

"But we talked about—"

Quinn interjected. "Maybe we should discuss this later. In private. Not at the breakfast table." He looked down the table at the Villa's residents. Most of them were staring wide-eyed at either their plates or at the argument at the head of the table.

Amarice stood, pushing back her chair with a loud scrape. She tossed down her napkin and stormed off. Quinn sighed. She hadn't touched her breakfast. Or her coffee. Lately, he often had to remind her to eat. When he did convince her to eat, she couldn't get enough.

He gave an apologetic half-smile to the rest of the table, then he took Amarice's coffee and an apple and left the dining room to find her. She had gotten worse in recent days, returning to her habits of no sleep.

He checked the study and their chambers. He tried the library and the baths. No sign of her. That meant she was likely headed for the forest. He looked at the items in his hands. There was no way he'd make it to the woods without spilling the coffee, and he hadn't finished his own. He downed it in one gulp.

"Quinn!"

He looked up to see Daisy running across the courtyard to him. He rolled his eyes. "Now's not a great time, Daisy. Can it wait?"

She shook her head. "No, you ass. It's about Amarice."

"What about her?"

"I'm worried about her."

"I am, too. That's why I'm trying to find her." He tried to hide the impatience in his voice. He wanted to make sure she was okay.

"She refused a sleeping tonic. I've tried every day. I've seen the dark circles under her eyes."

Quinn nodded. "I don't know what's wrong."

"She's got to get some rest, Quinn."

"I know." He pinched his brow between his eyes and recalled something. "Has she ever talked to you about Zayn?"

"Who?"

"Her childhood friend. Lover. I don't know."

Daisy shook her head. "Amarice doesn't talk about her childhood much. I'm her best friend, and I hardly know what her life was like before she came to Teleah at sixteen. Why do you ask?"

He shrugged. "I don't know. I asked about him the other night. She said he died, but when I asked how, she froze up. That was when she stopped sleeping again."

"You think all of this is about some boy who died over a decade ago?"

"Yes. No. I don't know, Daisy. I'm worried. Her magic—"

"I know. I can feel it. It's buzzing around her like a swarm of bees. I'm sure every Scholar here can feel it."

Daisy took the empty cup from Quinn's hand and handed Quinn a small bottle. "Make her take this. Somehow. If she doesn't sleep…"

"I can't drug her, Daisy!" It was wrong for anyone, but both he and Amarice had been drugged against their wills.

She gave him a wry smile. "Then convince her to take it."

Quinn slipped the vial into his pocket and nodded. Daisy flounced away, her red braid trailing behind her. Quinn shook his head and headed to the woods to find Amarice. He caught up with her halfway across the western meadow and jogged to stop her.

"Hey."

She turned to look at him but didn't slow her pace. "Hey."

Quinn held her arm to slow her down. She was trembling. He pulled her into his chest, wrapping his arms tight around her. "Amarice. What is wrong? Talk to me."

"I can't let them fight."

He tightened his embrace as her shaking worsened. "They're joining willingly, my love. They want to fight, to defend Elandria."

"But I swore to protect them."

"And they know that. But you can't stop them, love."

"Raymond is probably forcing them—"

"He's not, Amarice. He respects your wishes, and he is glad he hasn't had to resort to conscription. The Feast of Fire attacks mobilized them in a new way. They saw what will happen firsthand. They want to fight."

"I can't protect them. I can't protect anyone if they march off to war. I have to stay here, to keep everyone safe."

Quinn stepped back. He held Amarice by the shoulders at arms' length. "Amarice, my darling. Look at me." Her grey eyes were bright with tears. "You are not responsible for saving everyone. This war is happening. People are making hard decisions, but they are making them on their own, in good faith. Trust them."

"Some of them are so young." She choked out a sob, and Quinn pulled her close again.

"I know. I know."

Once again, he thought of little Melya dia Ishtani. He thought of his cousins' children, laughing and playing around the campfire, teaching him Deyoni jokes and colorful swears. A pile of stones weighed on his chest, making it hard to breathe.

He took a deep breath, grounding himself, letting his magic connect to the earth below him. "You don't have to do this alone, Amarice. You're not alone."

She didn't reply, and Quinn knew that she didn't believe him.

"My love, you must get some rest. When was the last time you slept?"

She shook her head. "I can't—I can't sleep."

"Is it the dreams?" They'd had a nasty one a few nights ago and received word yesterday of a fleeing Deyoni family who was mowed down by Lazori mercenaries. But otherwise, most of the violence of late had been battles. No Scholars or Deyoni were in the forces around Elandria, so the dreams were less frequent than before.

"No. I just can't—the thoughts—I can't..."

"Amarice, if you don't get some sleep, you'll lose control of your magic. Take a sleeping tonic. Please. We're all so worried about you."

She looked up at Quinn, lower lip quivering. "I don't like it. It's like when they drugged me."

"I know, darling. But I'm here. I'll keep you safe."

She swallowed, and a single tear ran down her cheek. Quinn wiped it away. "Just a little," she said.

"Just a little."

She allowed him to lead her back to the Villa. He guided her to their chambers. No one said anything, though everyone in the Villa stared with concern. Daisy raised an eyebrow as they walked past, and Quinn nodded at her.

Upstairs, she sat on the edge of the bed. Quinn handed her the glass vial. She took a small sip, downing only a third of the dose. He hoped it was enough because he needed her to feel better. He guided her up to the pillows and wrapped his arms around her as she curled into a ball. They said nothing, and he stroked her hair as she stared at the wall.

Her eyelashes fluttered. "Don't fight it, Amarice. I'm here."

"Don't leave." Her voice was weak with exhaustion and fear.

"I won't."

Moments later, she was asleep for the first time in days. Quinn didn't move, just held her close and wished her good dreams.

CHAPTER 25

AMARICE

Zayn had been avoiding her for a week, and she was tired of it. He ignored her at school, and when the schoolteacher released them, he ran toward home before she could leave the building. He slipped away to Brigitte-knows-where at lunch. Finally, at the end of the week, she cornered him as he came out of the outhouse after school. She wrinkled her nose. She couldn't wait until they were in Teleah with proper plumbing.

"You've been avoiding me."

Zayn looked up in surprise as he came out, lacing up his pants.

"Can't get away from you for long, can I?"

"Why would you want to?" She flipped her hair and smirked.

He rolled his eyes. "Fine. I've been avoiding you."

"Why?"

He lowered his voice and took her away from the nearby group of students by the elbow. "You know why."

"Because you fancy me?" She wiggled her eyebrows at him.

"Damn, Amarice. Sometimes you're a real bitch. Yes, because I fancy you."

Amarice dropped the smile from her face. "I've been thinking." When he didn't say anything, she continued. "Maybe it's not a bad idea."

"What isn't?"

"You and me." She examined her fingernails, trying to appear nonchalant.

Zayn sighed. "It's a terrible idea, and the fact that you're so disinterested proves it. I have real feelings for you, Amarice. I'm in love with you."

She snapped her head up, eyes wide. "You are? Truly?"

"But I already told you, I don't want to be your latest conquest."

Amarice straightened. "Rude."

"Sorry, but...you've got a reputation. And it's not wrong. I don't want that, Amarice. I want you. And if I can't have you, I would prefer we just stay friends."

She thought for a few moments, twirling her loose brown hair. "You're my only friend, Zayn. You always have been. And I think because we're so close, I just never considered you as anything more."

He snorted. "Great."

"Let me finish." She slapped his shoulder. "But when you said that last week at the pond, I thought about it, and I realized that I've been stupid. Everyone else, they don't care about me. They just want me for a little fun. But you—you see me."

Zayn closed his eyes. "What are you saying, Amarice?" he asked in a hopeful voice.

"I'm saying that I think I have feelings for you, too. And I'm willing to see what happens with us. I think...I think it could be good."

She gave him a little smile. A sweet one, not her typical flirtatious glance that she used on peers at lunch or young men at the market.

Zayn took her hand. "You're not just saying that?"

"No, I'm not. I'm a lot of things, Zayn. But I'm not a liar."

"I know."

The air grew heavy between them. Amarice's heart pounded. She leaned forward and pressed her lips against Zayn's. He gasped and kissed her back.

Weeks passed, and Amarice had never been happier. They found themselves in an isolated corner of the woods almost every day after school. She hadn't told him she loved him yet, but she suspected she did. How was she to know what love felt like?

Their horrid schoolteacher had finally retired, and a lovely Scholar fresh out of the Academy took over. For the first time in her life, Amarice enjoyed going to school. And her sixteenth birthday was just a few weeks away.

Zayn wasn't at school one morning, and Amarice was worried. She went to his house at lunch, but his bitch of a mother yelled at her to go away. He was back the next day. He said he'd been ill. But then he started missing more school.

The next week, he showed up at lunchtime. Amarice had her tongue halfway down a girl's throat behind the schoolhouse.

"What the fuck?"

"Zayn! You're back!" Amarice pushed the girl away.

He was pale, but his glare was stony. "What are you doing?"

"Oh. You know Larena."

"Get lost," Zayn said to Larena between clenched teeth. Larena looked affronted but ran off with a wave to Amarice. "I'm gone a few days, and you have to fool around with someone else?"

"I didn't know you expected us to be exclusive. How utterly rural."

"Of course I did! I told you I loved you!"

"Are you jealous? You shouldn't be. You know I only have feelings for you."

"You're a bitch." He clenched his hands into fists.

"Zayn. I'm sorry. I didn't know that's what you expected."

"Is Larena the only one?"

Amarice looked down. "No."

"Brigitte's tit. I knew this was a terrible idea."

Tears filled her eyes. "You don't mean that, do you?"

"Yes, I do. I knew you would hurt me."

"No! Zayn, please." She cried now at the hurt look on his face. How could she have been so stupid? "Please. I love you."

"No, you don't. You only love yourself." He turned and stalked off. Amarice slid down the building and sobbed into her arms.

CHAPTER 26

RAYMOND

The king rubbed his face as he sat behind the oak desk in the upstairs study. He knew that Amarice was going through something he didn't understand. He used to warn her that one day her façade would crack, and she would need to confront the shadows that lingered behind her bright eyes. Those shadows had sure picked an inopportune time to emerge. He was struggling to hide his frustration at her stubbornness. Her refusal to send Scholars to fight—and to fight herself—was naïve.

And now she was picking arguments in front of people at meals. They needed to present a united front to keep people's hope alive.

He looked at the thick stack of correspondence in front of him and sighed. It would be nice to have help with this, someone to sift through and figure out what needed his attention now and what could wait. He missed Andin. The valet had not come with the Telean refugees to the mountains. No one could tell him if the older man was alive or dead, and he hoped Andin had found his way to safety.

Raymond didn't think he could bear to lose another father figure, not so soon after Roland had died.

It wasn't safe to have anyone else take on Andin's duties, either. He trusted his guard, especially Erenia, but he needed them out training and receiving news from other units. Other than stacking letters on his desk, they had no need to be involved in his day-to-day obligations, but besides them, he had no one in his employ he could trust.

Erenia's investigation into the spy had yielded no fruit. He couldn't fathom who had betrayed him. Perhaps one of the Parliamentarians who had stayed on for counsel, but that would require them to play the long game and vote against Chamberite interests.

He opened the first envelope and began to read. It was an update from a captain on the southern peninsula. They had regained that territory, forcing the Lazori mercenaries to flee in their ships. He made a note to tell Amarice since she hailed from the peninsula.

His eyes glazed as he read more missives. Lists of numbers blurred in his eyes. Words ran together. He needed to get more coffee and stretch his legs. One more letter, he told himself. One more, and he would head down to the kitchen.

He froze. The next letter was addressed to Raymond, not "His royal highness" or even "King Raymond." He squinted at the sloping script. The handwriting was familiar. Could it be?

Andin.

That meant his old friend was alive. He smiled as he ran his fingers along the inked letters and turned the letter over to break the wax seal. It was an unmarked seal, which meant Andin was not in the palace.

His smile faltered as he read.

Dear Raymond,

I hope this letter finds you well. Please know that despite the words that follow, I have always loved you. I enjoyed watching you grow up into a bright young man.

However, I must confess that I have betrayed your confidence. Although I do not regret my actions, as I believe them just, I did not enjoy lying to you.

Scholars, including you, live a life of excess while so many in Elandria subsist in an honest fashion. Earth magic and Scholar culture have depleted Elandria of its morality. Gluttony and promiscuity abound, and it is detrimental to our grand society's history. These traditions have weakened the foundation of Elandria's honor.

I could not abide watching Elandria fall further into sin under your reign. Though I believe you have the fortitude to lead Elandria to greatness, the influence of the wicked Sage is too great. You lose yourself trying to impress her. But she will lead Elandria to ruin.

I learned the truth from Minister Samperian just a few years ago, and I have repented for my evil ways. I never wanted to put you in danger, so I ensured the palace would be taken while you were away.

You could become a great king if you would only do the right thing. Forsake the Sage and her lapdog. I pray to the Father and Mother every day that you will find the truth.

-Andin

Raymond clutched at his chest, trying to abate the sharp pain like a thousand arrows in his heart. He read the letter again and again. Heat rose in his neck and cheeks.

"FUCK!" He flung his arm across the desk, knocking the inkwell to the floor, which just angered him more.

How could Andin have done this? More importantly, how had Raymond not known? For all Andin's supposed concern about his soul, he had never tried to talk about it. Never once did he allude to the fact that he was religious, let alone a Chamberite sympathizer.

He stood, knocking over his chair. He pounded a fist into the wall and let out a loud roar of anger.

The door to the study flew open. Elaine.

"Raymond? What's wrong?"

He ground his teeth and hit the wall again. Her eyes were wide. She stayed in the doorway, her hand still on the door handle.

"My valet," he said with a huff.

"Your valet? Is he dead?"

Raymond shook his head. "Worse."

He turned and took the letter off the desk, holding it out to Elaine. "Here."

He couldn't watch as she read. He stared across the room and out the window, chastising himself for being so blind. So stupid.

"Oh, dear. Raymond, I'm so sorry. You had no inkling?"

"No, because I'm a fucking idiot."

Her hand settled on his back. "You're not. You're a good man. A good king. You're doing the right thing. Andin is the idiot because he doesn't see it."

Raymond swallowed. "He was like a second father to me."

Elaine wrapped her arms around his waist, placing her cheek against his back. She said nothing else as she held him, but it was enough. Tears streamed down his face. Though he was ashamed that he was crying in front of someone, he made no effort to wipe the tears away.

The pair stayed like that for a long time. Eventually, they made their way to the sofa. Elaine listened, one hand on Raymond's knee, as he went on a long tirade about Andin's betrayal. His angry monologue turned to wistful memories, and more hot tears fell. The pain in his gut didn't go away, but it eased as Elaine comforted him.

An ear-piercing scream from downstairs made them jump. Raymond rushed out of the study to the balcony overlooking the courtyard, Elaine on his heels.

All he could see were flames.

CHAPTER 27

AMARICE

Her dream swirled forward. Zayn hadn't been at school in two weeks, and Amarice hadn't gone to find him. The new teacher had asked her to consider applying to the Academy early, as she had mastered most of the curricula already, and she wanted to tell Zayn all about it. And to tell him she had said no. The two of them were supposed to go to Teleah together in two years. But she was still hurt and angry—and full of shame—so she didn't try to see him.

That evening, Zayn's mother pounded on the door of the shop. Amarice followed her mother down the stairs from their apartment. "Please. He's so sick. Please help."

Amarice's mother grabbed her bag full of medicines and supplies that she kept by the wooden door in their shambled apartment. Amarice's heart raced. He was sick. For his mother to be this desperate and seek help from Amarice's mother, it had to be bad.

"What's wrong with him?" Amarice asked as they rushed toward Zayn's home.

His mother shook her head. "I don't know. He'd been vomiting. I assumed it would pass in a few days. But then his fever spiked. He's barely left the bed. He seized this evening."

"For how long has he been ill?" Amarice's mother asked in her thick Deyoni accent.

"Three weeks."

That was when he first missed school, Amarice realized. Her mother glared at the woman. "Why are you just now getting help?"

"I didn't...I didn't know it was so bad."

The small cottage smelled of sickness. Amarice's mother knelt by his bed, placing her hands on him. "His skin is like fire."

Amarice froze in the doorway. Zayn, always so tall and strong, lay in his bed. His pale skin was drenched with sweat. She stifled a sob at the sight of his feeble frame.

"Amarice. Water," her mother said. She held out a pitcher, but Amarice didn't move. Her mother's voice was gentle but stern. "Now, Amarice."

Amarice felt as if she were walking through a haze as she took the pitcher. With one hand, she held the jug and made her way to the well. She hurried back, holding the container with both hands to avoid spilling any. Her mother was pouring a thick, brown tonic down Zayn's throat.

Amarice poured half the pitcher into a basin. She placed a finger in the water, chilling it. She dipped soft cloths in the cool liquid and began washing Zayn's skin. Her mother listened to his breathing and his heartbeat. Her face was grave. Zayn's mother watched from the doorway.

"Infection. It is far progressed." Amarice's mother glared at the frightened woman. "A week of tonics would have fixed this. Now, I do not know."

"Save him. Please. He's my only son."

Amarice's mother scoffed. "That's why you hit him and break his spirit? But I will try my best because I love him, too." She pursed her lips and barked at Amarice, "Heat the water for melaleuca tea."

Amarice placed a hand on the pitcher, bringing the water to a boil. Her mother poured it into a wooden mug full of leaves. The earthy, pungent scent of melaleuca filled the room. Amarice lifted Zayn's head as her mother tipped the hot liquid in his mouth.

Zayn sputtered, and his eyes opened. His throat was hoarse when he croaked out a word. "Amarice."

"I'm here. I'm here." She grabbed his hand. "Oh, Zayn. Why didn't you tell me you were sick? Were you so angry at me?"

"No." He coughed, a wet, loud echo. Amarice looked up to see her mother's brow furrow. "I was so mean to you. I didn't think..."

He fell into a coughing fit. Amarice rubbed his chest. "You silly boy. Does it hurt?"

He nodded.

"Where?"

"Everywhere."

Amarice's mother prepared poppy tea. He drank it down quickly, parched and desperate for a drink. He would fall asleep soon.

"I'm so cold."

That wasn't good at all. His skin was burning up. Amarice looked at her mother, who nodded, then used magic to warm the air around him. It was for comfort and nothing else. At this point, it didn't matter. He'd either make it through the night or not.

His eyes fluttered as he looked at Amarice. His eyes were glassy. "I'm sorry."

"No, you were right. I'm sorry." Tears burned her eyes as they fell.

"I love you."

"I love you, too, Zayn. Please. Please get better."

He drifted into a poppy sleep, though it was far from restful. He jerked and tossed. Amarice and the two women sat in silence around him. His breathing grew more labored as the cottage fell into darkness, and no one moved to light a candle.

An hour or so passed, and Zayn began jerking and seizing. His back arched as he thrashed. Amarice's mother tried to hold his head still against the violent convulsions. Amarice kept her hands on his arm, unable to move them. His mother grabbed his legs to keep him steady.

Then he stopped. His breathing steadied and weakened. His muscles stopped twitching, and his skin began to cool.

Amarice's mother spoke, her voice thick. "Coma."

Zayn's mother let out a horrible sob. She cried to him how sorry she was for everything, as if it would do any good. Amarice leaned forward and placed her forehead on his shoulder, her own tears soaking his clammy skin.

As the black night turned into the pale grey before dawn, Zayn drew his last breath.

۞

AMARICE WOKE two hours after she had taken the tonic, eyes flying open. She panted, and her heart pounded. She gripped the sheets to calm herself, trying to figure out where she was. As she blinked, her bedroom came into view, familiar yet stifling. The sounds of Quinn's stable breathing grounded her. She turned her head to see him dozing beside her, and her heart ached with guilt. He'd been so worried about her.

She was tired of hurting the people she loved.

She quietly pulled herself from the bed so as not to disturb him. It wasn't even lunchtime yet. Her hair was sticky with sweat, and she pulled it into a frantic braid before padding down the stairs. She had to get out of there.

She froze at the foot of the stairs, the dream that had roused her from sleep rushing back. Not a dream, she realized, but a memory. A memory she had spent a dozen years forcing from her mind.

People had died for her mistakes. For her stupidity and rashness and selfishness. Too many people, and now more would die. Quinn was right about the discord in Elandria. As Sage, she could have used her title to make relations better. But she had been too oblivious, too selfish to see it.

Magic boiled under her skin. She needed to get out of the Villa before wild magic destroyed everything in her path. She rushed across the sitting room and out the door into her study. The fire in the fireplace roared in response to her arrival, flames leaping over the grate. No.

She threw open the doors to the study. Daisy was kneeling over a large stone planter to harvest herbs. She looked up to see Amarice, wild-eyed and frantic.

"Amarice! Did you sleep?"

"I have to get out of here, Daisy."

"Where's Quinn?"

Amarice hurried to the northern door. Daisy followed. "Amarice, what's wrong? Talk to me, Amarice!"

Daisy grabbed the Sage's arm and screamed a bone-chilling scream filled with agony.

She leapt back. Daisy was clutching her right arm. Her right hand was as red as fire. Boils bubbled and erupted from the surface of her skin.

"No." Amarice's voice was barely a whisper. She hurt everything she tried to protect. And her magic was about to burst forth. "Daisy, no."

"Amarice. Amarice, let me help you." Daisy was yelling, even as the burns on her hand festered.

"Get away from me!" Amarice screamed at her. And then it happened.

Fire emerged from Amarice's fingertips, setting the nearest plants on fire. People rushed into the courtyard and panicked. A maid threw a pitcher of water on one of the bushes to no avail. The fire raged on, fueled by magic and anger and shame.

Amarice ran through the corridor before she set fire to anything else in the Villa. She had to protect them. She singed the door as she pushed out to the northern garden.

The fire kept coming. It followed her. It spread in front of her, scorching her fingertips as it left her body. She panicked. The river was to the east, but she'd risk too many innocent people in their camps. The forest was to the west. A forest fire was dangerous. But it was far enough from the people that maybe she could regain control.

Sweat dripped into her eyes. Her skin burned from the inside out. The blaze was building around her, even as it left her skin.

"Amarice!" she heard Quinn holler. "Amarice, stop!"

"I can't!" she screamed back. "It's too dangerous."

She ran.

The camps ignited. Flames engulfed tents as she tried to get past the inhabitants. People screamed and sprinted away. She heard water splashing but didn't turn back to see if it helped.

Just a little further, she told herself. She screamed in pain as magic seared through her veins, wild, out of control.

She ran until she reached the trees and moved as deep into the woods as she could. Soon, a ring of fire surrounded her. The blaze grazed the outside of her skin even as she felt the burn inside. Surely, surely her magic would weaken soon. Surely her power was nearly drained. But as the flames licked her skin, the magic poured out of her with more incendiary fury.

The fire was destroying everything around her. And it was making her stronger.

Stronger, with no control.

CHAPTER 28

QUINN

Quinn shielded his face as threw open the door to the study. The room was ablaze. At an ear-piercing scream, he had leapt out of bed only to find that Amarice was gone.

The path out of the study was narrow but clear. He had to put out the fire. He waved his hands, settling the flames into something more manageable. In moments, there were only a few burning pieces of furniture. He hurried through the study, the fire singeing the edges of his feet as he put out the rest before it spread.

He threw open the door to the courtyard and was met with a wall of heat and smoke. He coughed. The smoke was so thick he could barely make out the shapes of the screaming people. He dissipated it with his magic.

"The fire won't go out!" someone yelled at him. "Water isn't working!"

"It's her magic!" he heard Daisy cry.

The fire was contained for now on the plants, and he was glad most of the courtyard was stone. He had to prioritize, to conserve his magic for whatever destruction Amarice's wild magic was causing outside the Villa.

"Get everyone into the baths. The marble won't catch easily. Use your magic to shrink the fire and keep it at bay."

He shrank a few of the larger fires, then pulled the water from the fountain in a huge sphere. It multiplied and moved around the open area, raining down on the inferno. Smoke billowed, but the flames subsided.

He ran into the gardens. The fire had incinerated much of the life growing there. He coughed through the smoke and tried to figure out where Amarice had gone. Hopefully toward the river. He blinked against the sting in his eyes, desperate to find her path of flames.

The west. Of course. To save as many people as she could. He took off at a sprint, flailing his arms to shrink the fires and shouting at people to get the powerful Scholars. Only magic had a chance at stopping this destruction. He could at least make them smaller for the others.

But he had to get to Amarice.

He ran after her, flames hot against his skin. As he neared the trees, he stopped and looked to the sky. He hoped it worked, hoped it wouldn't drain him too quickly.

The Consort threw his arms to the sky, focusing all his magic on the clouds. The bright sky darkened with heavy clouds and a rumble of thunder. He dropped his arms, and the heavens opened. A deluge fell over the ground, soaking him and dousing the surrounding flames.

But the forest still burned.

He forced his way through, calling Amarice's name.

Her magic called to his, and he followed it deeper into the woods. He was drenched from the storm, his vision obscured by smoke and rain. The fires were lessening some, but the Sage's magic powered them. Only his magic possessed the necessary strength. He hoped.

A wall of flames appeared out of nowhere. Quinn threw his arms up in front of his face. He staggered back several steps. She was here. He knew it.

"Amarice!"

"Quinn!" He heard her voice, distressed over the roar of fire and the pounding of rain. "Go away! It's not safe!"

"I'll help you!"

"I can't control it, Quinn! It won't stop until it kills me!"

The air left his lungs. No. He couldn't let her burn here. "Amarice, no! Try, Amarice! I can't lose you!"

He couldn't see her. The fire was too big. He couldn't get rid of it, but maybe... He put all his effort into breaking the wall just enough to see her.

It worked. There she was, curled into a ball on the forest floor, a circle of angry dancing flames a foot from her.

"Quinn. If I let go, it will consume me. I don't want to go like this." She sobbed and shook with the effort of keeping the flames off her skin.

"Oh, love. Don't let go. I'll figure it out."

"No. It's too strong. I need you to finish this. I don't want to go like this."

"No."

"You promised me."

He had. Months ago, she had made him swear that he would do whatever it took if she lost control. He was the only one strong enough.

"No," he said again.

"Just make it quick, please. I love you."

He couldn't. The flames were growing again despite the magical storm. Amarice wouldn't be able to hold them off much longer. There had to be another way. There had to be a way to reach her.

That was it. It had only worked in dreams, but perhaps...

"Amarice. Close your eyes. Close your eyes and find me."

He closed his and cleared his mind. All he could see in his mind was the fire. He forced it out of his mind. This was dangerous, not looking at the flames surrounding him. If he failed, they'd both be dead.

He demanded his mind to empty until all he could see was darkness. "Amarice, find me."

He wasn't sure if he said it aloud or not. But far away, in his mind's eye, he could feel her. Her essence burned with fear and shame.

"Are you there, love? Focus on me." The fear subsided just a little; he could feel it, feel her very spirit. "Tell me what happened."

And then a flood of memories hit him, memories that were not his own. He saw a boy kissing Amarice. Zayn, he knew somehow, as if he had lived these moments. There was a fight. Zayn stormed off.

He saw Zayn on his deathbed. Quinn felt the grief heavy in his chest as if it were his own.

"I couldn't save him!" Amarice's voice was a scream in his mind. "I should have. And I didn't."

Quinn understood her in a new light. Understood her fear of Quinn leaving her when they first fell in love. Understood why she didn't want to send her people off to war.

"Amarice, he was sick. You were a child. A child, Amarice."

He could smell nothing but smoke and charred hair. Her fear spiked in his heart. The flames were getting closer to her, he knew. "Amarice, you were not born to save everyone. That is not your burden."

"But I'm the Sage."

"You're a guide. A leader. You have to let it go, Amarice. Let the shame go. Let Zayn go."

"I'm so scared."

"That's all right." He sucked in a sharp breath as his skin burned hotter. He wouldn't open his eyes. "It's all right. You can do this."

A flurry of emotions emanated from her, knocking the wind out of Quinn.

"Save yourself, Amarice. Release it all. Save yourself for me."

He heard her scream—out loud and in his mind. He clenched his eyes closed. Don't shut me out, please, don't shut me out, he pleaded.

And then the heat moved.

It no longer encroached on him, scorching his clothes and the hair on his arms. He froze, afraid to open his eyes. If the fire had stopped, it could mean only one of two things. He trembled in fear.

A hand touched his, warm and soft. He opened his eyes. Amarice stood before him. She cried, tears falling like the rain that soaked them. Quinn let out a breath he didn't know he'd been holding.

He pulled her into his arms and clung to her. Her skin was still hot to the touch, but her magic was no longer buzzing around her as it had for so many days. He wept into her smoke-scented hair.

"You saved me."

"Don't shut me out like that ever again," he said through thick sobs.

"I won't." She hugged him tighter. "I promise."

He blinked and looked around them. The forest was all ash and black and dead. He didn't know how far the blaze had spread. "Wow."

Amarice looked around, her hands still clasping Quinn's in a tight grip. "Oh."

He kissed her forehead. "No more shame. That's nothing that we can't fix."

She nodded and stepped away. She dropped Quinn's hands and turned her face to the sky. He could feel her magic again, not the furious festering from before, but a serene and powerful hum. He watched as her expression calmed.

Life burst forth around them.

The ashen forest floor bloomed with color—grass and flowers. The blackened trunks of the trees turned to warm shades of brown. Branches bloomed around them in every shade of verdant, vibrant green. The storm he had conjured cleared, and golden sunlight glimmered through the trees. Beyond, he could see cerulean skies, bright and full of hope.

Quinn gasped. He would never stop being in awe of her magic. Of her.

The Sage opened her eyes and smiled. A real smile, for the first time in a long time. It reached her eyes, and they shone silver in the sunlight. He pulled her toward him again, capturing her lips in a passionate kiss.

"You're back," he whispered against her lips.

"I'm back."

They walked back to the Villa hand in hand. Quinn had never felt more invigorated, his magic itching to burst forth. They brought back life to the destroyed land around them. Quinn laughed a little at the memory of Amarice showing how to revive burned, dead earth after the Forest of Seluya burned. Just the small circle of dirt had drained her to weakness.

Something had changed in that forest. *Tovari* magic, perhaps. He couldn't quite fathom that they had communicated mind-to-mind outside of their dreams. Their connection was stronger, and Quinn felt as if their magic was the same.

Amarice's shoulders dropped at the sight of all the burned tents and carts. That was something no earth magic could repair. He squeezed her hand.

"Do you think anyone was hurt?"

Or killed? The rest of her question hung weighty and unspoken on the air between them.

"I don't know. I wasn't far behind you, trying to get the fires under control."

"You never are." She smiled.

They passed through the small gate that marked the edge of the Villa gardens. The Consort Tree towered proudly, the lush leaves dancing in the wind. Cries of "they're back!" echoed around them.

Raymond was the first one to meet them, running from indoors. He didn't stop until he reached them and threw his arms around Amarice. He whispered something to her that Quinn couldn't hear. Then the king embraced Quinn. "You saved her. Thank you."

Corbin greeted Quinn with a hearty hug, and Janessa cried as she joined them.

"That was the scariest thing I've ever seen," she said.

Quinn and Amarice lost themselves in the embraces of Deben and Jack and Madge and Matthew and the rest of the house. Raymond was crying with his arms around Elaine, who spoke quiet words in his ear. She grinned when Quinn caught her eye. He smiled and nodded to her.

"Where's Daisy?" Amarice said.

Jack's smile faltered. "In her room."

Amarice pushed past everyone, and Quinn followed her across the Villa to Daisy's room. She threw the door open. "Oh, Daisy."

The head Healer from Teleah was attending to her. Daisy looked small and frail as she slept on her bed, right hand bandaged. The pungent, medicinal smell of salves and tonics filled the room.

"My lady Sage," the Healer said, bringing her hand to her brow. "My lord."

"Will she be all right?"

The Healer spoke in a low voice. "She'll live. I have her in a poppy sleep right now, and I've given her something to attempt to ward off infection. But her hand was severely burned. The damage is extensive. I don't expect she'll regain use of it."

"Oh, no."

Quinn grasped Amarice's shoulder to steady her.

The Healer continued. "I'll keep an eye on it, but if it becomes infected, amputation may be our best option."

Amarice turned and buried her face in Quinn's chest. He stroked her hair, noticing for the first time that the bottom of her braid was charred.

Daisy was right-handed, and Apothecaries depended on the use of their hands. She was one of the preeminent Apothecaries in the country. And she was a proud woman. She cared about her appearance, Quinn knew. As much as Amarice, if not more.

"She grabbed me," Amarice said, her voice thick with tears. "My skin burned her. Destroyed her arm."

Quinn swallowed. He didn't want her to fall into the same self-destructive shame as before. "Listen to me, Amarice. You lost control of your magic. It wasn't your fault."

"But it is. It's my fault I lost control." She looked up into his eyes. "But she's alive. She's alive, and she has a family here. We'll take care of her."

"Yes, we will."

The Healer cleared her throat. "She'll be asleep for a while. I'll apprise you of her situation."

The Sage and Consort slipped from the room. Only a Healer could dismiss the Sage, Quinn thought. Even the king couldn't do that.

"We smell like smoke," Amarice said, apropos of nothing. "I need a bath, a snack, and a good, long cry."

Quinn squeezed her hand. "That can be arranged."

CHAPTER 29

RAYMOND

A few days later, Raymond knocked on Elaine's bedroom door. It was early, and he hoped he had caught her before she went down to the kitchens to help Madge.

She opened the door bleary-eyed, hair poking out of two braids. She had a shawl wrapped around her nightgown. Raymond smiled. She looked lovely. Though he wished that shawl could move out of the way a bit.

"Raymond? What's wrong?" She yawned as she spoke.

"Nothing. I woke up thinking about you." Wanting you, he didn't say. "Wanted to start your day off with a kiss."

She stared at him in disbelief before a slow smile spread across her face. "You couldn't have done it at a later hour?"

He shrugged. "I didn't know what time you got up."

"Well, not five o'clock. But come here, you silly man."

She tugged on his loose shirt and pulled him forward, then stood on her tiptoes to kiss him. He liked this confident Elaine. Perhaps he should wake her up more often. He grinned into the kiss at the less-than-chaste thought that crossed his mind.

Elaine pulled away. "There you go. Now go back to bed."

"All right, fine. See you at breakfast. Love you."

He froze. She stared up at him with wide eyes. He hadn't meant to say it. The words had slipped out as if they said them all the time. He watched her swallow, speechless.

"I had planned to say it with a bit more romance," Raymond said. "I do, though."

Elaine blinked. Shit. This had blown up in his face.

"You do?"

"Yes." His heart pounded and a bead of sweat formed on his forehead. Stupid nerves.

"I love you, too."

"Really?" Had he heard her correctly?

"Yes. I love you, King Raymond." She laughed. "How strange my life has become."

"A good strange?"

"Yes, a good strange." Her eyes were light. Playful.

He dared himself to ask. "Do you still want me to go back to bed?"

"Get in here."

He slipped into her room. She glanced down the hallway, he supposed, to see if they were alone. He wouldn't get his hopes up. Well, not too much anyway.

She kissed him again, with more fervor, and he was glad to return it. Their kiss intensified, and he pulled her down to the bed. He moved that blasted shawl from her shoulders, and she let him.

He didn't leave her lips as his hands explored her body through her nightgown. She shivered under his touch. Her own hands grabbed at his arms, his chest.

He ventured lower, moving his kisses to her neck, and she gasped underneath him. He wanted her so badly.

"I'm not, ah, I'm not ready yet."

He pulled away. "All right."

"Soon, I think."

"I can wait."

She blushed. "You can keep kissing me, though."

He did.

RAYMOND RAN into Quinn when he slipped out of Elaine's room later that morning. Quinn raised his eyebrows. "That's going well, I take it?"

Raymond felt heat rise in his cheeks. They hadn't discussed whether they were telling people about their relationship. They hadn't even defined their relationship. "Yes."

Quinn chuckled.

"What are you doing up here before breakfast?" Raymond asked. "I never see you here anymore."

"Well, some king had to take over my study. But I was getting a hangover tincture from Jack. Amarice drank a bit too much last night."

"She's doing well, then?"

Quinn nodded. "Much better. It was a long week. And now that Daisy's awake, her mood is lighter. Happier." They walked down the hall together. "So. Sneaking out of Elaine's room like a schoolboy. It's a good look on you."

"Oh, fuck off." Raymond laughed.

"I'm surprised, though. I didn't expect... Well, the Elaine I knew is very different from who she is now."

Raymond stopped on the staircase and put his hand on Quinn. He glanced around to make sure they were alone. "It's killing me, Quinn. I haven't gone this long without taking a woman to bed since I was seventeen."

Red tinged Quinn's cheeks. "So, you haven't—?"

"No." Raymond gritted his teeth. "I'm being *patient* and *understanding*, and it is hard work."

Quinn clapped him on the shoulder. "You'll survive. Builds character."

They went to breakfast. Amarice braced her head on the table and grunted thanks when Quinn handed her the vial of Jack's hangover tincture. She poured it into her coffee and downed it in two swallows.

Raymond rolled his eyes. Some things never changed, but he would never want them to.

Elaine took a seat next to Raymond. They gave each other a secret smile, then she darted her eyes down, blushing. Raymond poured her some coffee, letting his hand brush hers as he set it down. He liked the way she shivered at his touch. Quinn met his eyes and snorted into his own drink. Cheeky bastard.

After breakfast, Raymond went to visit Daisy. She was propped up in her bed with a breakfast tray. Her food had barely been touched, and her brow was furrowed in concentration as she tried to use her fork with her left hand. He knocked on the door frame.

She looked up and smiled. "Come on in." She gestured with her bandaged right arm at the chair next to her bed.

He took a seat. "How are you feeling?"

She blew air out of her mouth, and it ruffled her loose hair. "Frustrated. Bored. I can't even turn a page in a book."

"I'm sorry."

"I'll get used to it." She pushed her breakfast away with her left hand. "It's good because I can still move the arm. But my wrist and hand—they're just dead."

"How's the pain?"

She shrugged. "It comes and goes. I don't understand why it hurts when I can't feel anything touching it."

"We miss you at meals."

Her smile faltered. "I miss you, too. But I look like a fool feeding myself right now."

"No one would care. No one would think you look like a fool."

"But I care." She shook her head. "How's the king life?"

It was his turn to shrug. "It's hard to tell who is winning a war. You know, it looks so much different than anything we studied in school. In books, it's always clear who was winning at which point."

"The path you traveled is always clearer when you turn around."

"Exactly."

"Did you figure out who the spy was?"

He swallowed and let out a long sigh. "It was Andin."

"No!"

"Yes. Samperian converted him a couple of years ago. I had no clue. He's been feeding them information since the beginning."

"They've been planning war for a long time." She looked straight at him, her eyes warm and kind. "I'm sorry. I know how much he meant to you."

"Yeah." He studied his hands. "I feel like an idiot that I didn't see it."

"Don't do that to yourself. You've been busy. Losing your father, running a country, fighting a war."

"How did it come to this?" Raymond asked. "I don't know how we were so out of touch."

"We're Scholars. We think we live in some ivory tower, high above the regular people. But that's our own making and our own undoing."

"You sound like the Lord Consort."

"What can I say? Amarice picks smart partners." She laughed. "Speaking of partners, I hear you've been cozy with Elaine."

"This damn Villa and its gossip. It's like the Academy all over again, but worse."

She raised her eyebrow at him, waiting for him to continue. He put his hands up in mock surrender. "Fine! Yes. We've been seeing each other. I don't know what else to call it."

"You love her."

"Yes." He recalled how the words had slipped out of his mouth that morning. "I do."

"Good." She giggled. "You and Quinn, just sharing exes, but you're so different. How strange."

"We have good taste." He winked, then turned serious. "Are we good, Daisy?"

"We are. You'll always have a place in my heart, Raymond. But we're better as friends. And I'm happy for you."

He stood and leaned over to kiss the top of her head. "Get better, Daisy. Anything you need, you let me know."

CHAPTER 30

AMARICE

Daisy had weaned off the poppy tea within a week and a half. The Healer and Matthew reported she was in good spirits, and she had a smile on her face whenever Amarice came by. But Amarice knew better.

Amarice leaned her head against Daisy's shoulder. She had climbed into the bed with her for their morning chat. "Be honest, Daisy. How are you really doing?"

Daisy sighed. "Honestly? I don't know, Amarice. I'm still in shock somewhat. And I'm sad, you know. Grieving. And..."

"And what?"

She stared at her hands. "And angry. But not at you!"

Amarice raised her head and looked her best friend square in the eyes. "You're allowed to be angry at me. I'm angry at me."

Daisy's face grew serious. "I'm angry at the situation. I don't blame you."

"But?"

Daisy dropped her eyes. "Do you remember when your mother died?"

"Of course!" Amarice didn't know how that was relevant.

"Well, do you remember how angry you felt at your grandmother? It wasn't her fault that your mother never returned to the Teyvana tribe. But in your grief, you thought it was her fault that your mother stayed in Davia and got sick."

"Yes, that's true. I did."

"Well, I'm not angry that your magic burned me. I'm angry that you wouldn't let any of us help you, and it got to such a—well, boiling point, if you'll pardon the pun. You wouldn't let me in. You wouldn't even let Quinn in."

Amarice nodded. "I felt like it would be a burden with everything going on."

Daisy rolled her eyes. "You would never let any of us get away with being so reticent. You'd push us until we talked." She patted Amarice with her good hand. "I say this with love, Amarice. But it's hard to be your friend sometimes."

Amarice swallowed. It was something she knew, deep down, but no one had ever told her to her face. "You know, I only had one real friend before the Academy."

"Zayn?"

Amarice looked up in surprise. "Well, yes. How did you know that?"

"Quinn asked if I knew anything about him before..." She waved her hand. "He suspected it might have something to do with whatever was wrong."

Amarice smiled. "Oh, Quinn. He knows me better than I know myself sometimes."

"But Amarice, I've known you since we were eighteen. I'm your best friend. I should know some of these things, like the name of the only friend you had in Davia."

Amarice nodded. "I know."

"What is it the Deyoni call you? Draba something?"

"*Drabekesala.*"

"Right. Magic earth mother?" Amarice nodded. "Amarice, that may be how the Deyoni see you. And you're a leader of the Scholars. But your loved ones don't need a mother. We need *you*."

Amarice blinked, trying to fathom this. She remembered the fights her mother and grandmother had when she was a young, insolent child. Her mother was too lax with her discipline while somehow still putting heavy responsibilities on Amarice's shoulders. Her grandmother believed she needed structure and boundaries.

"My mother knew what I was. The Deyoni talked of a day when the strongest *tovari* would come. They believed only a *tovari* could bring them hope."

"Like a prophecy?"

Amarice shook her head. "No, they don't believe in prophecies. More of a logical conclusion—someone had to be both Scholar and Deyoni to bridge the gap between them. It would be the destiny of whoever she was."

"Were they right? Or did you make it your destiny?"

Amarice cocked her head, considering. Like a candle lit in the darkness, everything made sense now. "I don't know. I never considered it. But my mother was the first to call me *drabekesala*. She knew it was me. It was clear early on that I had powers like no other."

"So, your mother called you magic earth mother?"

Amarice laughed. "Sometimes. And she let me get away with everything. She and my grandmother used to fight over me all the time. I was an awful child. Always mouthing off to my teacher and causing all sorts of riots to get attention."

Daisy giggled. "I can see that. I remember what you were like at the Academy."

"And my mother always sent me to the market. She was treated terribly because she was Deyoni. By the time I was old enough, my grandmother's health was poor. We didn't have much money. As a teen, I started sleeping with the merchants to get things I wanted or that we needed. Books. Herbs for my mother's medicines."

"I had no idea. Amarice, you had to grow up too fast. You were always taking care of other people." Daisy's eyes were full of tears. "Let us take care of you sometimes."

"I'm trying." Amarice smiled. "Now, quit changing the subject. What about *you*?"

Daisy sighed. "I'm only just starting to realize that my hand is gone. Well, the use of it anyway. And I don't know who I am without it."

Amarice fought the urge to say that she was still Daisy. Her friend needed her to listen without commentary. She couldn't imagine what Daisy was going through. She nodded and waited for her to continue instead.

"I can't be an Apothecary without my hand. It's not the same, giving others my recipes. There's an intuitive part of it, when picking the herbs and flowers, when stirring over a cauldron."

"You can learn to do a lot with your left hand."

"I know, but...I use both my hands all the time. I'm having a bit of an identity crisis." Her eyes filled with tears. Amarice squeezed her left hand.

"More than a bit?"

"More than a bit," Daisy agreed. "And Amarice, I use my hands for other things. Having a limp noodle on the end of my arm is far from attractive."

"You are beautiful, Daisy. Limp noodle or no."

Daisy smiled. "You're my best friend. You have to say that."

"No, I don't! I'm the Sage. I don't lie!" She bumped Daisy's shoulder. "It may not feel like it at this moment, but this will get easier in time."

"Or it will fester into a disaster of wild magic."

Amarice rolled her eyes and laughed. "But after that, it will get easier. Take it from an expert on disaster."

The Healer came in to change Daisy's dressing on her deadened right hand. The skin was healing nicely, Amarice noted. But as the Healer tested for feeling, Daisy didn't react at all. Amarice swallowed the guilt that bubbled inside her. She knew it was her fault, even if Daisy insisted it wasn't, but she wouldn't let it consume her this time, lest she hurt anyone else.

The conversation lightened after the Healer left. They gossiped about Raymond and Elaine and other people they knew. They reminisced about times from the Academy. Daisy had lived down the hall her first year, when Amarice was in her second and final year. Then Amarice had passed the fourth-year exams at eighteen and went to apprentice with the Sage of the time.

Amarice could have stayed in there all day. Even before everything had gone to shit, she and Daisy had rarely enjoyed each other's company since the war started. It was refreshing. But they were jolted from their bliss by a knock on the door from Madge.

"Amarice! You're needed in your study. There's news." Her eyes were wide; her tone was urgent. "Raymond and Quinn are already there."

Amarice hugged Daisy, then scrambled off the bed and across the courtyard. Raymond was bent over a map on her desk, pointing out something to Quinn and two of his captains.

"What's happened?"

Raymond turned to face her. His eyes were hard, and his jaw was set as he spoke. "We've just received word. The Chamberites and Lazori mercenaries are planning to march on the Villa in a week. They're waiting for another force from the north to arrive first."

Amarice felt the air leave her lungs. "How many?"

"Four thousand, give or take a few hundred," the captain of the guard said.

"We're marching on them first. We leave tomorrow at first light." Raymond held her gaze, challenging her.

Amarice blinked as she processed what he was saying. "Do we have enough people?"

Raymond crossed the room toward her. "I want to send a force to retake Teleah at the same time. That leaves us three thousand, with the Scholars who have been training. But I don't know if they'll fight without your blessing."

Amarice looked at Quinn. His lips were a straight line, but his brown eyes showed fear and something else. He gave her one nod. "This would be it, Amarice. This decides the war."

Amarice sighed. People would die. Many, possibly more than the Fire Massacre. Scholar blood would die, and their population was already dwindling. But this was the chance to end it all. The chance to avenge all the innocents who had been lost.

"They have my blessing. And I'm coming with you."

Raymond's shoulders dropped in relief. He pulled the Sage into a hug. "Thank you, Amarice. With you and Quinn, I think we have a chance."

She hadn't spoken for Quinn, though. She looked at her Consort, her wonderful partner. Her equal. Her lover. What if he died in battle? How could she go on without him?

He smiled at her. "I told you I would follow you to death itself, Amarice."

"Well, hopefully, it won't lead to that." She tied her loose hair into a knot and bent over the desk to study the map. "Now, tell me the plan."

CHAPTER 31

RAYMOND

Madge served them lunch in the study. Raymond nibbled on bread and cheese to calm his nerves as they strategized. The other captains had gathered and helped make plans. With luck, they would catch the opposing army unprepared. It was unlikely, they knew, but they should reach Beybrook within five days.

Elaine was in the back of Raymond's mind all afternoon, as well as the other residents of the Villa. If the battle turned against them, if they lost, there needed to be a plan. Otherwise, everyone who was loyal to himself and the Sage would be in danger.

He mentioned this to Quinn and Amarice. Quinn suggested they put Deben and Corbin in charge of getting the Villa residents to safety. Ilecin would be safe enough. And if they lost and Raymond and the others survived, they too could flee to Ilecin. They could seek refuge in the capital. Ilecin had been a trade ally of Elandria for a long time. If he reached the oligarchs before the Chamberites, they might offer him sanctuary.

These were thoughts he didn't want to think about, but a contingency plan was necessary. With the Sage and Consort riding into battle with him, the chances were good that they would win. If not good, then certainly improved. But he was too scared to be hopeful just yet.

Before dinner, he adjourned the meeting. He went down to assess the soldiers—the veterans and the new—and rally them to ride in the morning. He sat atop Sterling at the edge of the camps, the soft-peaked Sage's Mountains as a backdrop. The Sage and the Consort sat beside him.

"How is everyone supposed to hear me?" Raymond asked. Even years of oration training as a young prince couldn't combat this.

"Allow me," Amarice said. She closed her eyes, and Raymond felt a warm bubble of magic pushing past him. In moments, the ambient noise of thousands of people had faded, allowing only bits of conversation through. As the magical calm settled over the crowd, they stopped talking and turned toward Raymond.

He took a deep breath and spoke in a loud, booming voice.

"Citizens of Elandria, I stand before you today, not as your king, but as your comrade. Your brother. I am here to tell you that the moment has arrived. We will take back our country from those who seek to destroy it. We are all of us Elandrians, and tomorrow, we march as one front. We will show that Elandria's true wealth comes from its diversity and from the golden thread that unites us all.

"I will not lie to you. We will be outnumbered. Elandrian blood will be shed on both sides. But we have something that the other side does not. And no, I'm not talking about magic. I'm talking about heart. We are fighting for a better life, for a new Elandria. We are fighting for a country where everyone is valued, not in spite of their differences, but because of them. We are fighting for a country that honors equality and individuality.

"Tomorrow, we march. This battle decides the war. Your sacrifice will not be a footnote in the history books. Your service will change Elandria for the better. I am honored to fight alongside you. Your bravery and dedication inspire me every day. Rest well. Kiss your loved ones. For soon, a new chapter begins."

Amarice gasped as she released her magic, and cheers echoed through the mountains. These people were ready for war. The fight had become personal. Everyone had lost someone. Everyone wanted to return home, to return to their lives in Elandria. The Scholar refugees had fully embraced the Deyoni. And the nomadic tribes were ready for their day of equity. It was more than time.

Back at the Villa, Erenia took his armor and shield to polish. Raymond polished his own sword. He sat on a stone bench in the courtyard. Elaine sat beside him in a heavy silence. He tried to give her reassuring smiles, but he was certain they fell flat. After a while, she spoke.

"It was a good speech."

He grinned. "Do you think so?"

She nodded and was quiet for a few moments. "You don't have to ride into battle, you know."

He looked up at her. "What?"

"You're the king. You can stay behind and give orders."

He sighed. He couldn't lie to himself. The thought had crossed his mind. But if he wasn't willing to fight, how could he expect his people? That's why Amarice and Quinn were going. It was his battle as much as anyone's. "I could. But I won't."

"I know." Her eyes were full of tears. "You're so brave. You'd die for your people, and that's why you're a great king. But I had to try because I'm selfish, and I love you."

He reached for her hand. "I love you, too. And you know what you're to do in case the battle fails?"

She swallowed hard and wiped her eyes. "Yes."

"Good. I want you safe."

Dinner was a somber affair. Every time someone spoke, their voice became thick with emotion. Speeches and toasts were made, though no one cheered or clapped. Deben closed the meal with a ballad, a melancholy song of farewells.

Raymond declined wine with his meal and decided to join the others in the parlor. He needed a clear head and rest, so he excused himself early to his room.

He stared in the mirror above his dresser. This was it. He studied himself, trying to see the king that everyone else saw. Right now, all he saw was a scared little boy. He wished he could run into his father's chambers and climb into the big, overstuffed bed. Roland would tell him stories—great stories of Elandria's past kings and Sages. The heroes.

There was a knock on his door. He shook himself. "Snap out of it, Raymond."

He opened the door to find Elaine. Her pale brown hair was loose around her face. She wore a vibrant blue Telean-style gown, all draping fabric and swooping necklines. She was wringing her hands.

"You look exquisite," he said.

She smiled and tucked a strand of hair behind her ear. "I figured you had a lot on your mind and might want some company. But you're also probably very busy, and this was silly. I can leave."

"Stay." He opened the door wider and stepped aside, inviting her in. "I'm glad you came."

She ducked inside and sat in the armchair by the window. "How are you feeling?"

"Honestly? Terrified." He gave a dry, humorless laugh and pulled out the desk chair for himself. He straddled it backward to face her. "I'm sure that inspires a lot of confidence in the person leading this country."

"It does. I'd be far more worried if you weren't scared."

"Truly?"

"Of course." She grinned at him. "I'm reassured that you are, in fact, human."

"And you doubted that?" He raised an eyebrow and smiled.

She nodded. "Sometimes. Sometimes I think you must have come straight from my dreams. Or some tale of the old heroes." She looked straight at him, blue eyes gazing straight into his soul. "But sometimes you're so beautifully *real*. Vulnerable and contemplative."

Raymond swallowed, a hard lump in his throat. He didn't know what to say. No one had ever seen him like Elaine. "Elaine..."

She rose from her seat and crossed the small room to him. She took his hands and looked down at him. "I'm scared, too. Scared this is it, that I'll never see you again."

"Me, too."

She let go of his hands and straightened. She untied the gilded rope belt around her waist. Raymond's heart skipped a beat. If she unclasped the shoulders of the gown, the fabric would fall to the ground, and she would be naked in front of him.

"Are you certain?" he asked. His voice was hoarse with desire and emotion.

She lifted her chin, and Raymond fought the urge to lick his lips at the sight of her exposed neck. "Give me this. Give me tonight."

He rose and fumbled over the chair between them. She giggled, and the tension eased. He pushed the chair under the desk and took the step to close the distance between them.

He ran a hand through her long, silky hair and down her back, then he pulled her close and lowered his mouth to hers, and she shivered underneath him. She parted her lips, inviting him in.

Elaine's hands ran over his toned shoulders and back. As he deepened the kiss, she grew more curious. Confident. Her hands slipped under his shirt. He sighed into her as she touched him, her hands warm and soft.

He broke the kiss and pulled the shirt over his head, desperate for as much contact as he could get. How often had he imagined this moment? He'd wanted her for months now. Elaine studied his bare chest with wide eyes and a grin. She ran her fingertips down his stomach. He looked down, mesmerized by the contrast of her milky skin against his brown.

Brigitte's tit, she was going to kill him.

"You're gorgeous," she said.

"So are you." He took her hand and kissed it. "Absolutely stunning."

He walked backward to the bed, pulling her along. He sat and spread his legs, guiding her to stand between him. She bent down to kiss him as he ran his hands over her hips, up her sides, and to her breasts. She gasped.

"Still all right?"

"Yes, oh yes." She froze. "It's just...I'm nervous."

"I know it's been a long time."

She bit her lip. "And...and only once. I don't really know what I'm doing."

He pressed his hand against her cheek. "You're doing great, trust me." She blushed; he could feel the heat in his hands. "Do you want me to keep going?"

She nodded. He kissed her again until she regained her confidence. His hands moved to the clasps on her shoulders. "May I?"

"Yes."

Her dress slipped down to the floor and pooled at her feet. Instinctively, she tried to cover herself, but Raymond pulled her arms away. "Don't. You're perfect."

And she was. He couldn't help it; he licked his lips as he took in her curves. Like a man parched in the desert, he drank in the sight of her. He pulled her onto the bed and flipped himself over her. He took his time, kissing every inch of her, enjoying the symphony of her mewls and moans. Despite how much he wanted her, he moved achingly slow.

He ran a hand up the inside of her thigh, and her breath hitched. "Good?"

"Good," she said, her eyes half-lidded.

He couldn't hide the groan that came out when he finally touched her. Her back arched at the sensation. He explored her like a new, exotic locale, finding out what made her whimper in ecstasy. Heat pooled in his belly, and he forced his mind to calm down.

She gasped in shock as he moved his head lower, but she begged him to continue. He brought her to the edge over and over until she panted his name, fingers clutching the short curls of his head.

He came up beside her and kissed her hard. Her fingers clutched his upper arms, then moved to the laces on his pants, frantic. He shucked them off, and her hand wrapped around his length. He moaned.

"I want you, Raymond," she said. "Please."

He didn't have to be told twice. He kissed her as he sheathed himself inside of her. She wrapped her legs around him, pulling him deeper inside. They moved together in a steady harmony. He savored every moment—her feel, her smell, her sound. She shuddered around him, nails digging into his back, tipping him over the edge into release.

He collapsed onto the bed beside her and interlaced his fingers with hers. They lay together without words, only the sound of their breathing between them. Elaine snuggled against him, and he kissed her forehead.

He forced thoughts of tomorrow out of his mind, forced himself to be present there with the woman he loved. He focused instead on the way she felt against him and on the way he felt with her.

"Stay the night with me," he whispered.

"I'm not going anywhere."

Somehow, he slept that night. Elaine's presence calmed him. He woke early and looked at her sleeping face. Tears filled his eyes as he stroked her cheek.

She roused and opened her honey-golden eyes. She reached up to wipe his tears away. "It's time, isn't it?"

"Yes," he choked out. "I love you, Elaine, with every fiber of my soul."

She kissed him. When their lips parted, she said, "I love you, too. Come back to me, Raymond."

CHAPTER 32

QUINN

The sun wasn't up yet when Quinn and Amarice descended the stairs and went to the veranda for breakfast. They were to march north at first light. Madge was crying as she sat out platters of sausage, eggs, and fruit.

"Eat up, you need your strength," she said repeatedly.

The meal was a melancholy affair. Raymond was there in his royal finery, his right hand never leaving Elaine's thigh as he ate with his left. Daisy had joined them for the first time since the burn. Of the Villa residents, only the Sage, the Consort, and the king were heading to battle. Quinn had convinced his father and brother to stay and get everyone to safety in case the fight turned sour.

Two thousand soldiers were heading to Teleah to retake it on the morrow. Three thousand—mostly Scholars and Deyoni—were marching north under King Raymond's banner to meet the Chamberite forces head-on. He had sent out orders to retake other large cities.

The stablehands had Nivasi and Atsila ready when the Villa's residents poured into the northern garden. In the lands beyond the Consort Tree, Quinn could see the companies lined up, ready to march. He swallowed the bile in his throat and said his goodbyes.

Jack cried into his shoulder. He had taken over as lead Apothecary for the Villa and was needed here. "I refuse to lose my other best friend," he reminded Quinn through his tears. Quinn hugged him hard.

Janessa and Elaine kissed Quinn's cheek, then turned to say farewell to Amarice. Corbin held him in a long embrace and told Quinn how proud he was to be his brother.

"Avenge our mother," he said.

"I will. Take care of them."

"I will."

He said goodbye to his father last. "Are you certain I should not come?" Deben asked.

Quinn shook his head. "They'll need your hunting and travel skills should things turn against us."

Deben placed his hand on Quinn's face. "You are a good man. A brave man. I am honored to be your father."

A tear leaked from Quinn's eye as he wrapped his arms around his father. "I love you."

"And I you, my son."

He looked to Amarice, who had already mounted Atsila. She nodded at him, the Sage's diadem gleaming in the first rays of sunlight. He felt the weight of his own diadem like chains on his head. He swung his leg over Nivasi and patted the horse's neck.

"Raymond," Amarice said. "It's time."

Raymond continued to kiss Elaine deeply for a few more beats. He whispered something in her ear and wiped the tears from her face. Then he mounted his own stallion. With one final glance at Elaine, he rode off to meet the army and lead them to their fate, whatever it was.

They rode hard the first day, reaching the edge of the mountains. Quinn and Amarice didn't speak much at all. This was far different from any other journey. In just a few days, they would meet in battle and decide the fate of Elandria. Many would die, and that unspoken knowledge hung over the army.

The war camp was quiet, considering there were three thousand people. The people that spoke around the fires did so in hushed tones with their heads bent together. Amarice and Quinn made their way through the companies of Scholars, urging them to conserve their magic and start their fires the normal way.

They joined Raymond and his captains for a strategy meeting in the king's tent. Amarice held her head high and offered her input, but she stayed close to Quinn, her arm brushing against his. They needed more than one plan for this battle. One relied on utter secrecy. It was hopeful but unlikely. There were likely scouts along the route to Beybrook, and three thousand soldiers were hard to ignore. At this point, they just hoped the other side wouldn't find out in time for them to rally and organize too much.

And Quinn wasn't deluded. He knew whatever plans they came up with would be thrown out the second the battle started.

There hadn't been a battle with earth magic since Elandria's founding a thousand years before when everyone had magic. Brigitte had led the charge to push the Deyoni out of the valley. He saw the fear in Amarice's eye; she had never idolized the first Sage, and he knew she feared that she was becoming just like her.

They retired to their own tent for the night. Soldiers had put up a tent as grand as the king's with a large, plush pallet for sleeping. It didn't help. Quinn stared at the dark layers of fabric above his head for hours, trying to no avail to imagine what battle would be like.

He had loved his history classes from the time he was a boy. He devoured book after book about Elandria's history and that of the wider world. Military history had been one of his strongest classes at the Academy for Scholars, and he had engaged in many lively debates with Professor Quickthorn about the nuances of historical conflicts.

But now it seemed insipid, all the studies of war. He had fought before. He'd killed Charles Chambers with his own hands for his part in Rafe's death and Amarice's kidnapping. But those were a few people in a small village church. This would be a battle with over seven thousand soldiers, many of whom were professional swordsmen bought by Grellis's deep pockets.

He couldn't even be nervous at this point. It was still too unfathomable.

Somehow, Amarice had fallen asleep hours ago. He shifted in the bed and wrapped an arm around her side, letting her steady breathing settle his mind. He tried not to think that this could be one of their last nights together. They may be *tovari* with powers like no other on the earth, but were they really a match for four thousand soldiers?

He kissed her shoulder and closed his eyes. Exhaustion would not serve him well in battle. He began listing the ingredients of every medicine he knew in his mind. Within minutes, he was asleep.

MARCHING TO BATTLE WAS MONOTONOUS. Another thing the history books failed to mention. There was no friendly chatting, no bawdy traveler songs. An air of nerves covered the entire army, at least near the front where Quinn rode behind Raymond.

"We should practice the *tovari* mind connection," Amarice said on the second day. "It might prove useful during..." She waved her hand, as if refusing to say "battle" meant it wouldn't happen.

Quinn pulled Nivasi up farther so that he was right next to Amarice. "You don't worry it will drain us too much?"

She shrugged. "I haven't felt my powers drain as quickly since the fire. Have you?"

He shook his head. "No. That's true. I haven't."

Whatever had happened in the forest had strengthened them. More in tune with each other and with their own magical centers. Even Quinn's attempts to control the river had gone more smoothly than in the past.

"All right. How should we do this? The mental connection was more your discovery." She smiled at him, letting him know how proud she was of him.

Quinn grinned back. "Let's try this. Hold an image in your mind, and I'll try to see it."

She nodded and rolled her neck as if she were about to lift something heavy. Quinn chuckled.

"Ready," she said.

He closed his eyes, trusting Nivasi not to lead him astray. Then he pushed everything around them away. He tried to drown out every noise—the clip-clop of horse hooves, the rustle of armor, the tweeting of birds above them. He could feel Amarice's very essence in their connection and pushed the limits of his mind to overtake hers.

It was foggy at first. Covered in an ethereal smoky haze. He strained himself, trying to see what she was thinking of. He waded through layers of consciousness like sheets of spiders' webs that had wrapped her thoughts in silk. There was something there.

It took some time, but he unwrapped her thoughts like a Harvest Holiday gift.

"Blueberry pie?" he said aloud.

She giggled. "It sounded good. If we survive this thing, I'm demanding a blueberry pie the moment we get back to the Villa."

"I'm sure Madge will make you a dozen blueberry pies without you even asking." He took a hand off the reins and leaned over to pat hers. "We'll survive this, Amarice."

"Do you think?"

"I have to."

She nodded and sighed. "Your turn."

Quinn thought for a moment about something to hold in his mind. It took her longer because it was her first time reaching him instead of the other way around. He could feel her in his thoughts, the way it feels when someone is staring from a distance. Invasive, yet familiar.

"The willow tree in Corthy." Her eyes popped open. "That was a lovely night."

He grinned at the memory. "We caused an earthquake."

"We did." She cocked her head to the side with a smile, remembering. "My turn!"

They went back and forth for a long time as they rode. After Amarice's third food-based image, he tossed her an apple from his saddlebag. Something about this type of magic didn't deplete their magic; he imagined it was because they were pulling strength from each other's Gifts.

"I'm going to make it harder. More complex," Quinn told her verbally. "A memory instead of a stagnant image."

She was faster this time, and he knew when she was there. But she didn't say anything for several moments. She watched the memory play out.

He recalled the first time she took him to the palace. The black dress that showed her whole back. The softness of her skin when he fastened her necklace. The way his heart pounded.

He opened his eyes, still holding the memory in his mind, to see Amarice's face. Her own eyes were closed, but a smile lit her features. He sent her words. "I think that was the night I started falling in love with you."

Her eyes opened at that; she turned to face him and switched to speaking out loud. "Apparently, my feelings for you were apparent that night. I just hadn't realized it myself. Or tried to ignore it."

"I never understood why you were so afraid that I'd leave you or something. I get it now."

She nodded. "I still fight it every day, thinking something will happen to break my heart. That something will happen to you."

He couldn't reassure her, not when death was a grave possibility in the next few days. He didn't insult her by offering empty words. Instead, he changed the subject.

"Your turn." He flashed ornery eyes at her. "Make it something good."

Her memory was another one from the palace. They were dancing in the ballroom at King Roland's birthday. He could feel Amarice's love for him as he watched himself dance around her. Things could have been so different that night, but she had been drugged and kidnapped.

He could hear her voice in his mind, teasing and flirting. "I had big plans for you that night, you know."

"Plans?" he thought, feigning innocence.

"Plans. It's those leather pants of yours."

He laughed out loud. Erenia turned to look at them. Quinn shrugged and blushed. They must look ridiculous to anyone observing them, communicating without words.

"My turn," he said to Amarice.

It was much faster this time. When Amarice saw his image, she lost herself in a fit of laughter.

"How inappropriate, Lord Consort!" she chided him out loud.

Raymond turned around. "You two are having way too much fun back there. We are marching to war." But his face held a grin. "Care to let us in on the secret?"

"I have a feeling you don't want to know, my friend," Quinn retorted. "But if you want me to tell you…"

"I'm good, thanks." The king put a hand up. "Another hour and we'll stop for the night."

Quinn and Amarice acknowledged his words, then exchanged mischievous glances with each other. His heart was full. He was marching to war—and possibly death—and Amarice could make even that enjoyable. He guided Nivasi closer to Atsila and leaned over for a kiss.

"I love you, Amarice."

CHAPTER 33

AMARICE

The long days of marching passed quicker now that she and Quinn had their game. It was useful, too. By the end of day four, they could have entire conversations without speaking. Quinn had fallen back between other companies so they could practice at a distance. This was limited to a few hundred yards, no matter what they tried; only in dreams could hundreds of miles connect their thoughts.

As the battle drew closer, Amarice's terror soared. She held her head high to encourage the people she led, but she fiddled with her Scholar's pendant. Quinn was scared, too, and they discussed their fears in their minds, as it was easier than speaking it out loud.

Amarice had killed before. She had killed her attackers and some of the men who guarded Chambers. But that had been a direct assault on her. War was something different. The soldiers they would face were not necessarily zealots. And even if they were, this battle was initiated by Raymond and her. They were seeking out the violence to end the war.

Some of the opposing force—the Elandrians—had been enticed

not by ideals but by higher pay from Grellis and Azmar. Most of the Lazori mercenaries had chosen a life of war over a life of slavery, and she couldn't blame them.

And she was leading her own people to slaughter, too. Scholars and Deyoni. Just like Brigitte. And after Brigitte, magical peoples had left a life of violence. They stood for peace. Amarice had always stood for peace.

But when peace is threatened, values must change.

They were close to Beybrook and would stop to make their final camp soon. Raymond sent four scouts ahead. Two returned. The first deaths of this battle.

Amarice saw the way Raymond's shoulders had dropped upon news of their death. It was slight. Most wouldn't notice it, but she had known him well for a long time. He bore the grief of his country on his shoulders.

The two that returned had news; it wasn't exactly good news, but it wasn't bad, either. The Chamberite forces had received word late that the Elandrians were advancing. They were readying for battle but showed no sign of advancing. They would wait for the attack. A smart move, Amarice mused. Their troops wouldn't have any exhaustion from travel. Theirs were already at a disadvantage.

They refreshed their plans that night in Raymond's tent. Amarice and Quinn would lead a company of the most powerful Scholars into the heart of the battle. The other companies would try to clear a path for them. They had a mission, and if they succeeded, it would turn the tide of battle.

If they didn't, all would be lost.

Amarice set her diadem on a small trunk by their pallet bed. She stared at it—the silver, metal tree in the center surrounded by shimmering gemstones of emerald, sapphire, garnet, and diamond. She recalled how it had felt when she first took on the Sage's diadem.

Roland had beamed at her as the previous Sage, a woman named Marietta, had placed the diadem on her head. She stood on the stage at the Academy, surrounded by her professors and Raymond. Even her mother and grandmother had made the journey from Davia. It was the last time she had seen either of them.

Scholars had cheered as she made her speech about a new era for magical peoples. There had been fewer cheers as she talked about the rights of the Deyoni, but her mother had smiled from the front row.

She wondered now why the Sage's coronation was not a public event like the king's, open to all Elandrians regardless of their magic. Whenever the time came, she would change that. But it hadn't been much of a new era, except that discontent had grown. The Sage was a bridge between peoples, and she couldn't help but feel that she had failed.

Quinn came up behind her and wrapped his arms around her. "What are you thinking about, my love?"

"Have I failed as the Sage?"

"What? No, of course not."

She shook her head. "In my coronation speech, I had promised a new, better era for the magical peoples of Elandria."

"I know. I read it."

"Of course you did." She chuckled, then grew serious again. "But I was naïve. I didn't know what that meant. And now look at us. We're leading thousands of Scholars and Deyoni to their deaths."

Quinn kissed her cheek. "They're coming willingly. They're fighting for that future you promised because they still believe in it."

"Do you still believe in it?"

"I do." He spun her around by her shoulders to face him. "I believe that after whatever tomorrow brings, we'll usher in a new era for Elandria. For everyone, not just Scholars. Not just Deyoni. I believe in *you*."

Amarice pressed her head against his chest. She listened to the sound of his heart beating. What if this was the last time? "What if we die tomorrow?"

Quinn's arms tightened around her. "Then we die a noble death, fighting for a better future."

"Somehow, that doesn't comfort me."

"I know. Me neither." He kissed the top of her head. "I'm frightened."

"I'm sorry I dragged you into this."

"What in Brigitte's name do you mean?"

She looked up into his deep brown eyes, warm as chocolate, soothing as a dark ale. "I feel responsible for you. I named you Consort and forced you into this nightmare."

"You offered me the title of Consort. But Amarice, I would have followed you into the abyss the second I met you. And it would have been my choice. It's still my choice." He ran a soft hand over her cheek and placed it under her chin. "You've forced me into nothing. You've got enough to worry about without all this guilt. I do everything I do freely."

She nodded. He bent his head down to kiss her. It started as a promise, a vow to fight with her until the bitter end. It grew into something heated and wild. She felt their magic burn around them, between them, and through them.

Quinn moved his lips to her earlobe. Amarice sighed. "You know," she said, "we could die tomorrow."

"Mmhmm."

"We should make the most of our time tonight."

His voice was wet and husky in her ear. "My thoughts exactly."

Amarice tugged on his shirt. He lifted his arms as she pulled it over his head. The second it was gone, he was back on her. He sucked on the curve of her neck with frenzied passion as she ran her hands over his muscular, tight arms.

"Too many clothes," she panted. Her hands moved to the laces on his pants and pulled. He couldn't wait for her fumbling and dropped his hands from her hips to help her. Then he pulled off her tunic and riding pants, picked her up, and threw her on the bed.

They had fallen into a familiarity over their time together. Always enjoyable but never with urgency and desperation. Tonight was different. Tonight was like their first time. Frantic, hurried, with moments of conscious slowing to savor each other's touch. It was all hands grasping, teeth biting, tongues exploring.

They didn't hold back. Not tonight, with such an uncertain future. Their cries of pleasure mingled the way their magic did between them, like a double staircase to the highest point of the heavens, intertwined and inseparable.

Amarice's back arched as she lowered herself onto Quinn. He

gripped her hips with his strong fingers and gazed at her with loving, hooded eyes. They rode out each wave of ecstasy with gasps and moans. As she soared higher, she laced her fingers with Quinn's, grounding herself as she fell through euphoria.

Quinn flipped her over as her trembles stopped, increasing the pace and kissing her with wanton fury. She dug her fingers into his toned back muscles, and he stiffened and hollered her name.

They lay in a tangle of arms and legs on the soft, thick pallet, panting and dripping in sweat. Quinn held Amarice's hand and ran his thumb over hers in soft circles. For the first time in days, Amarice's mind was clear and unburdened. She focused only on the warmth of his touch, the smell of his skin, the taste of his kiss still lingering on her tongue.

Quinn yawned and stretched. Amarice turned on her side to face him. She traced random patterns over his chest. He had regained all of his lost mass from his kidnapping, thanks to Madge's cooking and his morning jogs.

He placed a hand over hers and smiled at her. "I'm sure the whole camp heard us."

She smirked. "Ask me if I care."

"Oh! I snagged us a bottle of wine from Raymond's tent." He sat up and rummaged through their belongings. "No chalices, though."

He opened the bottle and took a long swig of the firewine. Amarice held her hand out for her turn. "I knew I kept you around for a reason."

He winked and passed her the bottle. "Just the wine?"

"Among other things."

She let the smooth burn of firewine glide down her parched throat, not yet ready to consider tomorrow. She handed the bottle back to Quinn and wiped her mouth with the back of her hand.

"Tell me a story, Quinn."

"A story?"

"Something I don't know about you. I don't know."

She could see him thinking as he took another long drink. He pulled the bottle away with a pop. "Have I told you how Jack and I became friends?"

She shook her head. "No."

He regaled her with the tale of Jack's advances and Quinn's oblivion. Amarice laughed as he described how Jack had suddenly started spending all his time with Quinn. She could only imagine a younger, more innocent Quinn, fresh from Corthy.

"Your turn," he said. "Tell me something about young Amarice."

She smiled. Talking about her past was getting easier. "Have I told you about the time I was expelled from school for a month?"

"What? No! You?" He was genuinely shocked.

"I was a terrible menace. I was always showing off with my magic. My teacher hated Zayn and me. Especially me, which was at least partly my fault." She grinned a devious grin. "I certainly didn't give her a reason to like me."

"I cannot imagine."

"Oh, it's true! Anyway, there that was one day that I wasn't doing anything wrong for once. It was windy, and the books and papers kept blowing around. She thought it was me, which honestly wasn't out of the realm of possibility. But it wasn't this time.

"I told her I would do something far more interesting if it was me. Keep in mind, this was a bitter old woman, bent over with a bad back. But she was mean, and she kept trying to punish me. So, I retaliated. I conjured a gust of wind and blew her skirts over her head."

Quinn guffawed. "You didn't."

"I did. Everyone was laughing. Every time she tried to push them back down, I blew them back up. She was showing her old, stained bloomers to everyone and screeching. I've never heard such a noise."

Her lover held his gut as he laughed. "How old were you?"

"Oh, thirteen or fourteen, I think."

The wine helped them laugh and collapse in exhaustion and inebriation onto the pallet. Amarice's eyes were heavy. She curled against Quinn, who tucked the blankets under her chin. He kissed her forehead. She yawned.

Somehow, they slept. Somehow, they didn't dream of blood and violence. That would come tomorrow. As Amarice drifted off into sleep, she thought as far as last nights went, this was a good one.

CHAPTER 34

RAYMOND

He saw the line of opposing forces across a field of vibrant green grass that glittered in the morning dew. His stomach churned. Soon, this field would be covered in blood.

A mountain loomed behind the Chamberite army. Beybrook was there, though he couldn't see it, and the Great Silver Lake. He hoped the innocent citizens of the city had fled, hoped the Chamberites were compassionate enough to evacuate. His scouts couldn't get close enough to find out.

Amarice and Quinn rode up beside him on the front line. They looked strange in their armor. It glistened in the sunlight, giving them an otherworldly, exotic look, so different from their lightweight, loose clothing that allowed their magic to flow freely. They wore only breast-plates. A risk, but they needed their magic more.

"You remember the plan?" he asked them.

"Yes. Although I have a feeling it's about to not matter in the slightest." Amarice gave a dry, humorless chuckle. She looked up at the sky. Raymond followed her gaze and squinted at the bright sun.

It was a beautiful spring day, and the irony was not lost on

Raymond. But the sun was a problem. Although it would ensure visibility for his archers and sword fighters, it also complicated getting the Sage and Consort past the front lines and into the interior of Beybrook. Also, the Lazori mercenaries were trained in the desert. Anything that lowered their efficacy would help the Elandrians. He looked at Amarice.

"My lady Sage, set the mood for us, will you?"

"With pleasure."

She dropped Atsila's reins and raised both arms to the sky. In seconds, dark clouds filled the sky. Thunder rumbled overhead. Then the skies opened, and a deluge fell upon the valley.

As rain obscured his vision, Raymond realized he had just made this much harder for himself. But also, he hoped, much harder for the other side. He lowered the visor on his helmet and stared ahead.

"How do we start?" he heard Quinn yell over the raucous rainfall. "Who goes first?"

"Fuck if I know!" Raymond yelled back. He turned to Erenia on his left. "What do you think?"

Her armor clunked as she shrugged. "I think now is as good a time as any."

Raymond nodded. "Amarice, Quinn! Fall back."

"Be safe, Raymond." He could hear the quaver in Amarice's voice over the storm. "Please don't do anything too stupid."

"Don't you dare die," Quinn added.

"You, too." Raymond's heart pounded hard, as if it were trying to escape. This was happening. "I love you both."

He heard the soldiers part in formation behind him as the Sage and her Consort fell back to the interior. Their company of Scholars was fifty yards or so behind the front. His personal guard filled the space they left behind. He nodded at his captains. "For Elandria!"

"For Elandria!" they replied. Echoes of the cry roared behind him, reaching all the way to the rear of the formation. The sound pumped Raymond's blood. It was time to defend his country.

The other side thundered with their own battle cry. They sounded far away, and he wondered what their rallying cry was. Some of them thought they were fighting for Elandria, too, only their Elandria looked like genocide and discrimination.

As silence fell, save for the storm, anger surged through Raymond's veins. Good, he thought. He would need it. He would start this fight, and he would end it.

"ARCHERS!" he cried. The order repeated through the ranks. He held an arm up, signaling them to hold. He took one deep breath before dropping his arm. "FIRE!"

Arrows arched overhead through the air. They pushed through the rain, flying off-track but still soaring. A gust of wind from behind nearly knocked Raymond off his horse, but it forced the arrows further.

"Thanks, Amarice and Quinn."

He drew his sword with a loud yell and charged.

His ears rang with the shouts behind and ahead of him. His stallion galloped at full speed. Others began to pass him, their own weapons drawn. He allowed one more passing thought to Amarice and Quinn. Pictured Elaine in his mind's eye. Then lost himself to the bloodlust of battle.

The roar of the initial clash was deafening. Lazori pikemen comprised the front line. They faced Raymond down with no fear in their eyes, only hardened determination. He held tight to Sterling's reins so he could dodge them.

The first swipe of his sword took out a lance instead of a person. He ran his blade through the now defenseless mercenary, and blood splattered onto his armor. After that initial kill, he swung and screamed with no pattern, no method.

It wasn't long before the squelching of lost limbs and bowels became just another sound in the cacophonous symphony of death and war. If he was injured, he didn't notice. He could barely see in the rain. It blew sideways, obscuring the battle into swirls of red and silver and the blue of the Elandrian royal banners.

He pushed through the footmen, leaving bodies in his wake. Ahead was the cavalry. He could see only taller shapes atop horses. He bent low on his horse and kicked him to run faster. Shouts echoed as soldiers dodged the horses.

He reached the cavalry, his own mounted forces beside him. The other side charged. Raymond sheathed his longsword and pulled a shorter blade from the scabbard affixed to the saddle.

Clashing and crashing.

Screams and yells.

Red flew everywhere, painting the rainstorm. The king felt a slice land under his arm brace. He let go of the reins in shock. In that instant, another rider charged. His stallion spooked, and he threw off Raymond. The king tumbled to the ground.

His helmet fell off. Raymond groaned. A horse was about to trample him, and he rolled just in time.

He had to get up. Had to get on a horse.

With great effort, he pulled himself to his feet. Stinging rain pelted his skin. He looked around for his shorter blade. Gone. He looked up right as a Chamberite on horseback charged him. Without even thinking, he pulled his longer blade from his sheath and met the other's sword in a loud clank.

He dodged and swung wildly with both hands. He sliced the haunch of the horse enough to spook it as it turned around. The horse bucked its rider. Raymond darted to the fallen soldier and plunged his sword through his neck with a shout. A geyser of blood flew up, splashing Raymond in the face.

He wiped his eyes. The cavalry had gone past him. Soon he was engaged in hand-to-hand ground combat. He could only see his opponent. He had no idea how his own troops were faring. How Amarice and Quinn were faring.

He knocked the soldier to the ground with a body slam. The soldier was an Elandrian. A man who had served in Raymond's own command at some point. He might even know the man, have met him. As he went to land the final blow, something stopped him. The young man's eyes were wide.

"Please," he wheezed. "My mother..."

So much Elandrian blood. The man was unarmed, his weapon too far away for him to reach. Raymond stared into his eyes, frozen.

Moments later, smoke billowed through the battlefield. No, not smoke, Raymond realized as he looked up. He blinked against the cloudy white mist.

Steam.

Amarice and Quinn were alive, then. This was magical, and only they would be strong enough to cover an entire battlefield in steam. To what end, he didn't know. Around him, the battle paused as people looked on in wonder and confusion. It stung Raymond's eyes and skin, but it wasn't scalding.

He looked down at the soldier. He lowered his sword. "Choose Elandria next time," he said. He stomped the man's face, knocking him out and crunching his nose. But he would survive.

He ran forth, trying to fight through the hot, misty clouds. He was thankful the Chamberites had bright orange symbols on their armor because everyone was faceless now. More died at his hand. He had cuts and bruises all over his body. His dented armor dug into his skin. But he kept on.

Yell. Dodge. Slice. Dodge. Swing. Yell.

It was repetitive. A dance. A ritual.

At some point, the steam dissipated. Bodies littered the ground around him. He couldn't tell who was winning or losing. There were soldiers in orange and blue in infinite numbers. How would it end? How would he know?

"My king! King Raymond!"

He turned to find the face behind the shout. A captain was riding toward him. She pulled a horse by the reins behind her.

"Here!" She let go as she rode past Raymond and drew her sword. Raymond grabbed the reins and swung himself onto the back of this horse. He rode after his captain to the next wave of enemies.

But then they froze. Their opponents turned to see what was happening behind them.

A deafening roar. The earth itself shook, and he gripped the reins to stay astride. He was close to Beybrook now.

To the northeast, the Great Silver Lake swirled in a maelstrom. And then it rose, like a tornado of water high above the surface, forming into a massive sphere. Screams rang out at the sight, and the sound was like nothing he'd ever heard.

To the northwest, he swore the mountain shuddered. An avalanche began, and rocks and boulders rushed toward the city below. As they fell, the tower of water from the lake arced toward the city.

The city flooded from the east. Buildings on the west crashed as the avalanche and earthquake toppled them.

Raymond had never seen anything like it. He smiled at the beautiful destruction at the hands of the Sage and Consort. The Chamberite forces—Lazori and Elandrian alike—ran to the south, trying to escape the magical ruin, straight toward the rest of Raymond's army.

"Thank you," he said aloud as though one could hear him. He inhaled, ready for the final push.

CHAPTER 35

AMARICE

The Sage looked behind when she heard the orders for the archers to ready. She glanced up at the sky, the rain beating down on her face. Quinn pulled close and hollered at her over the storm.

"Won't the rain and wind knock those arrows down too soon?"

She nodded. "I should think so. But it's the first sign to advance."

She couldn't see Quinn's face in any detail through the downpour, but she imagined he was rolling his eyes. The order came to fire, and ahead of them, arrows loosed. She squinted and could barely see them launch, but the wind would blow them off course the second they reached altitude.

A vigorous gust of wind blew from beside her as Quinn aided the arrows with his magic. She smiled. Shouts sounded over the tempest, and the first lines charged. Captains nearby ordered their companies to hold, to wait until the first onslaught had passed.

The energy of battle buzzed around them. Raymond had rallied them. They were ready to fight for their people. For their country. And for a better future.

She nudged Atsila and followed Quinn and Nivasi to their company of Scholars. A small, mounted guard of Deyoni were there to deflect attacks while the Scholars made it to the interior. The rain made it impossible to see what was happening on the battlefield. She didn't know when they should ride forward or where to.

They waited a long time, listening to the horrid cries of death through the storm. This storm now fueled itself, the strongest Amarice had conjured. She was able to let it go from her magic. It raged on and showed no signs of dissipating. But now she was free to focus her magic on other things.

She felt Quinn in her mind as if he were knocking on an invisible door. "We should go soon."

"I know."

"I'm scared."

"Me, too."

She felt his hand squeeze her knee, and she looked at him through the rain. There was no point in delaying any longer. They had a mission, and the outcome of the battle depended on their success. She reached back into their mental connection. "East or west?"

She could feel Quinn weighing options in his mind of heading toward the lake or the mountain. "East."

They passed the orders on to their company. "Cause as much destruction as you can," Quinn told the fifty Scholars and twenty Deyoni. "If you feel your powers draining too quickly, fall back or hide."

"If you see innocents in the town, usher them to safety to the best of your abilities. But protect yourselves first," Amarice added.

"And send word if you find Azmar, Grellis, or Samperian." Quinn sent a thought along to Amarice. "Samperian is *mine*."

She pulled Atsila alongside Nivasi and leaned over to kiss Quinn. He placed one hand in her soaking hair and kissed her back with everything he had. Then they pulled away, gazed into each other's frightened eyes for a few moments, and charged.

The Sage bent low and whispered into Atsila's ear as they ran through the torrential downpour. Their own troops parted as they went past, but soon they were breaching the Elandrian front line.

They were in the fray now. She was thankful for the cover of rain and clouds hiding the bodies that her horse dodged and leapt over. She willed herself not to look down. Keep looking ahead, she told herself.

Following the Consort's lead, the surrounding Scholars used wind to blow soldiers off their feet. There was not much on their path that they could use. There were no trees, and they were still too far from the lake for any of the Scholars to use water. Some were able to make small snares from the grass the way Amarice had done during her kidnapping.

The Chamberite force fought hard, but she could sense their fear. Her magic pulsed in response, ready to burst forth. They were unprepared for facing magic in the battle. There were no Lazori mercenaries on this flank of the company.

They were so close to the back of the enemy lines. So close to Beybrook itself. She sent a tendril of a thought to Quinn, hoping he would notice even in the heat of the battle.

"Amarice!" he responded in her mind.

"They're terrified. We need to capitalize on that."

An image appeared in her mind, and she wasn't sure if it was hers or his. The connection to Quinn made their magic stronger and more unified. She sat upright in the saddle without slowing down. Her Gift of the Earth burned as fire flew from her fingertips.

It engulfed the foot soldiers. More balls of fire soared through the air. The other Scholars, who couldn't conjure fire, controlled the flames that already burned. Flames leapt around them, too hot and full of magic for the rain to douse.

She would never forget the screams or the smell of burning flesh in the rain.

But it worked. The Chamberite force ran. Some to the west into the thick of battle. Some north into the city. And others still ran toward the lake as if the water would protect them.

The rain was easing. She could conjure another storm or make this one come back in force. She turned to look around. So many were falling. Bile rose in her throat at the smell of shit and blood.

A captain of the opposing force was panting on the ground. Blood seeped from a wound in his abdomen; something had punctured through his flimsy armor. Amarice dismounted.

"What the fuck are you doing?" Quinn yelled with desperation. He rode up behind her. She held out a hand to show him she knew what she was doing.

She approached the dying captain. "Where are the ministers hiding?"

He coughed and sputtered. Blood oozed from his mouth. He had a matter of minutes. "End it."

"Answer me! The ministers! Azmar and the others."

She had to bend low to hear his response. "The council building on the high street."

"All three of them? Azmar, Grellis, and Samperian?"

"Ye-yes."

She pulled from her hip the small blade Raymond had insisted she wear. The man stared at her, eyes dull and begging. She placed the tip of the sword on his throat, and he closed his eyes.

"Find peace." She closed her own eyes as she pushed the blade upward through his throat to sever his spinal cord. It was quick, but more personal without her magic.

Blood splattered over her, and she let out a sob. Quinn reached a hand out to pull her away. "We have to go."

She mounted Atsila again. More troops were coming. The Deyoni were fighting hard around them, and Scholars stood with flames at the ready. "We need cover."

"Another storm?" he asked.

She shook her head. "No, we'll need visibility quickly once we get into the city."

"We're close enough to the lake. Fire and water?"

She laughed a painful, hysterical laugh. "I guess it was always leading to this. Fire and water. You and me."

"Until my last breath."

She hoped that wouldn't be soon. They pushed toward the edge of the lake. Their numbers were dwindling. People had died for her today. She would make sure their deaths were not in vain.

They reached the road closest to the lake, now emerged behind enemy lines. Quinn dismounted this time, needing to ground himself so his magic wouldn't lose control. He grunted, straining, as he summoned a massive sphere of water the size of a large building from the Great Silver Lake. Soldiers screamed as it floated overhead. No one had ever seen anything like it before.

Amarice blasted her fire magic at the ball of water. As it hit, the water erupted into ghostly clouds of steam. The other Scholars set to work magnifying them, spreading them, and pushing them out.

"Let's go!" she screamed at Quinn. "The council building!"

Her eyes burned in the hot steam as they rode into town. But as they made it to the center of the city, past all the soldiers, it dissipated. Most had blown over the battlefield, thanks to the other Scholars.

The Scholars and Deyoni knocked into houses to find people hiding. Amarice rode past as the evacuees rushed north. Those fucking Chamberite bastards, she thought. They had left all these people for slaughter.

Word spread through open windows and others fled their houses. Amarice turned Atsila hard onto the high street. They were almost there.

The Sage and her Consort dismounted in front of the council building. A line of Lazori soldiers stood between them and the door. Some hundred trained mercenaries. They needed to get past them. Needed them to abandon their posts.

She looked over at Quinn. "I think it's time for something dramatic."

He laughed. "I expected nothing less from you."

She grabbed his hand. His magic intertwined with hers and amplified. She looked at the mountain to the west. The high street sloped up to the peak and down to the lake. She forced all her concentration on the mountain.

A rumble built under her feet. It grew outward from her to the west. To her right, she could hear a roar of water. She dared a look, trying to keep her connection to the earth. Quinn had turned the entirety of the lake into a tower of swirling water, dozens of stories high. He squeezed her hand as he made it arc toward Beybrook.

A quarter of the Lazori soldiers ran. The rest trembled as they faced the Sage and the Consort, trying to stay upright against the earthquake.

The mountain shook, and the sound was deafening. Amarice raised her left hand higher as the vibrations moved outward through the city and the valley. She wasn't sure how she was still standing.

Then rocks began to fall. Boulders. A landslide made its way down the mountain straight for the high street.

"Move, you idiots!" she yelled in Lazori. "Move, or you'll be squashed like bugs!"

It worked. They ran, leaving the entrance clear. A flood hit the edge of the city with a resounding crash. Atsila and Nivasi bolted. They didn't have long before the avalanche arrived.

"Help me, Quinn!"

Together, they conjured a gale powerful enough to push against the avalanche and slow it. It was the hardest Amarice had ever pushed her magic. They had made it this far. She did not want to die now, not at her own hand.

It worked.

They fell into each other's arms, panting from the effort. "I'm getting weak," she said.

"We have to keep on. We're almost there."

By some stroke of luck, a few of their Scholar company ran up behind them shouting. Amarice wiped her eyes. They could do this.

The Sage and the Consort entered the council hall together, side-by-side. In the middle of the council chamber, a cluster of people huddled, clinging together.

Amarice's voice was an explosion of fury. "This ends now! Face me!" No one moved. As they drew closer, she heard them sobbing. "It's over, Azmar. Samperian."

"Azmar's dead," someone bit out. "Heart attack from your fucking earthquake!"

"Can't say I'm sad," Quinn said in a low voice next to Amarice.

Samperian broke away. His hands were up at his sides, palms turned to the sky. He muttered some prayer as he looked upward. Even now, he still clung to his ideology.

"Shut the fuck up, Darius! No one is going to save us!" someone else screamed. A Chamberite minister that Amarice vaguely recognized.

"My mission is holy!" Samperian said. "The gods have blessed me."

"Is this what divine blessing looks like?" Quinn asked. "It looks like failure to me."

Samperian charged. He drew a sword from his belt and rushed Amarice. Before she could react, Quinn had lunged in front of her, driving his own sword into Samperian's heart.

The zealot fell to the ground. Everyone stared. No one cried or screamed.

"We surrender!" It was Grellis who broke the stunned silence. "We surrender!"

The others put their hands up, weapons clattered to the floor. Amarice looked at the Scholars behind her. She nodded at a few of them. "Take the greasy fuck and spread the word. It's over."

Two women and one man grabbed Grellis and led him from the council building. She looked at the others who stared at her in fear. Azmar's corpse lay before them. For someone so intimidating in life, she was meek in death. Small. She sighed. Part of her wanted the rest of them dead, too. They had supported the Chamberite movement from the beginning.

But she was tired of death.

"Stay with them," she told the others. "I'll send soldiers to arrest them."

Then the Sage took Quinn's hand and left the building. Outside, her shoulders dropped in exhaustion. "It's over."

Quinn fell to his knees and sobbed, his body quivering from the tears. She was sure her own would fall soon, but not yet. She was too stunned.

When he composed himself, they walked south toward the battle-field. Amarice took in the damage as if she walked through a dream. Half of Beybrook was flooded. Many buildings near the mountain had crumbled from the earthquake and landslide. Yet somehow, at the edge of the city, standing in a foot of water, were two familiar faces.

Amarice laughed. Atsila and Nivasi were waiting for them. They huffed at the sight of their masters.

"Oh, Nivasi," Quinn said as he stroked her face. "You wonderful horse."

Atsila nuzzled Amarice's shoulder. "Are they this special? Or is this more *tovari* magic that binds us to these horses?"

Quinn shrugged. "Could just be the Deyoni blood."

"Whatever. I'm just glad we don't have to walk now. I'm exhausted." She placed her foot in the stirrup and swung her leg over the horse's back. Quinn mounted his own mare.

They walked through a field of death and devastation. The Lazori mercenaries were running north toward their home country. Mercenaries were only loyal to their money, and their bosses were dead or captured.

Amarice was nauseated at all the corpses in the field. It would take a long time to collect the dead. She dreaded hearing the final numbers.

Cheers erupted as the Sage and the Consort approached the Elandrian army. She let the joy flood through her. The war was over.

Elandria could be made whole again.

The troops parted for them, guiding them to where the king was in the center of the crowd.

King Raymond was surrounded by three of his captains who were tending to his wounds. His face was stained with blood and dirt and sweat, and his armor was covered in red. Someone had tied his left arm in a sling. But his eyes lit up when he saw Amarice and Quinn and waved off his attendees.

He stood, wobbling just a bit on his feet. Amarice and Quinn dismounted their horses in one motion.

"We did it," the king said in a hoarse voice.

"Yes, we did." Amarice threw her arms around her oldest friend, causing him to grunt in pain. "Oh, sorry."

CHAPTER 36

QUINN

The sun gleamed off the alabaster of the Villa, and Quinn's eyes filled with tears. He had never been happier to return home. As their banners were spotted, cheers resounded through the mountain air, echoing deep in his chest.

The war was over, and it finally felt real.

Raymond had sent news of the victory ahead of them to the Villa and throughout Elandria. On their second day marching back, a Messenger had arrived to inform the king that Teleah had been retaken. The prisons were full of the traitors who had taken the capital, and Andin, Raymond's valet, was dead by his own hand.

The cheers reinvigorated the exhausted warriors, and Raymond sped up his horse. Amarice and Quinn followed, eager to see the loved ones they had left behind. They rode through the camps to smiles and cheers and sobs of thanks. Quinn smiled and dropped his hand to those who reached up to him, squeezing their hands in return.

The residents of the Villa lined the edge of the northern garden in front of the brightly blooming Consort Tree. Quinn could see his father wiping his eyes.

Raymond all but leapt off his horse and into Elaine's arms. The others whooped and laughed as the king swung his lover around and kissed her with a never-before-seen vigor. Madge was the first to embrace Amarice, and the older woman wept loudly into the Sage's shoulder.

Corbin ran up first and squeezed Quinn tight. A lump grew in Quinn's throat, and he patted his brother's back. Quinn was mobbed by Janessa, Madge, Jack, and Matthew before he made it to Deben.

"My son, my son," said Deben through tears. "You are alive."

Quinn hugged his father close. The fear he had about never seeing him again—and so soon after meeting him—had not sunk in until this moment. He had pushed it away, deep down inside of him, in order to do what had to be done. But now, his own eyes were wet with relief.

"Brigitte's tit, Raymond! Put the poor girl down, or she won't have any lips left!"

Quinn turned at the sound of Daisy's chiding and snorted. Raymond still hadn't let Elaine go. He loosed one hand to make an obscene gesture in Daisy's direction, and everyone laughed. Daisy had her left arm wrapped around Amarice's waist, her right dangling life-lessly by her side. Amarice was leaning her head against her best friend's shoulder. She met Quinn's eyes and grinned.

Finally, the king let Elaine go. Her face was flushed, and she didn't meet anyone's eyes in embarrassment, but she clung to Raymond's hand as if she couldn't bear to let him go ever again. The others greeted Raymond with hugs and praises for his leadership.

"I think you know as well as I do that it was a joint effort. If it weren't for your Sage and your Consort, we wouldn't have succeeded." Raymond nodded at Quinn and Amarice.

"You don't know that," Amarice replied. "And it was a joint effort, but by several thousand people."

"Indeed."

Madge clapped her hands. "A feast! I am preparing a feast for tonight! All your favorite foods. Chicken and citrus pie for Quinn, and blueberry for Amarice!"

Amarice giggled. "I'd expect nothing less from you, Madge. I'm so glad to be home."

The returning warriors made use of the baths, soaking away the aches of battle and long travel. Quinn was quite certain he'd never be clean again and spent a solid hour in the heated, floral-scented waters. Amarice washed her hair no less than three times, sighing and moaning in pleasure as the grime rinsed away.

A few hours later, Quinn took Amarice's arm as they entered the veranda for dinner. Madge hadn't exaggerated when she said she was preparing a feast. She had outdone herself. Even the Feast of Fire and Harvest Holiday meals didn't compare to the spread. Platters were stacked high with roasted meats and vegetables. Hot loaves of fresh-baked bread made his mouth water. Mashed potatoes that smelled of garlic and bacon sat in a large pot. An assortment of the finest cheeses was displayed on a massive silver tray. And there were no less than five types of pie.

"Maybe we should win a war more often," Quinn said to Amarice as he helped himself to two slices of pie, his mother's recipe that Madge had improved and perfected. Amarice nodded in agreement, her mouth full of smoked meat.

The feast was a boisterous affair, and the wine flowed freely. Happy, lighthearted chatter mingled with the ambient sounds of the mountains. The returning soldiers, too, were feasting and celebrating with their loved ones. The celebrations among the camps grew more raucous as the night wore on. Quinn was content to stuff his face with meats and breads and piles of dessert, but Amarice insisted that they go outside to drum and dance among the Deyoni.

Stomach stuffed and head heavy with drink, Quinn followed Amarice out to the camps. Raymond and Elaine tagged along behind, and more Villa residents stumbled out of the veranda. Quinn held his drum in one hand and Amarice's arm in the other. She had donned her Deyoni garb, a skirt like flames and water, and her pounds of jewelry jingled as they walked. Jack ran up beside him to chat as they made their way to one of the bonfires.

Applause greeted them when they joined a large circle of celebration. Quinn looked around at the faces in the firelight. The lines between Scholar and Deyoni had blurred. The crowds were mixed, and deep friendships had been established.

This is what the new Elandria looks like, Quinn thought.

Amarice leaned up to kiss his cheek, then set forth to join the dancers. Quinn took a seat with the drummers. Someone passed Jack and Raymond spare drums, and they took a seat on either side of him. Elaine sat at Raymond's feet, knees folded up, eyes ensnared by the dancers.

"I don't know what to do!" Raymond shouted in his ear.

Quinn shrugged. "Just find a rhythm. Look to the man at the north of the circle. He'll determine whether the song is fast or slow."

He closed his eyes and cracked his neck as he got accustomed to the beat, letting the deep echoes flow through him. His hands flew over the drum's hide to play an upbeat, cheerful rhythm. Jack found an easy beat, and Raymond drummed along in an awkward, off-beat manner. It didn't matter. All the sounds melded together into a fluid, unified song of jubilation.

A blissful, surreal haziness fell over him as he watched the dancers. Deyoni dance magic. The powers of these people of the earth could create a trance stronger than the strongest liquors. Amarice's hips moved in an unearthly tempo, the coins on her belt glittering as they caught the firelight. Quinn's hands moved of their own accord, adjusting their rhythm as the lead drummer changed the beat.

The Deyoni women pulled several of their Scholar friends into the dance. He watched as Amarice pulled Janessa to her feet. His brother's wife shrieked and whooped as she tried to learn the steps that Amarice and the others demonstrated. Amarice removed two of her loudest necklaces of dangling coins and jewels and placed them over Janessa's neck. Quinn grinned.

Hours passed. It could have been moments or days, for all that time mattered in the drum circle. But soon, the circle shrank as couples partnered off and parents carried their sleeping children to bed. Jack had run off with someone he'd met that night. Raymond had led a yawning Elaine back to the Villa. He had no idea when Corbin and Janessa had left. Amarice panted as the last of the dancers broke away, her face flushed. She came forward and kissed a still-drumming Quinn on the top of his head.

He stood, tucking his drum under one arm, and captured her lips in a proper kiss. As they made their way through the camps, the first light of dawn crept over the horizon, illuminating the earth in glimmers of pale yellow. Amarice led him down to the kitchen to nick some food. They spoke in hushed tones as they ate leftover blueberry pie before tiptoeing off to bed.

This was what Quinn had fought for, not just in the battle, but every day of his life. He'd fought for a place in this world. For love and acceptance. For long nights with friends and days of fulfilling joy. He'd fought hard, and now he would never let it go.

CHAPTER 37

RAYMOND

"Are you certain, Elaine?"

She rolled her eyes. "For the last time, yes. I do not want to be the center of attention at your homecoming. I can't stand the thought of all those eyes on me, wondering who I am, when they should be cheering for you and your soldiers."

Raymond wrapped his arms around her. "You know, at some point, you'll have to have all those eyes on you."

She pressed her head against his chest. "You're certainly presuming a lot."

"Sorry," he said. "You know you don't have to come live with me. Or plan a future or whatever."

"I was teasing, Raymond." She pulled out of his embrace and planted a kiss on his lips. "I'm in no hurry, but my fate was sealed the moment you kissed me. And I'm not complaining about it at all."

He smiled, but it didn't reach his eyes, and Elaine noticed. She noticed everything about him. "What's wrong?"

"I'm scared of seeing the castle. My home. I have no idea what state it's in."

She took his hand and squeezed it. "That is scary. But you've just won a war. There's nothing you can't handle."

Raymond wasn't so sure, but he kissed her one last time before dressing in his finery. They were to leave for Teleah in a half hour. He had spent a few days recovering from the final battle at the Sage's Villa, but now it was time to return and rebuild. He had tried to get dressed earlier, but Elaine had distracted him. Not that he was complaining.

Elaine smoothed his tunic and grinned. "Very kingly."

"At least I look it. I don't feel it."

She planted a reassuring kiss on his lips and pulled him out of the room. They made their way to the front gardens, where the rest of the reverie awaited. Elaine waved and climbed into the carriage that would carry her, Janessa, Corbin, and Deben to the capital. Amarice and Quinn were already on their horses, waiting.

"About time," Quinn said, teasing. "We were about to send in a scout."

"Had important business to take care of, you know. Being king is demanding."

"Oh, I'm sure."

Raymond mounted Sterling. The dapple-grey stallion had been bathed and groomed, and someone had braided blue flowers, the color of the royal family, into his mane. He chuffed as Raymond took the reins and patted his shoulder. He heard the clatter of his guard mounting their own. Raymond looked at Amarice and nodded. "Here we go."

"Here we go."

The journey back home was pleasant. It was a crisp, bright spring day, and birds sang them along their path down the mountains. Everyone chattered happily, and Raymond caught occasional bits of songs from the soldiers farther back.

They stopped at the base of the Sage Mountains to stretch and water their horses. Amarice and Quinn had been quiet for much of the journey, and he suspected they were using their newfound powers of telepathy. It was unsettling knowing they could have whole conversations in their heads. Occasionally, they would burst out laughing for no apparent reason. None of Raymond's personal guard knew about their special magic, so he was certain the soldiers were confused. It added to the mystery of the Sage and the Consort.

As they neared the village outside of Teleah's walls, the captains called for proper formation. Amarice and Quinn slowed their pace to fall behind Raymond.

"No," he said as he turned his head. "This is a new Elandria. We wouldn't have won this war without the two of you. We enter as equals."

Quinn smiled and inclined his head. He pulled Nivasi forward to one side of the king and reached up to adjust his Consort's Diadem. Atsila brought Amarice to Raymond's other side. The Sage sat in all her power, her shoulders back, looking forward with a faint smile.

Shouts resounded as the villagers spotted the entourage. Raymond could see people rushing from their homes to line the road. Some of these people had sympathized with the Chamberite rebels, and he had no idea what to expect. He doubted anyone would try anything violent with the whole of the Elandrian army behind them. But was he returning in fanfare to jeers and boos? His heart beat like a frantic Deyoni drummer.

He had no reason to fear. They were met with cheers and applause. Citizens threw flowers onto the road. Children yelled for a chance to be waved at by Elandria's three most important people. Raymond chuckled as he waved.

Trumpets sounded from inside the walls of Teleah, and the city guard threw open the gates to welcome the heroes back from war. He wished he could be next to Elaine, to see her reaction at seeing Teleah for the first time. But then he thought about all the vandalized buildings that he had seen the last time he was here, even before the riot. Hardly the beautiful city he had grown up in.

A genuine smile spread across his face as they passed through the gates. Though damaged and broken, Teleah would always be his home. The crowds blocked most of the boarded up and vandalized buildings. Their cheers drowned out the trumpeters with sounds of joy. Even Sterling seemed to trot with pride through the familiar streets.

They followed the winding roads to the palace, waving and smiling to the citizens. Wherever the Chamberite sympathizers were, they were staying far away from the celebrations. Raymond knew that soon the task of trials and crowded prisons would face him, as well as rebuilding a new society. It was daunting, but for now, he enjoyed the hopeful spring air.

The parade ended at the palace gates, though his palace staff and loyal members of Parliament greeted the king and his entourage with applause. A twinge of guilt hit his heart when he noticed all the familiar faces that were absent, killed when the palace had fallen. And no Andin, whose betrayal still stung when he thought of it. He would mourn them and plan a memorial to the loyal staff. There was much to mourn these days, but there was also much to be grateful for.

He dismounted in front of the palace entrance. Amarice and Quinn matched him stride for stride as they entered the front doors to the grand entry hall. Raymond sighed and breathed in the familiar scent of his home. It was marred with a smoky smell. He looked around at the domed marble entryway. The skeleton staff had cleaned and repaired the hallway as best as they could, but chunks of stone were still missing along doorways and the balustrade. Scorch marks covered the doors, and soot stained many of the paintings.

Raymond thought he would be fine if he never saw another fire.

He had paused for a long time, he realized when Amarice lightly touched his arm. He looked at her concerned face, and he nodded to reassure her. Then he continued walking toward the staircase. A time would come for speeches and ceremony, but for now, he needed to get to work.

He wrinkled his nose against the smell of stale blood and smoke and tried to ignore the persistent red spots that had resisted the servants' cleaning in the corridors. The door to his rooms was new, replaced after the palace was reclaimed. He stopped and took a deep breath before turning the handle.

He smiled. The only smells in there were fresh paint and bouquets of lilies and herbs. Nothing looked out of place, save a charred corner of his desk. Firewine aerated in a decanter on a small table.

He collapsed in his favorite armchair. Amarice and Quinn sat on the small sofa. The Sage leaned against her Consort with her eyes closed.

"Wake up, Amarice," Raymond said with a laugh. "We've got work to do."

She groaned. "We just rode half the day. I'm tired."

A knock sounded on the door.

"Come in!" Raymond called.

A servant opened the door. She bowed her head and brought her right hand to her brow. "Your majesty, welcome home."

"Thank you, Amari. Everything looks wonderful in here."

She nodded with a smile. "Your other guests have arrived. Would you like them brought to you, or shall I show them to their rooms?"

"Bring them here, if you would. And Elaine will stay with me. You can have her belongings brought here."

"Yes, my king."

She disappeared and closed the door behind her. Raymond looked at his friends. Amarice's eyes were still closed, but Quinn was smirking.

"What?"

"Nothing."

"What, Quinn?"

Quinn shrugged. "I'm just...happy. Thinking about how much life has changed in a few short years."

Raymond laughed and stood. "Don't wax philosophical until I've had a glass or two of wine." He began filling chalices with the ruby liquid.

"Wine?" Amarice asked. She rubbed her eyes and sat up.

The men laughed, which made Amarice start chuckling. That's how the others found them when they entered Raymond's rooms. Deben and Corbin entered, deep in excited conversation. Bright-eyed Janessa had her arm linked through Daisy's. Jack winked at the servant and mouthed something to her that made her giggle. Elaine entered last, eyes wide and expression unreadable.

Raymond sat down the decanter of wine and folded Elaine into his arms. She returned his embrace.

He bent his head to her ear and whispered, "Are you all right?"

"It's a lot to take in, that's all." She raised her own head and kissed him on the cheek.

"It will look better when we finish repairs and painting, I promise."

"It's wonderful, Raymond."

He led her to the seat next to his, then handed out the glasses of wine. Everyone chatted about the parade and the positive reception of the citizens. Janessa and Corbin exclaimed about how massive the city and the palace were.

Raymond sipped his wine with one hand and held Elaine's in his other. He watched the room, the diversity of his chosen family striking him. The Sage and Consort. A Deyoni falconer. A self-taught builder and his wife from a small rural village. Elaine, the librarian. Two Apothecaries. So different and all united.

"This is it!"

Everyone turned to look at him with surprise at his outburst. Elaine raised an eyebrow. "What, darling?"

"This is it. This is how we fix Elandria."

CHAPTER 38

AMARICE

Two weeks later...

Amarice yawned as she made her way down to breakfast in the royal dining room. The council had a long day ahead of them. She and Quinn were to return to the Villa the next morning, and she had a lot to do today.

She ran into Elaine on the stairs.

"Good morning, Amarice."

"Good morning. It's so early."

Elaine nodded. "I told Raymond we should start later. He's absolutely giddy, though."

"And nervous, I'm sure. He used to wake me up at horrid hours before final exams. Banging on my dormitory door like the world was ending."

Elaine laughed. "Sounds about right. He's nervous, too, but I think it's mostly excitement."

"It is exciting."

They entered the dining room, and Amarice took her seat next to

Quinn. He leaned over for a kiss. He had woken up even earlier to get in a run through the palace gardens. Elaine sat opposite her. Amarice sipped the coffee a servant had placed in front of her and mused on how much had changed. She had been wrong about Elaine. She was bright and balanced, and she was good for her friend. In fact, she had found over the last two weeks that they had a lot in common.

"Nice of you to join us, my dear," Elaine said when Raymond entered the room and took his seat. "Since you set this meeting so early."

He rolled his eyes. "Good morning to you too."

After breakfast, the members of the Royal Council sequestered themselves in the room that had been repurposed for the council hall. Amarice had been skeptical of Raymond's idea at first, although Quinn had been on board from the beginning. Under Roland's reign, he had left Parliament unchecked, free to pass whatever laws they saw fit. Roland had trusted the power of democracy that Elandria had prided itself on. But left to its own devices, Parliament had been corrupted.

The king had the power to overturn any law he saw fit, and Raymond had exercised his royal rule for the war. But he feared becoming a despot. He alone did not want to stand against people. He was a royal and a Scholar; he was the first to admit he didn't understand the daily lives and struggles of his people.

Thus, the Royal Council was born. A diverse group of Elandrians would have the power to approve, deny, or modify the laws that Parliament passed. Amarice had been hesitant to break the Sage's precedent of becoming more than an advisor to the king, but Quinn had convinced her.

Deben represented the Deyoni interests on the Council. Though Amarice was half-Deyoni, she could never fully understand their plight, not the way one of their own could. She was glad to bow to Deben's expertise. Elaine understood the rural culture of the country better than anyone. Raymond had invited both Corbin and Janessa to join the council. They had declined—Corbin wanted to become a Builder, and Janessa said she needed time to figure out who she was. Jack had joined as well and brought with him a friend, Rina, who was not a Scholar and owned a business in Teleah.

They had the power to enact laws outside of Parliament, but they did not want to abuse it. After drafting the new plan, they had granted the Deyoni equal rights and overturned any anti-magic laws. In an attempt to get fresh blood into Parliament, every seat was up for re-election in two months. They had added four seats for Deyoni members. Elandria would be a true democracy again.

The council members took their seats at the large, round table. It would be a busy day; they had met every day for the last fortnight, but it was the last meeting for a few weeks.

Raymond cleared his throat. "I sent the final draft of the new constitution to the printers. I've also sent people to keep an eye on the elections in some of the larger cities. We don't want another Grellis or Azmar bribing and blackmailing their way into Parliament."

"Good. Rina and I have met with the business council and received estimates of repair costs," Jack said. He passed a piece of paper to everyone.

Amarice scanned the numbers. "Not as bad as I thought."

"It's mostly Scholar businesses."

"The hospital needs a considerable sum, though," Elaine said. "I met with the Healers yesterday."

"The Academy is helping with half of the costs," Amarice said.

Raymond cocked his head. "I thought they had depleted their Treasury during the war."

"They've had a sizable contribution." Amarice shuffled the stack of papers. "What about Beybrook? How are they on funds?"

"Amarice, what did you do?" She could feel Raymond's stare on her.

"Nothing."

"Amarice."

Quinn cleared his throat. "We gave a large donation."

"How large?"

"Large enough. And I turned down the portion of my salary that comes from the Academy for the next five years."

"Quinn!" Raymond exclaimed. "We could have made do. We have good credit with the banks, those in Elandria and elsewhere."

"Amarice and I have more than enough to support our lifestyle. The Villa turns a profit from farming and medicines."

"Still?" Jack asked. "I thought Daisy…"

Amarice's eyes welled with tears, but she cleared her throat. "She's not the only person who can make medicines, but the gardens supply many Apothecaries and Healers, plus we have the mountain residents' taxes and the royal allotment."

Raymond sighed. "Very well. What's next? Deben?"

"I am waiting to hear from the elders. I have sent letters to the largest tribes, and word will travel quickly."

"I met with the professors yesterday," Quinn said. "It…didn't go well."

Quinn wanted to restructure the Academy's organization to allow non-magic people. It was beyond radical. He had expected opposition, but Amarice knew how much his heart was invested in it.

She reached over to squeeze his hand. "Give it time. They'll see."

He nodded and cleared his throat. "What's next?"

৩৯৩

"I just wish they would see how elitist and unequal it is!"

Amarice sat on the bed in their usual chamber, which had been untouched by the raid, and watched Quinn pace the room. He had taken it much harder than she expected; indeed, she wasn't surprised at how the meeting had gone at all.

"It's a radical idea, Quinn. And they're quite traditional."

"I thought you supported this."

She put her hands up in defense. "I do! Wholeheartedly. But I'm not the one you have to convince. They're old and set in their ways. You want to upend a thousand years of history and tradition."

He stopped pacing and plopped down next to her on the bed, throwing his arm over his eyes. "I know."

Amarice leaned over and pulled his arm off his face. She looked into his deep brown eyes. "It will happen, love. Whether it's at the Academy or a new school, it will happen. But the war just ended. Give it time."

"The new school year is over half a year away."

"It might take longer."

He sighed. "It shouldn't."

"Your impatience sounds like, well, me." She smiled and planted a kiss on his lips. "We've got our whole lives ahead of us. And one day, we'll be the stodgy old ones who are set in our ways."

He gave her a little smile. "Perhaps. I'd like to think we'll always be open-minded, though. But I look forward to growing old with you."

"Me, too, although I'm in no hurry."

He kissed her and pulled her onto his lap. "You're a talented woman, but I think your biggest talent is distracting me."

"My *biggest* talent?" She raised an eyebrow. "We'll see about that."

She captured his lips in another kiss, eager to challenge his statement. She was on her way to disproving him when a knock interrupted them.

Quinn groaned. "I can't wait until we're back home."

"I know. This better be important." She climbed off the bed and adjusted her dress just as another knock sounded. She huffed. "Coming!"

Daisy stood in the doorway. "Hi."

"Daisy! I didn't know you had come back to Teleah."

"Yeah. Can we talk?"

Amarice glanced back at Quinn, who gestured at her to go on. "Of course."

The two friends walked arm in arm through the palace into the gardens. Amarice waited for Daisy to break the silence. It was several long minutes.

"I'm leaving."

"Somehow, I have a feeling you don't mean back to the Villa."

"No." Daisy stopped in front of a fragrant bush of white roses. Her injured arm hung loosely at her side. She wore long sleeves and silk gloves despite the warm sun. "I'm going home."

"To Te'eh?"

Daisy nodded.

"For good?"

"I don't know." She shrugged. "I have known that I wanted to be an Apothecary since I was eight years old. I've tried brewing again, and it's nigh impossible. Now, I have to figure out *who* I am without my career."

Amarice's eyes brimmed with hot tears. She blinked them away. "You can't do that at the Villa?" She knew she sounded like a petulant child, but she didn't want to lose her best friend.

Daisy shook her head. "No. I want a fresh start. My sister has children now, you know. I'm looking forward to spending time with my family. Being an aunt." She smiled. "My *other* family."

Amarice pulled Daisy in for a long hug. "You will always be my family. And you always have a place at the Villa."

"Thanks, Amarice."

CHAPTER 39

QUINN

It was quiet at the Villa.

Quinn was planting herbs in the courtyard, and he hadn't heard a sound from anyone else in nearly an hour. He chuckled when he remembered how noisy and crowded he used to think the Villa was when he first arrived. Now, everyone who didn't live here full time had left. The mountains had cleared out now that the Deyoni felt safe to travel again. He had to admit he missed the faint sound of drums as he fell asleep at night.

He and Amarice had slept a lot when they first returned from Teleah. The exhaustion of the war had caught up with them, but they were also at a loss of what to do. Now, a week later, they tried to find some semblance of their former routine. But as much of their role involved correspondence about research with other Scholars, there wasn't much to keep them busy. No one was diving back into research just yet. People were simply trying to rebuild their lives.

He was bored.

So often during the war, he had wished for quiet time to read or practice his magic in silence. Now, he had too much time and not enough to do. He worked on his book about Deyoni magic and was grateful that his father was there as a first-hand source. He gardened and helped restock the Villa's medicine stores. He dragged Amarice to bed often.

"Your thoughts are loud."

He heard Amarice's voice knocking at the door in his mind, and he could sense that she was close. He turned around to find her leaning against a marble column, arms folded over her silk dress.

"Only to the person who can hear them," he said out loud. He hadn't let her in to see his thoughts, though.

She smiled and shook her head. "No. You're musing. Everything about you radiates that the Lord Consort is deep in contemplation. Everyone's avoiding the courtyard so as not to disturb you."

He dusted the dirt off his hands and grinned. "Is that so?"

She shrugged. "Well, not the last part. At least, not that I know."

She crossed the courtyard and kissed him on the cheek. "What's on your mind?"

"I'm bored."

"I know. We go back to Teleah for a council meeting in a few weeks."

He nodded. "I'm not bored because we're back at the Villa. I like being home with you."

"But?"

"I've had an idea."

She smirked. "I could tell. What is it?"

"I want to take on apprentices. Not just one at a time like you do. But a few. I want to teach. I loved working with those Scholars on their earth magic."

A wide smile spread across Amarice's face. "I think that's a brilliant idea! You'll be perfect for it."

"Do you think so?"

"I know." She furrowed her brow. "It's only spring, though. The new school year won't start for eight months or so. What will you do in the meantime?"

"Write curricula. Figure out my requirements for who I accept. Correspond with the professors."

"It might put you back on their good side."

He laughed. "True. This is a far less radical idea than accepting non-Scholars to the Academy."

She took his hand and led him to the veranda for lunch. "I've been thinking about that. I think another school might be the way to go for now."

"But where would the funding come from? It's hardly the top priority for Elandria right now."

Amarice took her seat at the head of the table, and Quinn sat to her left. They were the first ones to the table. He helped himself to a large helping of Deyoni-spiced beans and brown rice. Amarice piled a salad on her plate.

"I don't think it needs to come from the Treasury. We have enough money to give a sizable donation. But I think we could get individuals to donate. And we could always charge a fee to attend."

Quinn cocked his head and thought. "I don't want cost to be a barrier. But if we kept enrollment small for a time, private funding could work."

"I can see it now." Amarice waved her hand in an arch. "The Quinn dia Gagiya Academy for...non-magical people?"

He chuckled. "Academy for Learning."

"Perfect." She took a bite, and he watched her chew with her brow furrowed. "Now we have to find rich people."

He shook his head and settled into his food. His father came and sat next to him, and he told them about this morning's hunt with the birds. Matthew joined them next. He was quiet lately. Sullen. He missed Daisy, and Quinn wondered if he would leave soon for a change of pace. He had another idea.

"Matthew, what do you think about an academy for non-Scholars?"

"I'm intrigued. Tell me more."

Quinn launched into his theory that most of the Scholar curricula had nothing to do with earth magic. Matthew nodded in agreement and asked questions.

"If this were to happen—"

"When it happens," Amarice said.

"When it happens, it would be best to put it in Teleah. My duties as Consort keep me here, of course. It would need professors."

Matthew's eyes lit up. "I've always wanted to be a professor. I'd love to take Quickthorn's place one day, but that lady will never retire."

"Not any time soon, that's for certain."

"Let me know what you need, Quinn. I'm interested."

Amarice smiled. "Do you know any rich people?"

❦

ONCE IN TELEAH later that month, they stopped for a late lunch at Corbin and Janessa's new home. They had rented a small townhome near the Academy. The outer façade was damaged from the riots, but the inside was quaint. The young couple was proud to show it off.

"I might have overcooked the meat," Janessa said as she sat a plate down in front of Quinn. "I've got a lot to learn about cooking. Corbin made the vegetables, though, so they should be edible."

"It's fine, Janessa. It looks great." He took a bite of the beef and tried not to make a face. It was chewy and dry. He swallowed and took a long drink of water before grinning at her. "Wonderful."

"Oh, good." She sat beside Corbin.

"What have the two of you been up to?" Amarice asked. Quinn watched as she cut her meat into tiny pieces. He followed suit to make it easier to chew.

"I've applied to the Builder's Guild. Raymond put in a good word for me." Corbin smiled, his head held high. Quinn's heart swelled with pride. "I've also been helping various shop owners and landlords rebuild. No shortage of work there."

"I should think not," Amarice agreed.

"And Janessa found work." He beamed at his wife.

"Jack hired me to help in his shop since he's serving on the Royal Council as well. His business is already booming. Some other shops are having trouble since re-opening."

Quinn nodded. "He was the most popular Apothecary on this side of the city before the war."

Quinn and Amarice stayed a few hours and promised to return before they left for the Villa. It was nice to see his brother thriving, and he knew that the city is where Janessa belonged. She would be making friends and hosting parties in no time.

At the palace, they spent the evening visiting with Raymond and Elaine. Quinn could hardly believe how much Elaine had come out of her shell. She acted as if she were already queen, being a gracious host and teasing Raymond. The staff appeared to love her.

Quinn mentioned his idea about the Academy for Learning to Raymond. The king leaned forward, his eyes wide with excitement.

"I think I have the investor you need."

"Oh?" Quinn asked. "Who?"

"Last week, I had a visit from Argent Grellis's niece." He held his hands up when Quinn made a face. "Hear me out. She was never a Chamberite. Loyal through and through. Her daughter is a Scholar. Anyway, she inherited every penny of Grellis's fortune when he went to prison and wants to—how did she put it?" He looked at Elaine.

"Invest in the new Elandria," she answered.

"Right. Invest in the new Elandria. I think this is a perfect opportunity."

Amarice grabbed Quinn's knee, and he put his hand on top of hers. "Is she still in town? Can you set up a meeting?"

"Yes, I'll do that tomorrow."

Quinn leaned back on the sofa and pulled Amarice against him. He sipped his wine, the high-quality stuff that Raymond always served, and savored the slight burn down his throat.

"It's happening," Amarice said. "The new Elandria we dreamed about. It's happening."

EPILOGUE

ne year later...

"Hurry up, Quinn! We're going to be late."

Amarice swore she could hear him roll his eyes. "They're not going to start without us, Amarice. We're the Sage and the Consort, remember?"

But he pounded down the stairs of their chambers. Amarice studied her Consort, clad in his black leather pants and sky-blue linen shirt. She bit her lip. She would never get tired of looking at her beautiful lover.

Together, they walked out of their rooms and out of the Villa. The late evening sky was painted with shades of pink and red and orange. A thousand people had gathered here for the anniversary of the end of the war. The Royal Council had declared it a national day of remembrance. The crowd was a mix of Scholars, Deyoni, and non-magic people. Elandrians, each and every one. One of Quinn's young cousins ran up to them, holding out two red chrysanthemums. Quinn bent low and thanked the boy. The Gagiya tribe had shown up two weeks ago to visit Deben and Quinn.

The crowd parted, and they walked toward a massive wooden pyre, too large for a funeral. Flowers and herbs decorated the symbol for all the lives lost in the war. Raymond stood next to it, Elaine to his left, and the rest of the Royal Council on her other side. Toward the front of the crowd, Matthew and Daisy were with the students from the Teleah Academy for Learning. Quinn didn't want his name on the school. Matthew had convinced Daisy to come teach after she spent several months in Te'eh. Corbin and Janessa were next to Quinn's five apprentices, having befriended them over the Feast of Fire.

The Sage and her Consort took their places in front of the pyre. She looked out at the crowd with tears in her eyes. How far they had all come in the last year.

Raymond nudged her. To her chagrin, the council had decided that she should speak. People were already calling the fight the Sage's War. Mostly, it was out of respect as her magic, along with Quinn's, had won the battle. To her, it weighed like the burden of responsibility.

She cleared her throat and stepped forward. Quinn's magic pulsed around her as he settled a calming bubble over the crowd so everyone could hear her. She felt his words in her mind. "You'll do great."

"My friends," she began. "We have spent much of the last year grieving. We lost much in the war. We lost friends and family. We lost our safety and security. At times, it felt as if we lost ourselves. We are right to grieve. And we will not stop. That grief is written into our collective memories. It challenges us to remember, to do better. To treat each other with kindness and empathy. It reminds us that we are not that different from one another.

"But today, we also celebrate. Elandria has come out stronger than ever before. Today, we honor those lives lost, and we hold them in our hearts. We remember the good times and the bad times. Today, we hold our new friends close. Our shared grief unites us in what is right. Our shared celebration unites us in what could be. With one foot in the past, and the other in our hopeful future, we build our present with a strong foundation."

She stepped back, and Quinn's magic dropped. Thunderous

applause broke out from the crowd. Quinn took her hand. She looked at Raymond, who grinned, his green eyes bright.

"Ready?" he asked.

She nodded and turned, and Quinn followed suit. She took a deep breath as she looked at the memorial pyre. Their magic lit up the pyre, a shining beacon in the setting sun. Quinn tossed his chrysanthemum in the flames, and she watched as the rest of the council did, too. Others gathered around the pyre to burn their flowers.

She studied the red flower in her hand. It didn't feel right. Instead, she removed the red rose she had tucked into her hair. A rose for Zayn.

With one foot in the past, she would remember her mistakes. She would stop forcing away the painful memories and honor them instead. The fire was warm near her face, and she tossed the rose into the blaze. With one foot in the future, the flames showed her what was possible.

Quinn put his arm around her waist and kissed her head. She looked up into her Consort's warm brown eyes, so full of love, grounding her in the present.

Past, present, future. Life was good, she thought. Amarice was the Sage of Elandria, and she would greet each day with passion burning like fire.

www.ingramcontent.com/pod-product-compliance
Lightning Source LLC
Chambersburg PA
CBHW031026260626
47153CB00017B/2402